ROBERT BARNARD

THE CORPSE AT THE
Haworth Tandoori

Scribner

SCRIBNER
Rockefeller Center
1230 Avenue of the Americas
New York, NY 10020

This book is a work of fiction. Names, characters,
places, and incidents either are products of the
author's imagination or are used fictitiously. Any
resemblance to actual events or locales or person,
living or dead, is entirely coincidental.

Copyright © 1998 by Robert Barnard
All rights reserved,
including the right of reproduction
in whole of in part in any form.

SCRIBNER and design are trademarks of Macmillan Library Research USA, Inc. und
license by Simon & Schuster, the publisher of this work.

Designed by Brooke Zimmer
Text set in Scala

Manufactured in the United States of America

10 9 8 7 6 5 4 3 2 1

Library of Congress Cataloging-In-Publication Data
Barnard, Robert.
The corpse at the Haworth Tandoori/Robert Barnard.
         p.   cm.
         I. Title.
PR6052.A665C59   1999
823'.914—dc21   98-39263
                 CIP

ISBN   0-7432-2427-2

For information regarding the special discounts for bulk purchases, please contact Sim
Schuster Special Sales at 1-800-456-6798 or business@simonandschuster.com

ALSO BY ROBERT BARNARD

No Place of Safety
The Habit of Widowhood
The Bad Samaritan
The Masters of the House
A Hovering of Vultures
A Fatal Attachment
A Scandal in Belgravia
A City of Strangers
Death of a Salesperson
Death and the Chaste Apprentice
At Death's Door
The Skeleton in the Grass
The Cherry Blossom Corpse
Bodies
Political Suicide
Fête Fatale
Out of the Blackout
Corpse in a Gilded Cage
School for Murder
The Case of the Missing Brontë
A Little Local Murder
Death and the Princess
Death by Sheer Torture
Death in a Cold Climate
Death of a Perfect Mother
Death of a Literary Widow
Death of a Mystery Writer
Blood Brotherhood
Death on the High C's
Death of an Old Goat

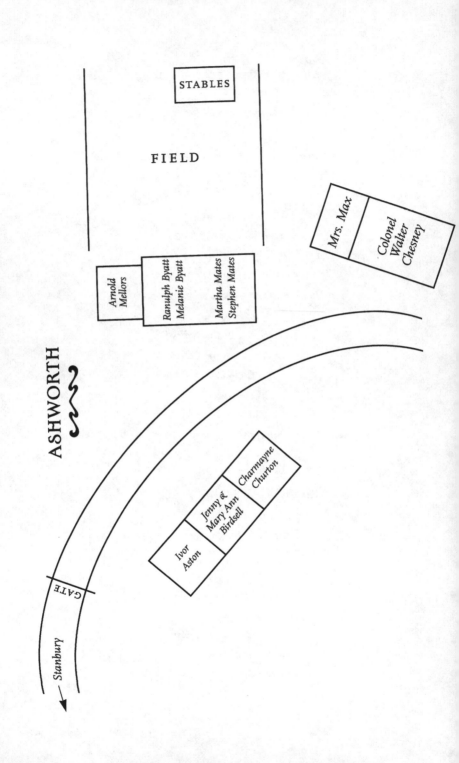

STABLES

FIELD

Mrs. Max

Colonel
Walter
Chesney

Arnold
Mellors

Ranulph Byatt
Melanie Byatt

Martha Mates
Stephen Mates

ASHWORTH

Ivor
Aston

Jenny &
Mary Ann
Birdsell

Charmayne
Churton

GATE

← Stanbury

AUTHOR'S NOTE

The Haworth Tandoori exists, and in the position I have placed it, close to the station in the town of Haworth in the north of England. It serves excellent Indian tandoori food, but I have given it a fictitious proprietor and waiters, and to my knowledge a corpse has never been found in its car park. All other characters, with the exception of the two ladies in the parsonage shop, are fictitious, as is the community of Ashworth, which I have placed on a greenfield site in the dip between Stanbury and Oakworth. Since this book was written a kitchen shop, called Tabby's Kitchen, has opened on Haworth Main Street.

THE CORPSE AT THE
Haworth Tandoori

PART I

The Corpse

I

THE BODY OF
AN UNKNOWN MAN

The last diners pushed away their plates of lamb biryani or chicken tikka masala, downed the last of their Tiger beers or their fruit juices, and began scrabbling in purses and feeling in back pockets as they made their way to the till. It had been a table for four, and they had arrived only shortly before ten o'clock. They had been talking incessantly, and had been quite unconscious that they had been watched for the past twenty minutes, that all the other tables were cleared and all the washing up had been done. The Haworth Tandoori was ready, indeed anxious, to turn off its lights and bolt its doors, but the late diners were quite unaware of the fact.

It was half past eleven at night.

"You two can go," said Mr. Masud to his two waiters as he shut the door on the customers. The young men had been constantly on the go from six until business had slackened off to those last four diners about half past ten. "See you tomorrow. I'll shut up."

Taz and Bash nodded gratefully and slipped out through the back door and up to the car park behind the restaurant. Mr. Masud went to bolt the front door and the side door, switching off all the lights in the dining area before going back to the kitchen. He was just about to bend down and switch on the dishwasher for its last load of the evening when he was frightened out of his wits— Haworth on weekends was a rough, unpredictable place—by banging and shouting at the back door. A second later he was relieved to recognize Taz's voice.

"Mo! Mo! Open the door!"

When he pulled back the bolts and opened it, he was confronted by a frightened face.

"There's a body in my car!"

"What? What do you mean, a body?" demanded Mr. Masud. "Some drunk got into it by mistake?"

"I mean a body! A dead body! In the boot!"

Mr. Masud swallowed and went out into the dim area of the car park. With reluctance in his steps he went over to Taz's ancient Fiesta and cast his eye down to the open boot: he saw first a hand, then the back of a head, then in the depths of the boot a scrap of white clothing that could have been underpants. Seconds later he was back in the kitchen and, seizing the receiver from his phone there, he pressed nine three times.

"Police. Keighley Police. . . . This is the Haworth Tandoori—you know it? Near the station. We've discovered a body. In the boot of a car. Yes, in the boot, left there. I think a man has been murdered."

By the time Detective Constable Peace had arrived at the little car park behind the Tandoori, the SOCO people were already beginning to assemble to collect the scene-of-the-crime evidence: there was, after all, little question of a dead man stuffed into the boot of a car having died from natural causes.

Lights were beginning to go up around the car. Not welcoming, warming lights, but a piercing, pitiless illumination of the scene. With less reluctance than when he had started in the force, but with a slight sense of shame underlying his curiosity, Charlie Peace went over to look at the body. It was a white man, young-looking; it was male, but the face was indistinct, tucked into the mass of limbs and trunk, so it would not be clearly seen until it could be removed from the boot. Charlie caught the same glimpse that Mr. Masud had seen and looked closer: yes, the body was naked except for a pair of white underpants. He stood back to look at the car: a very old, B-reg Ford Fiesta—one of only two cars in the car park. The other was an almost equally old Mini. From the little he had been told he suspected they both belonged to the waiters at the Tandoori. He conjectured that the proprietor must live close enough to walk to and from work.

Charlie walked away from the car and looked around him. The road he had driven down was the road to the station, which lay on the other side of the buildings he was looking at. The road then lay flat for a hundred yards to his left, though he couldn't see it, then began the steep climb up to what had once been the village proper—shops, church, parsonage on the edge of the sweep of moorlands, going southward to Hebden Bridge, westward to Burnley. Now the top of Haworth was taken up with cafés, shops selling tourist souvenirs, herbalists, and peddlers of the occult. Any real shops that sold things that people needed were at the bottom, around the station, and for anything except basics the people of Haworth had to hike up the hill to Crossroads or take the bus to Keighley. They had paid a heavy price for all the generations of their ancestors who had peddled tall stories about Branwell Brontë at the drop of a sixpenny piece.

Everywhere in Haworth, Charlie reflected, involved a stiff hike. He had a car, of course, but he wouldn't mind betting that this case would involve making door-to-door inquiries of shopkeepers and café proprietors up and down Main Street. He remembered a previous case at Micklewike, on the other side of the moors. That had involved fearsome climbs as well. One of the (few) good things that Charlie could think of to say about his native Brixton was that it was flat.

Two cars arrived, driving in from the road and parking behind the Tandoori. More SOCO people in one of them, his boss Mike Oddie in the other. Charlie recognized the car in the dim light, and walked over to it. Oddie put his window down and raised a hand in salute.

"What have we got?" he asked.

"I haven't got much more than I was told when I was called out," admitted Charlie. "Body stuffed in the boot of a car—but I expect you know that. Body in question is young, male, nearly naked. Caucasian, but I think the car belongs to one of the waiters here."

"Any connection?"

"I shouldn't think so. From what I heard when I was called out he found the body in the boot when he was going home, and went screaming to the proprietor of the place."

"Why his car, then?"

Charlie shrugged.

"It's an old bomb. The lock on the boot looked dodgy. Whoever dumped it may have thought it was abandoned."

"Well, let's get talking to him," said Oddie, climbing out of his car. "If you're right and the body was just dumped on him, we can let him go for the moment."

Taz had been waiting, with Bash his fellow waiter and his boss, in the kitchens of the Tandoori, compulsively drinking Cokes. His English was good, and his apprehension, which sometimes made him babble, seemed to spring mainly from his experience of finding the body and his reluctance to involve himself with the police rather than any irregularities in his status: he had been born in Bradford twenty-four years ago, he told Oddie, and he was a British citizen.

"So just go through what happened tonight," Oddie said.

"We finish 'ere— There's a party of four chatterin' away an' not carin' they're the last ones 'ere and everyone's waitin' to get 'ome. Anyway, they go— Arpast eleven it was. We'd cleared away, and Mr. Masud says we can go, Bash and me, and so we go out to Bash's car."

"Why Bash's car?"

"Mine's been out of order five or six days now."

"Why did you go to it, then?"

"To get me anorak. Some nights are nice an' warm still, but tonight's chilly. Bash drops me off on the Thornton Road, and I have ten minutes' walk from there."

Oddie nodded.

"I see. Go on."

"Well, I opened the boot, in the dark, and I felt in and—oh, God!—felt this body. Couldn't believe it, but there was still a bit of light from the kitchens and—well, I knew that's what it were. I ran to the back door, shoutin', and Mr. Masud opened up and called the police."

"I suppose you got no look at the man's face?"

"No—didn't even know it was a man."

"You've got no quarrel with any young man? Anyone been making trouble here at the Tandoori? Any other reason why a body should be dumped in your car?"

"I got no quarrel with nobody, except my mother-in-law, who's a pain."

"Well, we'll have to ask you to look at him when he's been removed from the boot, maybe tomorrow." Taz nodded unenthusiastically. "Just one last question: did you talk about your car with Bash or Mr. Masud in front of people who were eating here? Maybe said it was broken down and so on?"

Taz thought hard.

"Bash knew it was broken down because he gave me a lift the night I couldn't start it and every night since. I probably told Mr. Masud the next day before we opened. I could have said somethin' to Bash in front of the punters—like maybe I was goin' to get someone from me garage at

Thornton to 'ave a look at it on Saturday. . . . I'll 'ave to put 'im off now, won' I?"

"You will. Could you have said this in English, or—"

"Urdu. Could be either. We go from one to the other, Bash and me—don' know what we been talking 'alf the time. With Mr. Masud we mostly talk Urdu."

That was all they could get out of him that evening. He went off to accept, finally, Bash's lift home with perceptible relief on his face. The next day they took all three from the Tandoori to the mortuary at Keighley Police headquarters. They watched Taz's reaction in particular when he saw the face, which was still a horrible sight. He shook his head, first with pity. But he looked as closely as he could bear, then when he had looked away he shook it again as a negation.

"I've never seen 'im. He's never eaten with us while I was on."

He had a sharp, waiter's eye for customers, Charlie guessed. Assuming he was not personally involved, he believed him when he said the dead boy hadn't been a customer. His negative was confirmed by the other two men from the restaurant.

When they had gone Charlie talked to the young pathologist who would be doing the autopsy.

"Strangled, without a doubt. A nasty, slow death, as you can see from the face. There are signs that the hands had been secured, perhaps behind his back. It would be difficult to do it any other way, unless he was drunk or sedated. Will you be wanting some kind of artist's impression made?"

"Yes, I will," said Oddie. "It's the best hope we have of getting a lead on him at the moment. We can hardly show people a photograph of his face like *that*."

Charlie turned away from the body. Once again he had the sinking feeling that sometime in the next few days he would be seeing a lot of the daunting gradient that was Haworth Main Street.

Charlie parked his car in the Old Hall car park and went out onto the road. He was at the crossroads halfway up the hill. He had chosen to park here rather than at the top because he was the sort of person who liked to get the slog over first—in food terms a vegetables-first person rather than a meat-first one. So it was uphill to start with, calling at all the little tourist-oriented shops and galleries and cafés, then maybe he could give Main Street a miss on the way down and take the gentler road back to the Old Hall, passing the school and the park. Coming down Main Street, he knew, with its cobbled steepness, would be almost as grueling as walking up it.

The artist had done his best, but over the next quarter of an hour Charlie began to get the idea that his best was not good enough. It was the tail end of summer, and tourist trapping was on the wane, but though the proprietors and assistants were polite and had time to give him, the picture aroused no memories in anyone.

"If he was here in the school holiday period, there's Buckley's chance of his being noticed, unless he did something to make himself conspicuous, like buying something," said one disillusioned man in an art shop stuffed full of representations of Top Withens and sheep-populated moorlands. "You must know how chock-full of gawpers this place is then."

"He could have been here in the last few days," Charlie said.

"Oh, well, in that case, no, I haven't seen him, and he didn't come in here. Now you've got time, you notice."

That was the burden of practically all the interviews he had, as he went methodically upward, calling at establishments on both sides of the street. He concluded that the boy could have gone up or down Main Street (practically everyone except the halt and the lame did that), but that he didn't stop anywhere, perhaps because he had no money to spend, perhaps because he was not the type the trappers were aiming to catch.

There was, though, one flicker that could have been of recognition. Charlie had decided early on that the cafés were a better bet than the shops, because the shops sold nothing that a human being could actually *need*, but the cafés did. It was in a café called Tabby's Kitchen that the proprietress blinked and considered long, before disappointingly shaking her head.

"No, it wouldn't be right to say I recognized him," she said, handing picture back. "Just a vague memory that someone a bit like that was in here. But it would probably send you off on entirely the wrong track. After all, this picture's . . . well, not very *individual*, is it?"

"Not very," admitted Charlie. "We may be able to get a better one later on. What can you remember about this boy?"

"Not much. Not English, I seem to remember."

"Foreign? European?"

"No, I mean not *English*. Scottish, Welsh, Irish—I associate him with an accent."

"How long ago was this?"

"Oh, weeks. But I don't want you to think I'm talking about this boy here. That way you could go wrong. It's just a remote possibility."

"Will you think about it? Try to remember anything about him?"

"That never works with me. But if I don't try, things sometimes come to me. If anything does I'll be in touch."

Charlie had to be content with that.

It took him two and a half hours to get to the top of the hill, and do the clutch of establishments around the church. Not a café, shop, or pub admitted knowing him. He stood in thought: was it time to take the downward road and do the few businesses on the lower half of the hill, and then the station? The steam railway was a definite possibility: it was still running on weekends, and the boy could have come on it to Haworth from Keighley.

Then he remembered, with a guilty start, that there was still the parsonage. In the past the Brontës were what brought people to Haworth, though nowadays they often seemed to function merely as an excuse for purchasing a tea towel. But when he made his way along the path beside the church, then up the cobbles of Church Lane, he found the museum still presented in early autumn a busy enough front to the world—old people, young people, Japanese visitors, that cross section of the footloose and the driven that constitutes Britain's tourist trade.

A quick survey told him that the shop was the place to go. You came through the shop at the end of your tour of the Parsonage Museum, but you could also go into it without doing the tour at all. He saw souvenir hunters doing just that, emerging with postcards, mugs, and copies of

Wuthering Heights with special stickers on them. He pulled open the door and went in.

The shop was moderately busy, and a dark woman with large eyes was taking money behind the counter. As he paused, watching, listening to the voice on the educational video that was playing, an older woman with fair hair and a worried expression on her face hurried past.

"I've just heard from Grasmere there's a French school party on the way," she whispered to her assistant. "*What* a pity we can't nail everything down!"

The light-fingeredness of French school parties was legendary in police circles as well. Charlie went forward to get his inquiries out of the way before they arrived. He flashed his ID at the younger woman, then reached into his inside pocket and pulled out the by now dog-eared artist's impression.

"I wondered if you'd seen this young man," he said. "Not necessarily recently, maybe sometime over the summer."

She took it hesitantly, with the familiar uncertainty of all the other people he'd talked to that day, people who saw a great deal, perhaps too much, of transient tourist trade. She frowned over it for a moment or two.

"Mary!" she called, and the other woman came over. "He wants to know if we've seen this man."

Mary looked at it, then they glanced at each other.

"It could be," she said. "But I wouldn't want to be certain or get him into trouble."

"You won't," said Charlie, refraining from adding that he'd already been in all the trouble he could ever get into. "You are both speaking of the same young man?"

"Oh, yes," said Mary confidently, and the two women

gave glances at each other of perfect sympathy and understanding. "You're thinking of the singer, aren't you, Steph?"

Stephanie nodded.

"Singer?" Charlie asked.

"A young man who was singing for money, just outside here, at the top of the path that leads down to the car park. There's quite a lot of singers come to Haworth in the summer. This one had rather a nice voice, didn't he, Steph? A real tenor. He sang light stuff—folk songs, Gilbert and Sullivan, 'O Sole Mio,' that kind of thing. He had a guitar, but the accompaniments were a bit rudimentary."

"How long ago was this?"

They looked at each other again.

"It was the height of the season," said Stephanie. "There were lots of people milling around. But the height of the season is all the school holidays—"

"I'd say anything from four to eight weeks ago," said Mary. "But that's a guess, nothing more."

"Was he just here the once?"

"Oh, yes. Come to think of it, that's a bit unusual. They usually come back."

"And how long was he here?"

"About an hour," Mary said, surprisingly definite. "He was perfectly pleasant, as a singer, but some of the visitors inside the museum don't like it, find it distracting, so we generally ask them to move on after a time. Not that we've any right to do that, but they generally go."

"Did he say anything to you?"

"He didn't talk," Stephanie remembered. "Mary went out the door, and he'd obviously seen her behind the counter. He just raised a hand to her, grinned, and began packing away his guitar."

"So you had no idea, for example, what nationality he was?"

"No," said Mary, shaking her head. "But English-speaking, I would guess; wouldn't you, Steph?"

"Oh, yes. He put on an Irish accent for the Irish songs, and a Scottish one for the Scottish songs—not an awfully good one. He sang the Italian songs in Italian, but I'd say definitely English-speaking. His clothes weren't what you'd expect, sort of old-fashioned."

"Oh? What exactly was he wearing?"

"A tweed jacket, and flannels. He took off the jacket when it got hot. He had a white shirt on. It's not really what young people wear these days."

"No. . . . Is there anything else you can tell me?"

They shook their heads.

"I don't think so, do you, Steph?"

"No."

"Did you notice where he went?"

"Oh, yes," said Mary. "He went through the car park and down the steps beside the Weavers' restaurant."

"So he'd then be close to the Old White Lion and the tourist office and the post office?"

"That's right. But I didn't see if he turned in that direction."

"They have cards advertising jobs in the post office," said Stephanie.

2

THE ROAD TO ASHWORTH

As he passed the Old White Lion, with the King's Arms on his right and the Black Bull straight ahead, Charlie was very conscious that he could do with a pint. No such luck. He turned aside reluctantly from his plethora of choices. The window of the post office did indeed, down in one corner, have a board on which small advertisements and notices were pinned. He bent down to scan them. There were advertisements for bed-and-breakfast establishments ("Totally smoke-free zone"), for missing pets ("brindled and white, with damaged left ear and bleary right eye"), and, yes, jobs. Only one, though, and it looked as if it had been left up by mistake: one of the cafés, Tabby's Kitchen, was advertising for waitresses during the holiday period. Nothing more. Obviously late September was not the time when Haworth was recruiting casual staff.

Charlie straightened himself, changed focus, and gazed through the window. He had popped in with his picture while he was doing the top of the village, but neither of the women behind the counter had recognized it. There was a woman there now, but a new one: she was a large young woman, firm of manner, and, if Charlie judged aright, capable. He decided it was worth trying again. The afternoon was passing its peak, and there were only one or two loiterers around, gossiping after buying the odd stamp or collecting their pensions. He flashed his ID, and the little post office miraculously emptied itself.

When he showed the woman his picture she seemed, like most of the Haworth people he had shown it to, to be unimpressed.

"It's not very good, is it?" she said.

Charlie chanced his arm.

"As a picture or as a likeness?"

"Both," said the woman after a brief pause, considering and looking at it. "Yes, I think I have seen him, maybe talked to him. Not recently. It will have been over the summer. . . . Oh, dear, I can't say more than that."

"It's more than I've got from most. Could it have been in connection with one of your job ads?"

"Could have been. Or he could have been looking for a bed-and-breakfast place. Or just asking about trains and buses out. People come in here if the tourist office is crowded."

"You've only got one job advertisement up now, and it seems to be out of date. You would have had more up there in the summer, wouldn't you?"

"Oh, yes—waitresses in the cafés, bar staff and kitchen staff at the pubs and hotels, morning work at the B and B's. If he'd got any of those we'd have seen him around here. There was a general handyman job up there for a while, over at Ashworth. I wonder if it was that—"

"Ashworth? You don't mean Oakworth?"

"No, no. It's a little bunch of cottages off from Stanbury. Almost a community, you might say. Arty. One of them's said to be a real artist, well known. Name's on the tip of my tongue, but . . . I'm not into modern art."

"And they wanted a general handyman?"

"That's right. The ad was in the window for a while. He's very old, this artist chap, and they may have wanted help with him as well as help around the house and gardens. Wouldn't have suited everyone. . . . You know, I certainly remember *some*one coming in and asking the way to Ashworth. I don't say it was him—we get hundreds in here all through the summer rush period—but someone did. And it will have been a man, because they specified that."

"Is that legal?"

She grinned cheekily.

"We don't look too closely. And we're not lawyers."

"And what would you have told him, when he asked you for directions, I mean?"

"Go through Stanbury, almost to the end, and you'll find there's a path off to your right with a fingerpost that just says 'Public Footpath.' If you take that, veer a bit to your right; you can't miss Ashworth."

"He'll have been walking, I suppose."

"I expect so. My memory is that he had a backpack. Or he could have waited for a bus, but I don't remember him, or whoever it was, asking about times. There's not a lot of visitors go to Stanbury. In fact ninety percent of them never go off Main Street and Church Lane, where the parsonage is. If he went for the job, I expect he walked."

Charlie thanked her and took his leave. Outside the sun still had some warmth in it. It was an hour before the shops would close and Haworth would start to regain some semblance of a typical Yorkshire village. Charlie, on the spur of the moment, made a very untypical policeman's decision: the boy—if it was he—had walked, so he, Charlie Peace, would walk, to Stanbury. He turned right, in the direction of Hebden Bridge and Lancashire, and began walking, passing with regret one last pub, the Old Sun, and then leaving Haworth by the road that led him down into the valley.

It was a beautiful descent, but uneasy, due to the occasional nature of the pavement. Cars with farmers in them, or retired people, or tourists sped past him in both directions, sometimes driving erratically. If he had known the footpaths in the area he would have chosen one of those. Low down in the valley there was a row of attractive cottages, off from the road, with flower gardens in front that bordered on the showy. From the corner of his eye he had spotted a man deadheading near his gate. Charlie slackened his pace, then stopped, took out his handkerchief, and wiped his forehead. He raised his hand to the gardener.

"Need to get my breath before I do the upward stretch," he called.

"Oh, aye?" said the man, pausing willingly. He was small, wiry, and had the look of an animated garden gnome. "Or 'appen you'd like to ask a few questions about a picture of a boy?"

Charlie grinned.

"I stand out."

"You do. If you'd been Japanese I wouldn't ha' thought twice."

"Someone from Main Street has been talking."

"O' course they 'ave. We used to have a shop in Main Street, the missus and I, 'fore we retired. People still there, shopkeepers, get on the blower when it's quiet and tell us what's going on. Now, where's your picture, young man? Because we're old doesn't mean we don't notice things."

Charlie, seemingly for the hundredth time, dug in his pocket and handed it over. The little man out of early Walt Disney stood and considered it for a few seconds.

"Margaret! Come out here, girl!" A buxom woman twice his size came out, having probably been watching from the kitchen window. "Here's that black copper Arthur rang us about. Wants to know if we've seen this young chap. An' we 'ave, 'aven't us?"

She too considered the picture, frowning.

"Aye, we 'ave. I don't recall where, exactly—"

"The Grange, girl, the Grange."

"Oh, aye, 'appen."

"The Grange? Where's that?" Charlie asked.

"Pub in Stanbury. You'll see it—can't miss it. Stanbury's only got one street."

"And you saw him there when?"

"Over t'summer sometime. Mebbe July, mebbe August—don't rightly remember."

Charlie was curious.

"Why do you remember seeing him then? You get thousands of tourists around here in summer."

"Not so many in Stanbury, and not of an evening. But he wasn't just a tourist. I remember seeing him because he was wi' the Ashworth lot."

"Ah! Who exactly are you talking about?"

"Oh, Mrs. Birdsell, the Mates boy, Arnold Mellors . . . don't remember exactly because they're often in the Grange, different ones of them."

"And you remembered him *because* he was with them?" Charlie persisted.

"Aye," said the man, a glint in his sharp little eyes. "I thought, Poor, bloody lad, getting involved wi' that crowd. Because he were a nice-enough-looking chap."

"And the Ashworth crowd?"

"Don't like 'em. Don't trust 'em. Outsiders, every one of them. Wouldn't give them the price of a loaf of bread and expect them to come back wi' one."

"Creepy too," volunteered his wife.

"That's right—creepy. Unnatural, like."

"I see." Charlie stored this information away, adding the mental proviso that he mustn't be biased before he even met the Ashworth people. The problem could just be that they were artistic, and therefore different. "And was that the only time that you saw him?"

"'Appen I saw him driving past in their old car. Or mebbe waiting for a bus. That were it, at a bus stop. But in the pub were the only time I saw him close to, for any length o' time."

"Did you get the impression that he was working at Ashworth?"

The man thought.

"Aye, I did. It were like he were part o' the group, or getting to be that way, poor bloody lad."

It was said in the same tone as earlier, not as if he knew that the boy was dead. Still, it must be suspected soon, Charlie realized, that his investigation signaled something more important than a mere missing young person. Charlie gave them his thanks, said he hoped he wouldn't have to trouble them again (while realizing that they very much hoped he would), and then began his walk up the hill toward Stanbury.

Stanbury, he already knew from driving through it, was a street and not much more. It was what Haworth was in people's imagination but had not in fact been for centuries—a small Yorkshire village. It was sleepy, inward-looking, and liked basking in the twilight sun. The doorway of the Old Co-op stood open, and a woman who had the air of a sprightly bird sighting a particularly attractive worm watched his approach.

"Just past the little church and off to your right, where it says 'Public Footpath,'" she informed him. She felt no need to explain how she knew where he was going, so he accepted it as a matter of course as well, merely raising his hand in acknowledgment and proceeding on.

A little community where everyone knows everyone else, where every tiny item of news is transmitted by a constantly humming bush telegraph, and yet this boy could disappear and cause not a ripple of comment or query. It was eerie.

And yet when he thought about it, it was not so remarkable. The people of Ashworth, the boy's employers, presumably, had only to say "He's taken off" for that to be an end of it. Young people did take off these days. They had casual not regular jobs; they were at the expendable end of the labor market. Say that, for reasons unknown, this boy had come to seem expendable on a permanent basis in somebody's eye. The story could be put around that he'd just moved on, slung his hook, sought pastures new—whatever phrase was most convincing to the listener—and people would have accepted the story.

Past the church and then, here it was, a footpath, signposted, leading down into the valley. It was only a footpath but tire marks showed that it could be used in a pinch by vehicles, and had been fairly recently. Charlie turned in off the road, feeling as he left the shelter of houses that exposed sensation that townies feel in the open countryside: me in a landscape, not me in a peoplescape. He passed a lone farm, with chained, barking dogs. Farm dog, he thought, a different, more unsettling creature altogether than the fireside pet. Down, down he went, with the sound of cars becoming more and more distant, until he started to turn to his right and saw in the middle distance a collection of houses. This surely was the object of his search.

As the bend in the path began to get more pronounced he got a better view. A jumble of houses, like children's model houses scattered rather than arranged over the floor. One house decidedly bigger than the others, probably originally the farm. Built on to this was one of the small cottages. Around it, in no particular order, several other cottages—Charlie thought he could discern five front doors, three in one terrace, two in another. There were little gardens, clotheslines, a car left in a field behind the largest house, near what had once been stables. The field needed mowing, and one or two of the gardens were unkempt, though others were almost indecently showy and one had a garden gnome and another had a ring enclosing a large chunk of coconut at which birds were pecking.

This then was Ashworth. And it was—what? A colony of artists? A great artist with disciples? An artist who was something of a commercial concern, and who surrounded himself with a limited company—market men, publicists, accountants? It was, at any rate, at least in the locals' eyes, a unit—a colony, a community, a clan.

He went down farther, toward a gate that divided the little knot of dwellings from the path. The sun disappeared behind the hills, and seemed to alter the look of the place. The big house now looked forbidding, the gardens all slightly forlorn. Charlie's partner was doing a doctorate on Browning, and a line she often quoted came into his mind: "Childe Roland to the dark tower came."

Had the boy, Charlie wondered, had something of the same feeling when he'd come to Ashworth earlier in the summer?

PART II

The Boy

3

ARRIVING

The boy raised his hand in greeting to the fair-haired woman from the museum shop, scooped the coins from the tweed cap at his feet, and began putting his guitar back in its case. It was time, anyway, for a bite to eat. He grinned at the women whom he knew were watching him from the shop, turned on his heels, and went down the steps, through the car park, and down the little passage by the side of the Weavers' restaurant. He walked toward the precipitous descent of Main Street, but dallied as he passed the post office. Notices. Someone wanted his washing done, someone wanted cleaning work, pubs and cafés wanted waiters and bar staff. Handyman . . . that could be interesting. He could turn his hand to anything, he thought. Ashworth, near Stanbury. Singing in the street was pleasant, but it didn't, at least in Yorkshire, bring in a lot of money. He walked down the tourist-thronged street, and decided to try Tabby's Kitchen.

The money earned from Irish and Scottish folk songs, interspersed with bogus Neapolitan ballads, stretched to a Welsh rarebit with egg on top and a pot of tea. When the waitress brought it he ate ravenously, wiped his mouth clean of yolk with the paper napkin that had been wrapped around his knife and fork, then sat thinking. Being footloose and fancy-free was an Irish tradition, and it suited him. Still, one big disadvantage was that you never knew where your next meal was coming from, and whether it would satisfy your youthful appetite. This handyman job was probably only for the summer, but it would give him regular wages, and if he didn't like it he could simply up and leave. It certainly wouldn't do any harm to check out the place and see if it would suit.

He got up, paid the woman at the till with a dazzling smile and £3.25, and went out into Main Street again. He looked down the thigh-tormenting slope. He had known nothing like this in his native Ireland—nothing quite like it in England, either, in his five weeks in the country, though the blackened stone was becoming familiar. After the towns, after the tourist venues, where he functioned as a one-man machine for screwing money out of the unwary, a small place would be nice. Maybe it would be a farm . . . pleasant, restful. On an impulse he went into the post office and checked. Yes, Ashworth was a farmhouse near Stanbury, with a few cottages around. Declan felt a tug that was all but irresistible.

He had been in Haworth long enough to know where Stanbury was. He retraced his steps until town suddenly gave way to moorland and fields, then took the road down the hill and followed it when it turned upward again. Stanbury, when he gained it, was approved of. The boy liked villages, came from one and felt at home in them. He stopped to ask an old man toiling along the street past the church how he could get to Ashworth, and had the path silently pointed out to him. As he turned off the road, to his right, his heart rose again: a broad, green valley. A farm with a cottage and dogs—just what he was used to. He was traveling, adventuring, but he was carrying his history with him, and was conscious of the fact. A conviction grew in him that Ashworth, when it was gained, was going to be somewhere where he could feel at home.

As he descended and rounded a corner he realized that he must be there. It was exactly as the woman in the post office had described it. Not just a farm, but a hamlet centered on a farm. That looked wonderfully promising. The boy knew he got on well with people, that his appearance predisposed them to like him, and that that didn't change when they got to know him better. He came to a gate, swung it open, and found himself among the little knot of cottages.

There was a woman bending over to weed in the front garden of one of the little cottages—a cottage in the middle of a little terrace of similar ones, with roses and gladioli in the garden and a JESUS LIVES sticker in the window looking out on the lane. The boy cleared his throat.

"Excuse me."

The woman straightened. She was wearing an old cream blouse and an even older tweed skirt, once green and brown, now generally muddy. Her face, unmade up and not particularly clean, showed a similar disregard for the opinions of others. She smiled, but he got the impression that strangers here were not frequent, were not particularly wanted, and were evaluated.

"I'm looking for Ashworth."

"Well, you could say this is all Ashworth. We take the name from the farm."

"Maybe it's the farm I want. There was this advertisement in the post office in Haworth."

She nodded, obviously interested.

"Oh, yes. You're the first. It only went up Monday. . . . Well, you look sturdy enough."

"I can do most things."

"Mind you, it's not just physical stuff you'd be doing, not with Ranulph. You need strong mental qualities as well—tact, cheerfulness, friendliness."

"Well, I think I've got those," said the boy, with the confidence of his twenty or so years.

"I hope you have. I'm Jenny Birdsell, by the way." They shook hands, then she leaned forward to impart information. "It's Ranulph you'll have most to do with in the house, if you get the job. What I've said probably has given you the impression that Ranulph is difficult. That's not really fair. He's demanding. But then, as his physical powers fail he *needs* more attention, for his art's sake. To get the vision onto canvas. He has to be helped, moved, have all his things to hand."

"He's a painter?"

"Ah, you didn't know? I thought the name Ranulph might have alerted you. But then, you're young. Ranulph Byatt is his full name, one of the country's greatest living painters. If I were you I would say when you go to the house that you've heard of him."

"I will. Thanks for the suggestion."

She put her head to one side, considering.

"Perhaps you'd better not pretend to know his work. You might be found out. It's the womenfolk there who are in charge on a day-to-day basis, them you would be dealing with."

"Is that his wife?"

"Wife and daughter. Melanie is younger than Ranulph, but she's getting on herself, and she has her problems— arthritis, just like him. Lady Byatt we call her when we're in an irreverent mood. She was desperate for Ranulph to accept the knighthood when it was offered to him. It's Melanie who's really in charge. Martha's her daughter. Such a *drab* name she gave her. Almost . . ."

She faded into silence, having made her point without actually voicing it. The boy looked at her, in no way put off.

"So it's them I have to deal with?"

"That's right. Satisfy them that you can do the job—all the jobs, rather—and you'll be in. I'd put in a word for you, but Melanie wouldn't take any notice of *me*."

"Who had the job before?"

"No one. They moved Ranulph round as best they could, and sometimes got in outside help for the garden and the handyman tasks around the house. Stephen helped, of course, when it suited him, or when he wanted something."

"Stephen?"

"Martha's son. Stephen Mates. But he'll be flying the nest quite soon, and, anyway, he's getting very Bolshie."

The boy almost smiled at the dated word, but he damped the smile down at its source. He didn't get the impression that Jenny Birdsell had much of a sense of humor. Her way of talking about the job gave him the impression that he was wrong to regard this as only a summer job. It was meant to be permanent. Well, it didn't have to be permanent for him. That was entirely up to him. He could take off whenever he liked.

"I'd better be getting along," he said. He turned around. "I suppose *that's* the house, isn't it?"

"That's right. The gate and the front door are just around the corner. . . . It's a pity you don't know more about art, you know."

"I don't know much about a lot of things," said the boy, but, optimistic by temperament, he added: "I expect I'll learn."

"I hope you do. It will be such a *waste* otherwise. If you *can* learn you'll understand the greatness of Ranulph's contribution to contemporary art." She smiled brightly. "Maybe you'll come to *worship* him, as we all do."

The boy repressed the instinct to say "Maybe," and instead delivered a cheerful "I'm sure I shall."

The farmhouse, on the other side of the lane, sprawled invitingly. It was a low, stone building with narrow windows upstairs, more generous ones on the ground floor. Leaving Mrs. Birdsell and rounding a corner in the lane the boy found a small front garden and, central to the block, an old oak front door with a genuine bell that, when the rope was pulled, gave out a fearsome baritonal ring. He had thought he heard, on the instant of ringing, the sound of raised voices from a distance. Now there was silence, and as he stood there in the sun, in the little garden of shrubs and border plants, he began to hear strong, young footsteps approaching the door inside the house.

"Yes?"

The door had been opened by a young man, about his own age, much darker in coloring, though, with beetling eyebrows and an angry manner. He was wearing jeans and a check shirt, but they set uneasily on him: they were the clothes of a farm boy, but he did not have a farm boy's manner or speech.

"I've come about the job."

It took a moment or two to sink in.

"Oh, the *job!*" The boy was not quite sure what the intonation suggested: that only a hobo would consider a job like that? That it could hardly be considered a job at all? That it was some kind of cover for something else?

"That's right," he said, with the determined good humor that he had always found got results. "The handyman's job."

"OK, OK," the young man said, as if temporizing. "What's your name?"

"Declan O'Hearn."

The young man gave him a tight smile.

"Right you are, Declan. . . . Well, you'd better come in, hadn't you?"

He led the way down a wide hallway, over threadbare carpet, until at the far end he flung open a door.

"Mother. Grandmama. This is Declan O'Hearn, come about the handyman's job."

The young man, apparently feeling he had done more than enough, threw himself on an old sofa under the window, and prepared to watch the scene sardonically. Declan stood uncertainly by the door. The young man's manner had unnerved him a little, made him socially uncertain. He had the impression he had interrupted something—probably a routine family row, something with which he was familiar. Standing by the mantelpiece were two women, one old, one middle-aged. By a bookcase adjacent to the mantelpiece was a man, tweed-jacketed, with a pipe and a mustache. He looked like a solicitor or a bank manager, and certainly not like a painter.

"Thank you, Stephen," said the older woman, speaking distinctly and with immense condescension. "Come over here—Declan, is it? That's an Irish name, isn't it?"

"It is that. I come from County Wicklow."

"A beautiful country, yours. Ranulph did some wonderful work there in the summer of sixty-seven—landscapes, of course." She beckoned, and Declan moved somewhat hesitantly over to the fireplace. She looked him over like a cattle buyer. "Well, you appear capable enough. Farming stock?"

"That's right. Peasants, I suppose you'd call us."

"Good. Call things by their honest name. Used to physical work, then?"

"Sure, I've done plenty of that in my time. But I've an education as well."

"Splendid. Then you'll have heard of Ranulph Byatt."

"I have." The boy registered that he was telling nothing but the truth, though his intention had been to convey a lie.

"My husband," she said, sinking down into a chair. "Now, quite a lot of your work would be for and concerning him. Moving him, helping him to mix paint, moving his easel, stretching and setting up canvases, and so on. Being there, in short, while he paints, and assisting in every way."

"I'm sure I can manage that. It would be an honor."

She nodded complacently.

"It would. But you see, Ranulph can only paint for limited periods. Two, two and a half hours at most. Sometimes he will have a little nap after lunch and then manage a little more, but mostly not. The rest of your job would be outdoor work—in the garden, the stable, doing shopping, some handyman jobs around the place when things go wrong."

"I could do all that."

She looked closely at him.

"You seem to be very confident. What's your situation? You look as if you're traveling around. You don't have a job at the moment?"

"No, I'm traveling the country, as you say. Getting a bit of work where there's anything on offer." In a burst of confidence he added: "Singing for my supper sometimes, in the street. I have quite a nice voice."

"Just so long as you don't irritate Ranulph with it," said the old woman. "He has no ear for music."

"Tell him about Granddad" came the voice from the sofa. Stephen was still lounging there sardonically, looking at the little group around the fireplace.

"I *have* told him about your grandfather," insisted Mrs. Byatt. "I've made no secret it's heavy, difficult work."

"Tell him what Granddad is *like*," insisted Stephen. "Tell

him about the rages, the sulks, the tetchiness. Tell him about the sheer bloody-mindedness."

"Declan said that he was educated, Stephen," said his grandmother. "He will know that artists are . . . different."

"Oh, Granddad is different, all right. He lives by different rules to other people's. But don't blame it on his art. Plenty of artists have looked like bank managers and behaved perfectly decently. Art shouldn't be used as some kind of excuse. That's a nineteenth-century fallacy. And Granddad would have been a monster whatever his profession."

"Stephen!" The middle-aged woman spoke for the first time, her conventionality outraged.

"Mother, Declan's going to find out. Best tell him now so he can walk straight out of the door if he feels like it."

"To talk about your own grandfather like that—"

"Tell it like it is. That was one of your generation's mottoes, wasn't it? Make it clear to Declan that he'll be abused, harried, hectored—kicked, if there's any strength in his legs."

"But you'll have the satisfaction of knowing that, in a very small way, you are contributing to the work of one of this country's great artists," said Stephen's mother, turning to Declan with a misty look in her eyes, an almost exaggerated devotion in her voice, which contrasted oddly with what seemed like personal uncertainty. "Surely that is *some*thing, isn't it?"

"It certainly would be," said Declan, but more for something to say than because he had any such ambition.

"You'd have a room to yourself," said her mother, more practically, "and all your evenings free. You can eat with us or go off with your friends."

"He'll have lots of friends round here, coming from County Wicklow," said Stephen.

"He'll make friends, of course. A pleasant young man like Declan will always make friends."

"Unlike your grandson," said Stephen.

"Yes, unlike you, Stephen, who *repel* friendship." Stephen remained irritatingly silent, as if disdaining self-defense. "At least this will have told you, Declan," she went on, turning back to him, "that this is not an *easy* job."

"No, well, I'll just have to see if I can cope," said Declan. "I haven't always had it easy so far." In a sudden gush of honesty he added: "I like the idea of a room to myself. It's something I've never had at home."

"Lots of brothers and sisters?"

"That's right. I can put up with a lot for a room of my own."

"Then you'll take the job?"

"I'll take it if you're offering it," said Declan, with the mental proviso that they were "on liking" quite as much as he was, if not more so.

Suddenly the man with the pipe spoke for the first time.

"They've been exaggerating about Ranulph. His bark's worse than his bite. And he can be as meek as a lamb for weeks at a time."

"Granddad is *never* meek as a lamb."

"Comparatively. When he's not painting anything major."

"When he's meditating a picture," said Mrs. Byatt. "When the next painting is taking shape in his mind."

"It's when he is trying to get that picture in his mind

47

onto the canvas that frustration sometimes turns into rage," said his daughter. "The gap between vision and reality, you know, that's how he describes it. Every time he feels he has failed, because he can't match the painted pictures with the ideal conception. Can you, as a layman, understand that?"

"I think I can," said Declan.

"We just have to hold our breaths and wait until it passes."

"Till we can just be his doormats again, instead of the targets on his shooting range," said Stephen. There was a moment's silence.

"Well, that's settled, then," said Mrs. Byatt, with a forced naturalness. "Now, you'd better get to know us, since you're going to be part of the household. I'm Melanie—*please* try to call me that, it's so much more friendly. On the other hand it's perhaps best to call Ranulph Mr. Byatt, at least to start with. He'll make it clear what terms he wants to be on with you."

"*Quite* clear," said Stephen.

"And I'm Martha," said Stephen's mother. "Martha Mates. I'm Ranulph and Melanie's daughter. Stephen is my son. And this is Arnold Mellors."

The man with the pipe came over and shook Declan's hand.

"I live in the cottage built on to this house," he said. "You must feel just as at home there as you are here."

"Thank you," said Declan, not quite feeling at home anywhere yet.

"Arnold took early retirement," said Martha Mates.

"Before I was pushed. Nobody wants experience or mature judgment anymore in the business world. I paint myself, in a small, amateur way. But living close to Ranulph is—well, a breath of life, artistically speaking."

"I'm sure it is," said Declan, who was undergoing a crash course in discretion.

"Well, I think the sensible thing would be to show Declan to his room," said Melanie Byatt, getting up from her chair by the mantelpiece. Getting a good look at her for the first time Declan saw the remains of a very good-looking woman indeed—full of figure, erect of carriage in spite of what he took to be her arthritis, and beautifully dressed in a creamy-brown frock with a vivid rose-and-orange shawl. Why dress so well in a rather drab farmhouse on a weekday in midsummer? The answer was perhaps in the face: handsome, chiseled, with wide mouth and striking hazel eyes, the whole effect just touched with a suggestion of a bird of prey. The boy's diagnosis, with only an intuitive understanding of the world he was sliding into, was that Melanie had always been beautiful, and that she had used her beauty to exact homage or obedience.

Certainly beside her, her daughter looked drab—dressed sensibly, inclined to dumpiness, with a moon-shaped face innocent of makeup. It was as if she was making a statement that she was not in competition.

"I can show Declan to his room, Mother," said Martha Mates.

"No, no. You know I like to do the honors of the house, as long as it is mine. . . . You'll eat with us, Declan?" she asked, turning to him and widening her painted lips.

"Thank you very much."

"Ranulph eats in his room. He's very tired today so I think, you know, the best thing will be to prepare him tonight, and for you to meet him for the first time tomorrow."

"'Sufficient unto the day . . .'" came from the sofa.

"Stephen, if you were not about to go up to Oxford I would seriously consider forbidding you this house," said Melanie Byatt. "Come, Declan."

She went slowly, painfully through the hall and up the dark stairs, leaning on a stick with an ivory knob on top, then along an almost equally dark landing, at the end of which she threw open a door.

"Here we are."

It was a small room with a single bed, a chest of drawers, a tiny wardrobe, and a desk. It had not been decorated for many years, though the wallpaper had originally been unusual. Declan went over to the window. It looked out over a long field at the back of the house, with stables at the far end.

"It's heaven," he said.

"Hardly that. But I hope you can make it your own. The bathroom is there and your lavatory over there. There's another one at the other end. We eat at half past seven. Make free of the house until then, and the grounds too, but best not to come upon Ranulph before he's been prepared. I do hope you'll be happy here."

And sitting on his bed, Declan looked around him oozing contentment. This was *his* room. Not his and Patrick's, or his and Stephen's and John Paul's, but *his*. He felt sure in his mind he could cope with the people in the house, their oddities, their animosities, their passions. He sat there for all of twenty minutes, savoring his luck, then he got up and looked out the window again: a long field, horses in the distance, high hills beyond them. This was good, this was natural, this was like home. He could have sung out one of those deceptively simple Irish ballads he had charmed the paying customers with in Haworth. More than the people in the house, this room, the field outside his window and the hills beyond, made him feel immensely contented, at peace, secure.

4

THE ARTIST AT HOME

Breakfast next morning was a slightly uneasy affair, as dinner the previous evening had been as well. Declan sensed that it was nothing to do with his own relationship with the people around the table, only apprehension about how things would go when he encountered the only member of the household he had thus far been kept away from. He reserved judgment on the situation at Ashworth, but his initial impression was that they were all terrified of that unseen presence—and that included

Stephen, the only one who was willing to formulate anti-Ranulph sentiments.

Was he the only one, he wondered, to feel them?

It was made clear to him that, today at least, he would be wanted only when Ranulph Byatt was ready to paint.

"Daddy paints when he *needs* to paint," said Martha Mates, with a metallic brightness in her voice. "Of course we don't know when that will be, but probably around mid-morning. I'm sure you can find things to do until then."

Declan decided it would be impolitic to just mooch around, and still more so to practice his guitar. Still, he needed something to calm his nerves. Nervousness was not usually a problem with him, and he concluded it was something he had caught, as one might catch the flu, in this house. When he had had his last piece of toast and marmalade he told Melanie (as he had studiously been calling her) that he would be in the front garden weeding when they needed him.

He enjoyed working in a garden: it was something he was very used to, it was conducive to thought—he had always been accustomed to think through any situation he found himself in—and he had considerable expertise at it, never for a moment being in doubt as to what should be torn out, what left to flower. He had been at it for nearly an hour and a half, and had come to the conclusion that if Ranulph Byatt was at all tolerable he could well stop at Ashworth for quite a while, when Melanie came to the front door and beckoned him. He went to the kitchen and washed his hands, and then together they proceeded again slowly up the dingy staircase. Declan felt a bit like a minor functionary accompanying the Queen.

"He's quite excited, you know," said Melanie, unable to keep the surprise out of her voice, or a sort of nannyish condescension. "I think it's the prospect of seeing a new face."

At the top they turned left instead of right, and progressed nearly the whole length of the landing. Eventually Melanie stopped at a door, gave Declan an encouraging smile, then tapped on it and opened it.

It was the atmosphere of the room that struck Declan first—or more accurately, the smell. It was an invalid's room, and an old-fashioned invalid's room at that. It breathed sickness and decrepitude. Embrocation, herbal inhalers, all manner of ancient remedies that some would call natural, others would call quack, gave the room a close, sickly feel.

"We air it as soon as he goes out," whispered Melanie.

The next thing that Declan registered was the invalid. He was dressed—shirt, waistcoat, trousers—and sitting in an armchair, his daughter, Martha, standing beside him. He was the remains of an impressive, even intimidating man. Now he was long, very skinny, and his gaunt face was fallen in, only the intensely living eyes bearing witness to the force his personality had once had. But the glow that came from them was a burning, not a warming one, and Declan, educated by priests and nuns, immediately thought of hellfire.

"Hello, sir," he said.

Ranulph Byatt harrumphed, and even that sound showed Declan that there was force in the voice as well as the eyes. It was a voice that he would have associated with a general more readily than with an artist.

"Come and help me up," the voice said, after regarding

Declan intensely for a second or two. "They've dressed me, you notice, my womenfolk. Why, you ask? Because they don't want you to be revolted on your first morning by the sight of my ancient flesh."

"I wouldn't be that, sir," said Declan, going over. When Martha Mates made to take her father's other side, he said: "I think it'll be easier if I do it on my own. I learned the technique with me old gran."

He put his arm around the stooped shoulders and gently but deftly raised the old man to his feet. Once standing, Ranulph Byatt needed to pause to get his breath.

"So, I'm the successor to your old gran, am I?" he asked with the first trace of bitterness in his voice. "Well, you seem to have learned a thing or two. Forward now."

Together they walked slowly to the door, then turned right. Martha and Melanie lingered in the background. The next door down, at the end of the landing, was open, and light was flooding out of it. Step by step they approached the light, then turned and entered the long room. Declan was astonished at its size. Two bedrooms had been made into one large studio by the removal of a wall, and also of the ceiling. The windows had been enlarged by making them into one long one, and part of the roof had been turned into a massive skylight. All this Declan registered only subconsciously, because he was helping Byatt slowly forward to a high-backed padded chair in front of an easel. Finally he positioned the old man directly in front of the chair, then eased him down into it.

"Well done, boy. You'll do," said Byatt.

Declan registered a glance passing between mother and daughter, one that mingled gratification and surprise.

"Sure, you're no problem at all, sir," he said.

Ranulph Byatt was again out of breath, and it was some time before he spoke.

"Now," he said, "I want you to watch this carefully. We'll only show you this once, mind. It may look difficult but it's not. Martha!"

Martha Mates came over and took up a palette that stood on a stand beside Ranulph's chair. There followed a process, which Declan followed intently, in which the artist gave instructions and Martha obeyed expertly.

"More of the blue—too much—a dash of the green. A little more. I'll need some of the yellow."

The process took ten minutes or more, and Declan registered carefully the paints that were currently in use. Martha was good at the job, but Declan had an odd sense that she was doing it without understanding and that this irritated Byatt. Yet her words always suggested that she loved and admired her father. Perhaps she was jealous of his art? Loved the man, hated the distraction of his genius? And perhaps it was because she did it without the devotion of the artistic acolyte that the job was now to be taken over by himself. If so there was a real danger that he would be found to be inadequate.

"Sometimes you have to sit in front of him and hold the palette close," whispered Melanie. "Often for quite a long time."

Declan nodded.

"*Right,*" said Ranulph Byatt. "Did you get that, boy?"

"I think so, sir, most of it," Declan said. Then he added modestly: "I expect I'll get things wrong at first."

"I expect you will. Well, let's get on with it. Shoo!" Byatt turned his neck painfully to look at his womenfolk. "Don't come back unless you're sent for." Then he turned to the easel, as if he had put his wife and daughter entirely out of his mind, and was glad to have done so. He took a broad brush from a jar beside the easel and sat considering.

Declan didn't know much about art, and wasn't even sure he knew what he liked. He recognized that the half-finished picture on the easel was not an abstract, but beyond that he could make no judgment on it. The colors were predominantly green and blue—a natural scene, then—and they were in great blocks of color: blue toward the top, a central section of green, with some yellow to the sides and at the front. Fields, Declan thought, and sky. But when by a natural association of ideas he raised his head and looked through the long window, he could see no resemblance between the picture and the long field and stables behind Ashworth, which the studio overlooked.

"Keep your mind on what you're doing, and not on what I'm doing," snarled Ranulph. Fine, thought Declan. Except that I'm not actually doing anything at the moment.

He soon was. Byatt eased himself forward, took a more delicate brush from the pot, and gazed intently at the picture. There was silence in the room for a minute or two.

"Take the palette and keep it close to my hand," directed Byatt at last. "Kneel or sit—whichever is easier."

Declan sat with his back to the canvas, holding the palette immediately under it. Now he had the best possible view of Byatt, who did not seem to mind, or even to register his gaze. Declan amused himself by trying to imagine the man as he had been in his prime. There were one or two photographs around the farmhouse, but he had not yet inspected them closely. He knew all about the effects of aging, though, from his own family, who were long-lived.

He saw Ranulph Byatt in his forties as tall—maybe six foot two—upright, with a good pair of shoulders and a decisive manner. The face had probably always been gaunt, and the gauntness had inevitably given him a forbidding air. That, combined with the glinting devilment in the eyes, must have made relationships difficult. Had he been capable of softness, of tenderness? Declan reserved judgment on that. Certainly Byatt seemed capable of inspiring devotion, discipleship. So had Adolf Hitler.

He kept returning in his mind to the eyes. They were not things Declan could study closely, because it seemed like impertinence while Byatt was painting, and Declan sensed that impertinence was something the man would never tolerate. But he did, finally, manage to get a sidelong look at those eyes, and it struck him still more forcibly that they were the last things to age; pale blue, piercing, merciless. If Byatt had been a schoolmaster, children would have quailed beneath that gaze. Headmasters too. He stared ahead at his picture, seeming to analyze, dissect as he painted. To him, Declan thought, nothing else seemed to exist as the brush—slowly, calculatedly— applied strokes sometimes bold, sometimes delicate. Nothing else exists, least of all me, he thought. So he was surprised when Ranulph Byatt spoke.

"Not *the* field," he said. "Not the field I see in front of me. *A* field."

Declan was quiet for a moment, then realized he was responding to his first action when looking at the picture.

"I see," he said.

"I am brought down to painting imaginary landscapes," Byatt went on, his voice harsh as he paused between strokes. "*My* field, a field I've seen, a field in a photograph, a field in someone else's painting. Then they come together to become a field picture. . . . Pap. That's all I can paint now. Small-gallery fodder. But I have to paint."

"Do you never paint portraits?" asked Declan naively. The eyes were turned momentarily on him.

"Never! Cash-on-the-nail, painted-to-order stuff. I wouldn't prostitute myself. I sometimes paint—how can I describe it to someone like yourself?—I paint my reactions to people, what effect their personalities have on me, pictures *based* on people, springing from them. Events, happenings too: I paint the impression they have on me, the force with which they impress me. But rarely, rarely . . ."

"And when you do that, would they be a more abstract kind of picture?" Declan asked.

"You could say that." Byatt started painting again. Declan had the odd sense of being played with, as an angler plays with a fish. There was relish in the performance, as if Byatt enjoyed talking to someone totally ignorant of art more than he would have enjoyed talking to a fellow artist or a connoisseur. "I did think of ending my days painting hundreds of different views of that field outside, like that charlatan Bacon and his bloody popes. Couldn't face it. And they wouldn't even be gallery fodder. No one would have been interested at all. No, better as it is. Perhaps that fool Stephen will make me hate him so much that I can get a picture out of my hatred. . . . All right. That's enough. Now I must sit and think."

He waved Declan away. Not quite knowing what he should do, he got up and stood beside the palette stand.

Ranulph Byatt sat back in his chair, gazing at the easel. Time passed. There was a total silence. Not even a clock ticked in the studio, and the rest of the house seemed to Declan almost exaggeratedly quiet. Declan felt as if he were mounting guard at some enormously impressive state funeral. When Byatt spoke, however, it was in tones of dissatisfaction and frustration.

"Why do I bother? Why do I plan tomorrow's work? This stuff is on a level with my art-student work just after the war. I should be ashamed. . . . Come on: lift me up."

So the earlier journey from room to room was done in reverse. Declan first put his arm across Byatt's hunched shoulders and eased him up. The old man seemed already to be used to the routine, happy to rest his depleted height and weight on the young man. When, slowly but confidently, they reached the landing, Byatt paused: he had heard, as Declan had, a slight sound from the bottom of the stairs. He waited to get his breath, then roared:

"You don't need to spy on us. He'll do. You're redundant for the moment, Martha. You can come and teach him about care of the brushes, then you can take your cards. Resume the husband hunt. I'm well suited with the lad here."

As they continued with their walk, Declan's mind registered two things: first, that Byatt's hearing was as acute as his sight; second, that he dismissed his daughter from her place as his helper with all the relish of a Victorian mill owner sacking his hands. Whatever inspired his womenfolk's devotion to him, it was not considerate treatment.

*   *   *

That evening Declan went with Stephen to the Grange. They picked up Jenny Birdsell and Arnold Mellors on the way. They had been standing by the big gate, talking and gesturing, and they volunteered their company rather than waiting to be asked. Stephen looked as if he could gladly have done without it.

The Grange was a nondescript pub, but one with angles and crannies, and the Ashworth party made for a corner that seemed to be theirs by tradition. While Stephen made for the bar to get the first round—and probably because he was not with them, Declan thought— Mrs. Birdsell said, "I hear things went awfully well today."

"Not so bad," said Declan.

"That's wonderful. Because Ranulph doesn't take to everybody."

"No, I suppose not."

"It must feel such a *privilege* to be approved of by him, and to be able to help him." She looked up, and saw Stephen handing over a note at the bar. "But I mustn't say any more, or I'll be accused of sentimentality! The most terrible of crimes! Isn't it odd to be called sentimental when you *care* passionately about England's greatest living artist?"

Declan said nothing. He felt himself on unknown terrain, where silence was the best policy. He had an odd sense of being drawn into a conspiracy that he felt was nothing to do with him. People who said they cared passionately about something usually were using this as an excuse for any kind of shabby conduct or dirty trick. Stephen's sardonic expression when he sat down with them showed that he knew the direction the conversation had taken.

"Now tell us about yourself," he said, handing Declan his half pint. "And about Ireland. If you went by your countrymen's reputation, you wouldn't think there was an Irishman alive who drank half pints."

Declan was relieved—and he saw Jenny and Arnold were disappointed—by the change of subject. He started hesitantly. He didn't tell them about his drunken father, or his drunken uncle, or, come to that, about his occasionally drunken aunts, but he got into his stride when he talked about growing up in rural Ireland, the perpetual fight against poverty, the struggle for education, the still-powerful priests. Soon he was talking well: in that respect, at least, he was the Englishman's stereotypical Irishman. When he finished it was time for the next round.

"I'll get these," said Arnold Mellors, getting up. "Same again, Stephen? Declan?"

"And I'll have another vodka and tonic," said Jenny Birdsell. "Then my daughter won't smell it on my breath."

"That's a *legend*, Jenny," said Stephen with a world-weary sigh. "Anyway, she guesses you've been drinking when you fall upstairs."

"Sure, it's a terrible thing," said Jenny in a stage Irish voice, and smiling at Declan, "to have a pious daughter who's always shakin' her head at her ould mother's lapses from grace."

Declan smiled noncommittally.

When Mellors returned with the drinks he was followed by a short, squat, waddling figure in a frilly navy blue frock; she in her turn was followed by a man, slightly taller but hardly more easy on the eye, dressed in baggy trousers that seemed to date from decades past, with shirt open at the neck, and a straw hat at a rakish angle that did nothing to dispel his air of bile and self-preoccupation. He was carrying two glasses.

"Mind if we join you?" the woman said. Jenny Birdsell nodded unenthusiastically.

"Charmayne Churton, and her brother, Ivor Aston," said Mellors, and then gestured toward Declan.

"The new handyman, Declan O'Hearn," interrupted Charmayne, a strong element of gush in her voice. "We've all heard about you."

"Not an easy job you've taken on," said her brother. "We hear that you've made an excellent start."

"Charmayne and Ivor have cottages on either side of me," said Jenny Birdsell. It seemed something of an effort to keep her voice as neutral as it was.

"We're devoted to Ranulph," said Charmayne, sitting down and producing the statement as if it were some kind of certificate or passport. "We agree on that. We sometimes *tiptoe* to the studio—with Melanie's permission, of course—just to see the work he's been doing that day."

"We'll rely on you to tell us when we can do that without disturbing him," said Ivor Aston. "Which means when he's asleep, basically. Ranulph has very acute hearing."

"Yes, I've noticed."

"We wouldn't think of trying to watch him at work. It would be intrusion. Quite apart from the fact that he would hear, and have one of his rages. To be the object of one of them would be shattering to someone of my temperament."

"Isn't it remarkable," said Stephen to no one in particular, "that my grandfather inspires such devotion?"

"Not really surprising," put in Arnold Mellors quietly, "considering he's one of the country's great artists."

"Was," said Stephen. He turned to Declan. "Grandfather feels no affection, you know. He's incapable of it. That's why it's remarkable that he manages to inspire it in others. Even my mother, whom he treats like dirt, seems genuinely fond of him. To me it's a great mystery."

"Not really a mystery," said Jenny Birdsell, her manner quite schoolteacherly, "when what we really feel—what we feel *primarily*—is not affection but admiration."

"Hmmm," said Stephen, considering that. "Partly true, I suppose, like most things. But it's not true of my mother, for one. What she feels is affection—love. It's incomprehensible."

"Love often is," said Declan feelingly. "People love the most terribly unsuitable people—husbands and wives, parents and children, brothers and sisters. And it *is* incomprehensible to outsiders. There's no logic to it, or it wouldn't be love."

Stephen shrugged.

"Maybe, maybe. But I hope when I love I don't waste it on someone who's incapable of feeling affection herself."

"Maybe someone who's incapable of loving back is a lot safer than the other kind," said Arnold Mellors.

"Safer?" said Stephen, his voice rising. "You don't understand much if you think loving my grandfather is safe. You watch it, Declan, or you'll fall victim too. Because he has one other clever trick that can be deadly—absolutely deadly."

"What's that?"

"He makes you know what he wants done without having to tell you in words. And he makes you want to do it for him."

5

IN THE BOSOM
OF HIS FAMILY

The next morning Declan took over the male nurse part of his duties for the first time: he helped Martha to get her father up, then alone he helped him to shave, dress, and relieve himself. He had had a great deal of advice the night before from Martha about what needed to be done, and what Ranulph Byatt liked or disliked in the doing of it. In the end he just went his own way, doing things as he had done them with his elderly relatives back home. Only once did he displease his charge, when he pulled the old man's trousers on little by little.

"Put them around the ankles, then pull them *up!*" he roared.

"Oh, is that how you like it, sir?" said Declan, unfazed. "Then that's how it'll be done."

The getting ready process tired Byatt, and he sat for some minutes getting his breath.

"Does my ancient body nauseate you?" he asked suddenly, looking at Declan with a loathing that seemed to be directed not at him but at himself.

"Not at all, sir," said Declan truthfully.

"Well, it ought to, a young man like you. It nauseates me. And it used to be a body capable of giving pleasure. Not just what you're thinking of, but pleasure to look at. Difficult to believe that now."

"Growing old's a nasty business, sir. The only thing nastier is *not* growing old."

It seemed touch-and-go whether Ranulph Byatt would dispute this piece of folk wisdom, but in the end he just looked at Declan thoughtfully and said, "Ye-e-es."

At around half past ten Byatt was ready for work. It was about the same time as he had been summoned the previous morning, and Declan concluded that Martha's words about not knowing when inspiration would strike were so much flimflam; it was production-line stuff he was painting, and he worked to a routine.

The couple of hours in the studio were different from the first session only insofar as Declan on the second day had to prepare the palette. He decided that the best course was to be polite, even obsequious, but firm. He never wavered in calling Byatt "sir"—indeed, it came naturally to him, so old, so different, so commanding did the artist seem to a twenty-year-old Irish boy. On the other hand, when Byatt asked for a "dash" of this color or a "dab" of that, and then bawled "too much!" Declan waited a second and then asked to be shown specifically how much a dash and a dab were. Ranulph Byatt looked at him speculatively, and then took a tube of paint and demonstrated, insofar as his shaky, pain-wracked hands were able.

The blocked shapes of the picture began to gain more substance, to look less like a scheme, more like a picture. Declan decided that if this was production-line art it was good for its kind. He did not reflect that for the first time in his life he had made an artistic judgment. When he was asked to squat, palette in hand, in easy reach of Byatt's hand, he decided that the old man's features, regarded closely again, revealed a new access of liveliness, the mouth in particular more mobile. So he was not entirely surprised when, out of the blue, the old man said, "I might go down to dinner tonight."

Without hesitation Declan came back with, "I think we can manage that."

The old man chuckled: "Surprise them."

"It will that," said Declan. "Though I'm not sure we can manage to *creep* down the stairs."

"No, they'll hear us starting down and gather at the bottom like a flock of squawking hens."

The relish and contempt in his voice were unmistakable.

"If that's what you want," said Declan.

"It *is*," he said emphatically. Then, after a pause, "I don't get much chance to spring a surprise. These days."

"If you'll just tell me what time to come and get you," said Declan, studiedly neutral.

"They bring me my tray at seven-fifteen," said the old

man. "Say a half an hour before that. One of them will be in the kitchen getting it ready. The rest will be having their sherries and their gin and tonics. I'm not allowed sherries or gin and tonics. Half a glass of gnat's piss now and then is the most the doctor will permit. I'll insist upon it tonight."

I bet you will, thought Declan to himself, and as he took the old man back to his bedroom he thought he detected a sense of pleasurable anticipation in the tired, old body. He's looking forward to making trouble, Declan decided.

Unusually, the old man demanded a second session in the studio in the afternoon. As a session it was short and unremarkable, lasting no more than half an hour, and resulting in no more than a few dabs at the fields picture. Declan assuaged his boredom by watching through the window an upright, vigorous man training a young dog at the far end of the field, not far from the stables. Declan could see him snap an order at the dog, who would then crouch down, paws forward, gazing intently at the man, who would then turn, walk away, pause, then turn back to face his animal, pause again, then bark an order. The dog would bound up to him, and be rewarded by a second-long pat on the head. Then the whole process would begin over again.

"Colonel Chesney," said Ranulph Byatt, contempt in his voice. "Bloody fool. Should have bought himself a mechanical toy. Cost less to feed."

At seven o'clock prompt Declan presented himself at the door of Byatt's bedroom. The old man had been lying down, but had not taken off any of his clothes, apart from his waistcoat and slippers. With mischief in his voice he insisted Declan put on his tie for him, and a proper jacket.

Shoes, he said regretfully, he did not think he could get on any longer. Once dressed "respectably for dinner," as he called it, they began the long walk along the landing to the head of the staircase. There they paused. Voices were coming from the sitting room where Declan had been interviewed on the first night. The door was open, but neither man could hear what was being talked about. After a minute or so Ranulph Byatt nodded to Declan and they began their descent of the stairs.

Declan had already noticed that the third stair from the top had a creak to it that a horror film producer would have coveted. The pair of them together made it more noticeable than ever. Talk stopped in the sitting room. They progressed down another stair. It had a high-pitched squeak to it. There came the sound of footsteps from the sitting room. First Martha, then an unknown man appeared in the doorway. Colonel Chesney, Declan suspected, from the determined set of his shoulders and the small military mustache. The two of them advanced to the foot of the stairs and Melanie, slower, appeared in the sitting room doorway. Of the three she seemed the least concerned, merely regarding them with a stately interest.

"Daddy, what *are* you doing?" Martha cried. "We'll be bringing your tray up in a few minutes."

"Don't bother yourselves. I'm here."

"But you know what Dr. Dinsdale says about overdoing things—"

"Are you sure this is wise, Ranulph?" asked Colonel Chesney. Then, as if retreating even before he had advanced, he added, "Would another arm be of any assistance?"

"I have a perfectly adequate arm helping me already, Chesney," said Byatt. They made the last two steps down into the hallway, and Byatt looked around him triumphantly.

"Well, Declan *has* done you good," said Melanie.

"He has. Get back to your drinks, all of you. I suppose Stephen is doing my tray. Go and tell him not to, somebody, and tell Mrs. Max there'll be an extra to dinner. And *wine*. I want wine! We'll go straight into the dining room, Declan."

Such was the force of his personality that Martha and Colonel Chesney, after a word or two of expostulation that were aborted as soon as uttered, turned and retreated back to where they had come from. Declan wondered whether Chesney was the husband that Martha was said to be hunting. Melanie watched them, amused, then hobbled through to the kitchen to alert Stephen and Mrs. Max, as the cook was always known, that there would be an extra place needed at table for dinner. Declan and Ranulph proceeded slowly along the hallway from the sitting room, then turned into the door of the dining room. Ranulph paused and looked around, seeing it for the first time in some while.

"Dark and drab and dreary and dusty," he pronounced.

Declan, who was not especially sensitive to his surroundings or critical of them, could only agree. Dark, old furniture, heavy and unstylish, drab reproductions on the walls, dismal fawn wallpaper, peeling in places. If he had been asked to describe what a prominent modern artist's home would look like, it would have been nothing like this. The room—the whole house, with the exception of the studio—was caught in a time warp and called for explanation.

The only one that Declan could come up with was that

the house had been bought, or perhaps inherited, with the existing furnishings, and that Ranulph Byatt was quite indifferent to his immediate surroundings—an indifference that had communicated itself to, or been shared by, his "womenfolk." But even if that were so, how could an artist be happy with faded and shabby old prints on his walls when in the corner of his studio, as Declan knew for sure, canvases of his own were stacked unseen?

Declan's thoughts were interrupted by Mrs. Max, who bustled in with a steaming plate of soup.

"I thought you might like to get this down you before the others come in," she said to Ranulph. "I know you have problems with soup, and the boy can help you."

Mrs. Max had problems with the name Declan, which she was unfamiliar with. Declan thought her action showed great delicacy: Ranulph would certainly not like to be spoon-fed soup in front of his family.

"I'm very much afraid 'the boy' *will* have to help," he said ruefully. "Thank you, Mrs. Max."

"It's a great pleasure to see you down again, sir," she said, turning at the door. "I hope it's to be a regular thing."

"We'll see, we'll see," said Byatt, taking his first mouthful of soup from the spoon held by Declan. "At least you're not telling me not to overdo things."

"As if that would be of any use!" said Mrs. Max. "I've known you too long to try that one. If I'm any judge you've been overdoing things since you were in nappies."

Ranulph Byatt enjoyed his soup. At one point he took the spoon from Declan and tried to feed himself, but as the spoon approached his mouth his hand began shaking and the thick brown liquid spilled back into the bowl and onto the polished table. Shaking his head but saying noth-

ing, Byatt handed the spoon back. He had not quite finished the soup when voices were heard in the hall. He
pushed the plate away from him, as a sign that he had had
enough.

They all came in, a little awkward, uncertain how to
behave in a situation they were no longer used to. Mrs.
Max hurried in first, with an extra place mat, glass of
wine, and cutlery, followed by Melanie, Martha, Stephen,
and Colonel Chesney.

"We asked Walter to stay to dinner," said Martha fuss-
ily, almost apologetically.

"He's welcome," said her father briefly, then added: "I
suppose you thought I'd behave better with him here."

"Don't be silly, Daddy. Of course you'll behave well.
Anyway, we'd asked him before you came down."

"I can attest to that, sir," said Colonel Chesney.

"Oh, you can attest to that, can you?" asked Byatt,
unable to keep the scorn out of his voice. "Then of course
I accept your attestation."

Mrs. Max brought in a heavy pewter tureen and they all
helped themselves, still awkward, to soup. Declan guessed
that if Ranulph hadn't come down Mrs. Max would have
brought in a tray of plates already filled with soup. They
began eating, Melanie being the most insouciant and normal, Stephen the least. The latter crouched over his plate,
ate as if eating was done in obedience to an order rather
than as a pleasure, and stared ahead of him in a glowering
manner as if auditioning for the young Heathcliff.

"Well!" said Byatt, watching them all without affection.
"It must be over a year."

"Since you came down to dinner? I think you're right,
Ranulph. Maybe eighteen months," said Melanie, pausing

in her eating and still the most normal in her behavior of all of them.

"And yet here everything is, exactly as it was—apart from Declan, of course. Here's you, my dear, still queening it at the head of the table, nursing the consciousness that you are the wife, soon to be the widow, of one of Britain's great artists, and trying to forgive me for refusing that knighthood that would have given you the ladyship you've been in training for all your life."

Melanie smiled pityingly.

"Dear me, Ranulph, do we have to celebrate your return by going over all those old canards? For the thousandth time, I merely thought you should accept the honor that you richly deserved, that's all."

"*More* than richly deserved. *Over*deserved!" said Byatt, his eyes flashing. "If it had been a peerage, as it should have been, I would have accepted."

A shadow briefly passed over Melanie's face, disturbing for a moment her queenly placidity. Declan decided that the emotion that prompted it must have been regret.

"You will have to be content with posterity's verdict on you as my muse, my inspiration, my sheet anchor to the world," continued Byatt. "Posterity, as a rule, can be relied on to get it wrong, but in that they would be right. You have been my inspiration, *and so much more.* . . . And then there's dear Martha—still the same, still devoted, still a martyr to duty. Where do you get that from? I wonder. Duty is a thing I've always tried to bypass, to forget about entirely, and I've found that very easy to do. Duty hasn't loomed at all large either in my dear wife's scheme of things—her moral universe, as you might say, though with the rider that a universe has never been smaller than my wife's moral one. I suppose we shall have to blame the grandparents as usual. My father was a dreary little man, the sort of person who worries if he's five minutes late at the office, and works five minutes over to make it up."

Declan, who was cutting up the steak, which was the main course for his employer, flushed. He was used to family rows, but cruelty in the O'Hearn household was direct, brutal. This cruelty nestled under a civilized, urbane exterior. It was, he sensed, the more deadly for that.

"But at least there's something now in your life since I was last in this room, isn't there? The husband hunt! And that really is something new and important, because it can go on for the rest of your life. It will give you an interest until senility breaks out, and you may be on your deathbed and you will still not have got anywhere with it."

Martha Mates looked down at her plate, flushing, and began to cut determinedly at her meat.

"You're cruel," said Stephen Mates.

"Yes," said Byatt. Declan thought he was going to leave it at that—as well he might, in Declan's view—but he added: "To be realistic is to be cruel."

"You can be realistic but simply make the judgment in your own mind," said Stephen.

"But that would be to dodge the issue, wouldn't it? Silence assumes consent, assumes complicity with lies and fantasies. Such as that you, Colonel, will ever be a painter."

"There is no such fantasy on my part, I assure you," said Colonel Chesney in clipped yet somehow heartfelt tones. "Pure dabbling, I realize only too well."

"Yes, you are to painting what Florence Foster-Jenkins was to singing and William McGonagall was to poetry," said Byatt, his meal pushed aside, sitting in a pensive and somehow doubly dangerous pose. "Or Stephen is to any intellectual endeavor."

Stephen sat still. He had, his body language suggested, been waiting for this, and now his burning eyes showed only an eagerness to get it over.

"Stephen's delusion is rare," said his grandfather, with the magisterial wisdom of old age and long experience. "It's common enough to come across people who are convinced they can sing, or act, or paint, when they haven't the first idea. But it's very seldom that someone with a mediocre brain is convinced he's one of the world's great minds."

"Of course Stephen doesn't think anything of the sort," said Martha.

"But how else can one explain his determination to grace one of the world's great centers of learning? It's not as though he hasn't had people trying to get the message of his mediocrity across to him in the course of his life. Schoolmasters have tried: his reports were uniformly unenthusiastic, and his exam results pretty much what those reports predicted. Family and friends have taken him aside and tried to tell him he'd be happier if he didn't aim so high. But to no avail: the message has never got across. My grandson's education has to culminate in Oxford, no less."

"It's hardly an outrageous ambition," said Martha. "Lots of people have it, and Stephen's father went there."

"Oh, yes, indeed. If Stephen's father hadn't gone there he'd have had no chance at all of going there himself. Leeds offered, Reading offered, Essex—God help us— offered. But, no, it had to be Brasenose College, and since their enthusiasm for the son of their undistinguished old boy was minimal, it had to be done by the usual sordid bargain which has secured mediocrities a place at Oxford over the years: the bribery in this case being a large—large to *me*—sum of money to refurbish the library, and the gift of one of my best paintings."

"You swindled them," said Stephen, the contempt in his voice undisguised. "The picture wasn't from your red period, as you claimed."

"The whole deal was a swindle," said Byatt complacently. "Swindling swindlers is a venial sin in my book. And so in October Stephen will go up to Oxford, with all the prestige that that implies, and with a self-assessment as a first-rate brain. And I, who have shelled out the bribe that got him in there, will shell out his upkeep there, and probably shell out for debts he incurs by mixing with the sort of fast set outside his class that he probably thinks all brilliant young Oxonians have to be in with. What a prospect! And all because Stephen, who is the child of mediocrity, has convinced himself that he has a great brain and deserves a place among the great minds of this country."

Stephen sat for a moment, considering his response. Then he stood up, crumpled his napkin, and made for the door. In the doorway he turned. He had at least, Declan decided, a considerable sense of drama, of using his body and his hatred to make an effect; he looked, standing there, surprisingly large, menacing, and forceful. He directed his gaze with loathing on his grandfather.

"If I was a mediocrity I would probably worship you. Because that's the type you attract: people who are nothing very much, and people who are weak, pliable, mal-

leable. That's the sort all tin-pot dictators surround themselves with. You can't stand me around because I'm not
like that. You're willing to buy me a place at Oxford
because I'm the only one here who sees you as you are:
sheer poison. You're cyanide made flesh. You're vitriol in
human shape. You kill the spirit of everyone around you.
That's why I have to get out."

The door banged behind him.

"He doesn't mean it," said Martha feebly. "He's just
going through a phase." Her father ignored her.

"Well!" he said, in a voice that sounded almost happy.
"The boy is developing a vocabulary. I expect he's set himself the task of studying the thesaurus for half an hour
over breakfast. That's the sort of thing mediocrities do."

And as they were toiling up the stairs when the meal
was over Ranulph said nothing about the scene he had
just manufactured, still less apologized for it, but he did
say cheerfully, "I think I'll begin a new picture tomorrow.
Something a little less factory-made. Something *angry*."

6

THE DISCIPLES

As he pottered around Ashworth and the surrounding country in the days that followed, Declan began to fall into a routine. He realized as he got his bearings on the place that he now knew people in all the dwellings that made up the little community. Mrs. Birdsell, in the row of three tiny cottages, had Ivor Aston on one side of her and his sister Charmayne Churton on the other. The siblings were together yet not together, it seemed. Declan had a strong impression that Jenny Birdsell did not relish the closeness of the pair. Arnold Mellors had a rather larger cottage built on to one end of the main farmhouse. He asked Declan in for a drink one evening, and they talked in a relaxed and general way—politics, weather, painting, but nothing directly about Ranulph Byatt. The relaxed nature of the talk was something Declan never felt with Colonel Chesney, mainly because the man himself never was. He lived in a semidetached cottage, the other half of which was occupied by Mrs. Max. They nodded to each other if they passed or met on their front doorsteps, sometimes chatted in the lane, but they did not seem close in any way except geographically.

Stephen was someone Declan saw little of. After the scene at dinner he seemed to make himself as scarce as possible, ranging the fields and moors, his camera slung over his shoulder, or shut up in his room reading. Any "natural" closeness between two young men, both apparently without any circle of friends, was avoided and when they met he was polite to Declan, no more. His hobby, photography, was not one that could bring them together, Declan being ham-fisted with a camera. If Stephen went out to a pub it was with people from Ashworth, and Declan felt he did not want to get involved with any drinking set in his immediate vicinity. So he avoided the pub in Stanbury and roamed the district if he fancied a beer after the evening meal, sampling pubs in Crossroads, Oakworth, and Oxenhope. There he found uncomplicated conversation, companionship that might or might not blossom, and even now and then an audience: with a badly out-of-tune piano to accompany him he sang Irish ballads and folk songs in Oakworth, and was told by more than one beery customer that he ought to go professional. After that he sometimes took his guitar with him on these excursions.

It was in a pub in Crossroads, oddly enough, that he met Jenny Birdsell's daughter, Mary Ann. She came in in full Salvation Army gear, in the company of an older man wearing the male equivalent, and together they went around the two bars rattling their collection boxes and selling *The War Cry*. Declan was among the last to have the box thrust under his nose, and he was surprised when the girl said, "I know you."

"Do you?" he asked, looking up at a pleasant but insignificant face behind round rimless spectacles. "I don't think—"

"You're the new help at Ashworth, looking after that dreadful old sinner."

Declan felt awkward.

"He's probably that, but he treats me fine and we get on OK. How do you know?"

"I've seen you around. From my bedroom window. I'm Mary Ann Birdsell, by the way."

"Declan O'Hearn."

Mary Ann made a quick decision, handed her box to her partner, and sat down.

"I've finished for the day, Jack. See you same time tomorrow."

Declan thought he ought to buy her a drink, and he got up, feeling in his pocket for coins from his first week's wages.

"You don't have to," said the girl. "They won't turn me out or anything. Well, a Coke if you must."

When he got back from the bar with her drink she was sitting on her bench seat, her mouth primly set, her hands clasped in front of her on the table. She was looking around her at the locals, nearly all of whom she seemed to know.

"Do you often drink in pubs?" Declan asked.

"Quite often. Why not? I go round pubs twice a week, trying to bring people to salvation."

"No reason, of course. What else do you do?"

"We bear witness in Keighley market twice a week, and we do a lot of work among the homeless—"

"No, I meant what else do you do apart from, well, this?"

"Apart from my Christian witness? I work in the SPCK bookshop in Keighley. I have decided that my whole life must be devoted to Jesus. It's the only way I can give it a meaning. You don't find that?"

"Well, no."

"You will," she said with serene confidence. "I'm sure you *will* find Him, perhaps quite soon. You must feel the need to, to get you out of the terrible atmosphere at Ashworth. I'm there as little as possible—that's why we've never met. We call on sinners to repent, but to be always in their company is to invite contagion."

"I'm not sure I see the Ashworth people as sinners," said Declan.

"Then you can't have met them yet. But you've seen Ranulph. He's the greatest sinner of all."

"He's nothing but a poor old man sliding toward death," said Declan with conviction. Mary Ann shook her head vigorously. "But there's one thing I have noticed about the Ashworth people."

"What's that?"

"Almost all of them are alone," said Declan. "The two old men, Chesney and Mellors. The brother and sister, living close but not together. Mrs. Max, who Martha tells me has a son, but he's not with her. Even the four at the farm seem to live in separate worlds: you'd think there'd be something between mother and daughter, mother and son, but there's really practically nothing, not a spark. You and your mother—"

"We're the most alone of all."

"That's what I suspected."

"Of course, I'm not alone now I've found the path to Jesus. You can't be alone with Him, can you? But before that . . . And when we're together in the house we . . . we have nothing to say to each other."

"Why is that, do you think?"

"Why is what?"

"Why does Ranulph Byatt seem to attract these lonely types around him?"

She shrugged.

"I suppose he is a sort of false messiah. Mrs. Max is different: she has a son, like you say, and he's grown up, got a job in Burnley, and moved away. Nothing odd there. They're close, even if they don't live together any longer, and they're quite normal. But the others seem to need something in their lives, and they've chosen him. They need to find the True Way, but they blind themselves to it."

"How long has the community been in existence?"

"Community? That's not a community. Just a collection of sad, lost people. Ranulph inherited the house and cottage from an admirer about fifteen years ago. An old lady who loved his early landscapes. He moved then, and the rest of us have moved in over the years. But I think many of them have been sort of around him for years before that."

"What do you mean 'around him'?"

"I mean known admirers of his work who were sometimes admitted to the Presence. People living off of the crumbs from his table. My mother is typical. She went to an exhibition of his work at the Hayward Gallery in 1982, and she's been a sort of groupie of his ever since. It's pathetic."

"So let me get this straight—Ranulph Byatt inherited the farm and all the cottages from an admirer?"

"Yes, an elderly spinster, as you might have guessed."

"Right. And all the cottages were empty?"

"Derelict, more like. Ashworth hasn't been worked as a farm since just after the war."

"So he had them done up and let them to admirers?"

"Yes, bit by bit. Sometimes they did the renovations themselves: Chesney did, and my mother did all the interior decorating. People use words like 'striking,' which is their way of avoiding saying it's embarrassingly awful."

"And they all pay him rent?"

"Of course. Ranulph likes money and Melanie *adores* it. The rent they charge isn't exorbitant, but it's certainly at market level."

"I'm beginning to get the picture. He needs admiration, and currently he needs money as well. He's managed to get both. And have Martha and Stephen always lived with her father?"

"Pretty much so, I think." She wrinkled her brow and looked very young indeed. "Certainly since Stephen's father took off. But I'm not sure they weren't all living with him and Melanie even before that."

"He keeps his hold on people," commented Declan.

"Not on me, he doesn't," piped up Mary Ann. "I've escaped." She beamed around. Declan wondered whether escape was possible: whether she might still be chained by hatred and opposition, like Stephen, or whether she might simply have jumped from one bondage to another.

"But what are we talking about us for? You'll find out everything about us soon enough, and by then you'll probably want to leave. Tell me about yourself."

But Declan wasn't going to tell her any more about himself and his family than he had told the other Ashworth people. That was something he always preferred to keep under cover. And he'd found that if he talked about Ireland—about small Irish villages, about the priest and the schoolteacher, the pub and the church—he could flannel most people into thinking he'd been telling them about himself. In general folks were interested but had little idea about the country, apart from notions picked up from *Ballykissangel* on television. They usually liked his stories, and Mary Ann certainly did. The topic lasted them through another half for Declan, and on the walk back to Ashworth. But as Declan watched Mary Ann inserting her front door key into the door, she said, "You really must tell me about yourself some time."

As he waited till she was safely in, then turned back toward the farmhouse, Declan meditated that the fact that the girl had got a bad dose of fundamentalist religion shouldn't lead him to assume that she was stupid.

His working hours as well as his free time were developing into a routine. Outdoor work, which came before and after his sessions with Byatt if it was fine, came to be a matter of seeing what needed to be done and doing it. Melanie and Martha did not intervene, unless there was something needed doing, like repair of furniture in their bedrooms, which he could not know about. His independence seemed to suit not just him but the ladies as well:

they had their own business and their own preoccupations, though Declan had no idea what they were. So he pottered around the house, mending things that were broken, giving emergency first aid to things that were going in that direction, and on fine days he gratefully took himself out into the open air.

In the gardens and field, though he was often bent double, he could better observe what he still thought of as "the community." He was also more exposed to advances from its members. These advances did not change his opinion of the essential loneliness of everyone at Ashworth: it was because they were solitary that they pestered him with unwanted attention. But he also began to get the idea that each of them had some kind of function in the group of acolytes. From glimpsing the mail on Mellors's table when he had been there, and from seeing him drive off in the Byatts' car with canvases stored on the backseat, he got the idea that Mellors was Byatt's intermediary with galleries and other potential sellers. That car, though unreliable, seemed to be the only car at Ashworth. It was very old, and Stephen tinkered unconvincingly with it now and then in the stables. Charmayne, sometimes with Mrs. Max in tow, seemed to do most of the shopping, to collect prescriptions and get them made up, and to take anyone who needed anything major such as clothes or books or new electrical appliances to Bradford or Keighley to get them.

Jenny Birdsell was used as a second-string nurse when Melanie and Martha were exhausted. She was called on less often now that Declan was installed, but he still found her officiating upstairs from time to time when he came back of an evening. She had that artificially bright tone he associated with nurses of a bygone era ("Before I was born," he said vaguely to himself, being too young to have much idea of time or history). He himself instinctively preferred a lower-keyed, more natural approach when he was around his charge, and he thought it both more appropriate and more modern.

The function of Colonel Chesney and Ivor Aston in the little community he reserved judgment on, only registering that Chesney appeared to serve as a butt for Ranulph Byatt's blackest jokes, yet didn't seem to resent it, and that Ivor Aston was the only one whose pictures showed any signs of talent. Another artistic judgment, but he made it the more confidently because he was so sure everyone else's pictures were self-evidently awful. Also he told himself that he seemed to be getting an eye for paintings.

It was Charmayne Churton who showed herself most keen on having the sort of chat that might go any deeper than conventionalities or mere Ranulph worship. She watched Declan when he was mowing the back paddock one day, and when he came close to her side of the field, she said, "You look as if you could do with a break. Feel like a tea or coffee?"

Declan paused. He was certainly feeling tired and sweaty. He detected no lust in Charmayne's voice. He had no taste for being lusted after by middle-aged women, particularly (it had unfashionably to be said) by fat middle-aged women who had all the fleshly allure of a tugboat. He was conventional in his tastes.

"Thanks," he said. "That would be great."

He took his muddy shoes off on the doorstep, and once he got inside saw that this had been the right move. The ground floor of the tiny cottage had been turned into a combined living space and kitchen, and the decor was twee in the extreme: flowery curtains and furnishings that were definitely pre–Laura Ashley, frilly lampshades and antimacassars, with cozy and humorous pictures of animals covering the walls. He was willing to bet that the china would be decorated with tiny flowers and very thin, and when Charmayne came back with a tray, that was exactly what it was.

"This is cozy!" she said cheerily.

A sight too cozy, thought Declan gloomily. The only thing that wasn't cozy was Charmayne herself. Changing the image in his mind, he told himself that her body had all the grace of a concrete mixer, even though it was clad in a billowy navy dress with the odd tape or streamer hanging down in the same material from random parts of it, suggesting that if you pulled one the dress would either fall to the floor or draw apart, like curtains. Declan put the thought from him.

"You take sugar, I bet," said Charmayne in a conspiratorial, brown owl sort of voice. "Help yourself. How are you getting on at the big house?"

"Really well," said Declan with rather more confidence than he felt. "Mr. Byatt and I don't have any problems with each other. Not so far, anyway."

"Call him Ranulph. We all do, when we are not in the Presence." She giggled. "What is he painting now?"

"He's just finished a painting of fields. He's looking at old pictures of his now, and photographs. I think it will be a painting of a seashore with cliffs. Though he's also talking about painting something angry. He was going to begin last week, but he says he's got to meditate it a lot more."

"How exciting!" said Charmayne, relentlessly girlish. "I would so like . . . but it's naughty of me to ask!"

"What?"

"To *tiptoe* in some time when Ranulph is asleep and won't be disturbed, to have a peek at the work in progress."

"You mentioned that. You'd have to ask Melanie. It's her house."

"I suppose so. It's just that she always asks my brother at the same time as she asks me. I'd so like to *drink* in a new painting on my own."

"You'd have to sort that out yourselves," said Declan doggedly, ignoring the disappointment in her pale green eyes.

"If you say so. Of course, I do realize that Ivor is much more of an artist than I am. My own work"—she waved her arm around the room—"is popular art, and it doesn't even have the merit of being particularly popular!"

She laughed, a hollow sound that embarrassed Declan. He got up to hide his discomfiture and looked at the pictures which crowded the walls to an extent that suggested their unsalability. They were all of animals—moles, badgers, foxes, hamsters, mingling with the more frequent dogs and cats—and even when the creatures were not wearing aprons or policemen's helmets or chefs' hats they were given a human touch that some might have thought delightful, others might have considered landed the pictures in no-man's-land where the animals were interesting neither as animals nor as humans. Declan sat down again and took up his tea.

"I do sell some," said Charmayne, unnerved by his lack of the conventional politenesses. "To greeting card manu-

facturers, or people who make pottery for children. I make
no claims for them."

"They're . . . very pretty," said Declan.

"Oh, they're nothing. Of course as I say, I realize that
Ivor is much more of an artist, but I always feel . . ." She
paused, threw him a look that was birdlike, and could be
imagined coming from a carrion crow, and then leaned
unpleasantly forward in her chair. "I don't know whether
you've *heard*."

"Heard?"

"About Ivor. Well, you're bound to hear sooner or later,
so I may as well tell you." Declan was not so innocent of
the big world that he didn't recognize this ploy. He found
the relish with which the woman thrust herself still farther forward distasteful. "He's been inside. For quite a
long while."

"I see," said Declan. He felt himself being willed to ask
what for, so he said nothing.

Charmayne looked disconcerted, but then flicked her
tongue all the way around her lips.

"For possessing and disseminating material calculated
to deprave and corrupt. Child porn. Kiddies doing awful
things and having unspeakable things done to them.
Doesn't it make you sick?"

"It's . . . very unpleasant," ventured Declan. It was a
subject on which you could hardly say less.

"I brought him here to live with me because he needs
*some*one, but . . . well, we've never *jelled*, if you know what
I mean. And it's always seemed to me that in Ivor's pictures there are . . . traces of his obsession, his tastes, if you
catch my meaning."

It would be difficult not to.

"I must be going," said Declan, setting his cup and saucer down on the table and beginning the process of getting up. Charmayne Churton ignored him. She was gazing ahead of her in a pose of deep thought, as if meditating a pronouncement.

"I can accept that depravity can contribute to great art," she said, as if she were fulfilling an engagement at Delphi. "But when it contributes to third-rate art it neither enriches it nor excuses itself."

Declan slipped out to return to his mowing. He did not meditate on Charmayne's words because he had already decided there was no meaning to them. What did interest him was her relationship with her brother: being jealous of him, broadcasting his unsavory past, yet sticking close to him, in some way *needing* him. There were relationships in Declan's own family that made him recognize the twin, contradictory impulses, though he could not explain them.

That evening Ranulph Byatt was too tired to go down to dinner. Having heard the women go down the stairs Declan went along to the bathroom to put a flannel over his face, only to find Stephen there cleaning his teeth.

"Hi," he said, waiting.

"Hi." Stephen spat out toothpaste and water. "I saw you going into Charmayne's cottage this afternoon. George medals have been awarded for less."

"Just for a cup of tea."

"I should hope so. Well, at least you got out alive."

Declan grinned, playing it cool.

"She didn't make any advances. In fact, I didn't get the idea that was what she was interested in."

"No, straightforward lust isn't the Ashworth gang's besetting sin."

"Isn't it?" said Declan. Then, feeling rather daring, he added: "But husband hunting is what your grandfather accuses your mother of."

Stephen stood up and looked at him, an expression of amused incredulity on his face.

"Isn't language a strange thing? Is that the idea you got? That my mother is desperate to find a new husband?"

"What else could I think? That is what your grandfather said, isn't it?"

"It's what he said. But his meaning was quite different. He wasn't saying she was desperate to find a new husband. He was saying she was desperate to find her old one."

7

STRAWS IN THE WIND

"So what do you think?" said Ranulph Byatt to Declan about a week later, during a morning session in the studio.

Declan toyed with the idea of buying time by saying "Think?" but rejected it. Byatt was old, but he was not a fool. By now they understood each other very well, could almost be said to like each other, and Declan knew that he was being asked his opinion of the situation at Ashworth.

"I think you've got yourself a little group of disciples here," he said, "without . . . without seeming to want them."

Ranulph laughed wheezily.

"You were going to say 'without doing anything to deserve them,'" he said, in a tone of good humor. "That's not true. My painting got me my disciples."

"Of course," said Declan. "But you don't feel the need to be nice to them, treat them well."

"I don't. They're fools. Admiring my paintings, or anybody's paintings, is no guarantee of high intelligence. Fools they remain. Encourage fools and you confirm them in their foolishness. What else do you think?"

Declan considered. He realized he was being asked to bring into the open any stray thoughts he had about his employer's habits and situation.

"You're a painter, but you don't seem to care about your surroundings."

"You mean the house I live in? I'm too old, I don't care any longer, I don't like fuss. As you probably know by now I was bequeathed this place by a silly old thing who thought I painted beautiful landscapes, and I just left it as it was."

"Yet you've a stack of pictures in the corner there, and others around the house just piled up. For some reason you don't feel the need to put them on the walls."

Ranulph Byatt shrugged.

"Now you are sounding naive. Not every picture is to be lived with, certainly not all of mine," he said. "And most of the recent stuff is not worth hanging."

"Yet you go on painting."

The old man stared up fiercely, waving his paintbrush in Declan's face.

"Of course I go on painting. It's my whole existence, the thing everything in my life has been *about*. It's the only thing that keeps me alive, mentally alive. If I couldn't paint at all I'd—take something. And who knows? Something may come back, the spark light itself again, or whatever silly, inadequate image one uses for the glory of being able to paint. Meanwhile"—he gestured at the canvas—"the junk keeps the wolf from the door."

"I'm sure you're not in want."

"What would you know about it? Do you think I should just live off the old age pension or something?"

"No, of course not."

"I've always been used to the best—well, not always, but for years now: the best wines, the best food, someone making sure of my well-being. Living comfortably is what Melanie expects, and she's right. Even that fool Stephen is right in his way: the grandson of Ranulph Byatt should go to Oxford, even if the college has to be bribed to take him. It's a matter of pride, my boy, knowledge of my rightful place. I'm not having a grandson of mine going to the Polytechnic of Solihull, just as I wouldn't be fobbed off with a mere knighthood."

"I see, sir," said Declan, who found the sentiments prehistoric.

"But it all costs money," said Byatt ruefully.

"Maybe Stephen shouldn't be thinking about university at all."

Byatt grinned bitterly.

"Maybe you would be right—if he had other skills. He hasn't even got what today they call 'social skills.' He can't get on with people, and nobody likes him. He's no bent for selling things, or making money out of thin air, like the yuppies used to. And he hasn't got a smidgen of creative talent. No, universities are made for people like him.

If you've got the responsibility for a boy without any of the talents, you buy time, and maybe a third-class degree to boot, and you hope you're dead by the time a decision has to be made. . . . If only Catriona had lived."

"Catriona?"

Byatt was looking ahead, a sharp, unfathomable expression on his face. Declan looked at him as intently as he dared, and wondered if what he was seeing, for the first time, was a sign of love. If so it was not a sort of love he recognized.

"My other daughter. The brilliant one dies, and the fool lives on. Punishment, do you think? It's like a sort of bargain: I'll give you all *this*"—he waved his hand around the studio, as if it symbolized all his creative gifts—"and I'll surround you with fools. Beethoven seems to have had plenty of fools around him, and Dickens too. I bet Shakespeare did as well, and he *married* one, which no one could say I did. . . ."

Declan registered the sort of artistic fraternity in which Ranulph Byatt would like to include himself but he was in truth only half listening. He was watching the man's hands. On the canvas was suggested the broad outlines of a cliff landscape, but they were outlines only: nothing had been filled in when they resumed work that morning. But in the past few minutes Byatt had been worrying at the blue and white and gray tints on his palette, and now he began in the bottom right-hand corner of the picture to paint a boiling, surging foam, a sea both angry and destructive, and he did it with strokes that had an energy and range such as Declan had never seen in all the twenty or more sessions they had had in the studio thus far.

Byatt didn't speak again, but worked in silence until he

signaled that he wanted to be taken back to his room. Once there he made Declan take him straight to his bed, where he lay down, still fully clothed, and immediately went off to sleep. Declan diagnosed complete exhaustion, and tiptoed to the door. It was a revelation to him of how creative work at a high pitch could drain body as well as mind.

That evening Stephen came to dinner, knowing that his grandfather had said that he was too tired to. He made no contribution to the conversation, and sat immersed in his own thoughts—not glowering (which he could do very powerfully, when he had a mind to), but mentally absent on other business.

"I see that work has started on the new picture," said Melanie in her social voice, over a starter of duck pâté.

"Yes, isn't that marvelous!" chipped in Martha. Both women looked toward Declan.

"He started on the sea quite suddenly," he said. "I'd thought it was going to be a summer scene, but he seized the brush and suddenly I saw it was a very rough sea—stormy, wintry, all froth and foam. He was going at it with great energy for twenty minutes or so, using actions I didn't know were in him, not any longer. I'm afraid he tired himself out."

Melanie nodded wisely, asserting her role as the one who knew him best.

"That's the problem," she said. "But of course if he's doing good work that compensates him."

"Of course."

"What had he been talking about?"

"Oh—" Declan stopped when he realized that if he mentioned Ranulph's dead daughter, he could distress her mother and sister. "Oh—old family matters."

Melanie was not deceived or put off.

"Was it Catriona?"

"Yes, it was."

Martha made a noise into her plate. Declan decided it was a sob. Melanie looked at her, then went back to her food.

"What was the letter you had this morning?" she finally asked Martha, as Mrs. Max cleared away plates.

"Oh, just my man in Peckham."

"Your private detective in Peckham," said Melanie with scorn in her voice. "Doesn't it sound seedy? Something out of Muriel Spark. I presume he had no news?"

"He thinks I ought to go down and have a talk with him before too long," said Martha. "Discuss strategies."

"He has no news, but he's stringing you along."

Martha pursed her lips.

"You really ought to be glad, Mother, if I can save Daddy some of the expense of Stephen's education."

"To do that you will have to first find Morgan, he will then have to be in reasonable financial circumstances, and you will then have to begin the process of extracting money from him. Stephen, if he gets a degree at all, will be graduated and, one would hope, started in a profession before we will see a penny."

Martha's face assumed an expression of obstinacy, or rather its habitual expression was intensified.

"I don't anticipate it taking anything like as long as that. In any case, we can recoup the money retrospectively. It's right that Stephen's father should pay for his education."

Melanie sighed. Her attitude resembled her husband's when he talked about being surrounded by fools.

"You've been happy enough to rely on your father for the last twenty years, Martha. Even when he was around, Morgan was hardly a whiz kid financially. He found it difficult to earn anything, and if by any chance he did he was reluctant to let go of it any way except across a bar. You're on to a very bad wicket, Martha."

"That's not what my man in Peckham says."

Melanie sighed theatrically.

"He wouldn't, would he? I really don't know why you need this. You've got plenty of interests."

"The Women's Institute," said Martha, her voice tinged with bitterness. "Oh, yes—I do get a great deal of stimulation from the Women's Institute."

The rest of the meal passed largely in silence, but as they got up after the gooseberry fool, Melanie turned to Declan.

"Catriona was our elder daughter. She died in an accident many years ago."

"He told me she was dead, but not how."

"It is better Ranulph doesn't talk about it."

"He brought it up himself. It's difficult to—"

"Of course Ranulph is not to be contradicted," said Melanie, as if this were something laid down in the Pentateuch. "But don't bring it up yourself, and if he does, try to lead him tactfully away from the subject."

"I'll try," said Declan, mentally adding that in his view Ranulph Byatt was the most unleadable person he had ever had to do with. Declan lingered behind in the dining room while the women went out slowly, Martha adapting her pace to Melanie's, her bitterness seeming evaporated. At the door they turned toward the living room. Declan followed Stephen up the stairs.

"Do you remember your father?" he asked him. Stephen paused at the bend of the flight, his face a mask of blank mystification. Declan realized he hadn't the slightest idea what had been talked about at dinner. At last he said, "I suppose if I do at all it's as a *presence*, a shape. Anything I know about him comes from things I've been told."

"That wouldn't necessarily be reliable."

Stephen shrugged.

"A child's memories wouldn't necessarily be reliable either. Everyone seems to agree he was nothing very much, and if my mother does succeed in finding him she'll be in for a big disappointment. Someone has said that his most likely address is cardboard city. Still, I suppose it gives her an interest."

"Is that what she needs?"

Stephen shot him a look that said he was getting much too interested in family matters.

"It's a lot healthier than being obsessed with her own father."

He turned abruptly, marched up the remaining stairs, and went to his bedroom, slamming the door.

Declan had thought to go out that evening, but then decided against it. He lay on his bed reading Wilbur Smith until he heard Stephen leave his bedroom, closing the door more quietly this time, then tripping down the stairs and out the front door. Declan lay his book on the little table beside the bed.

The women, he was sure, were still downstairs. He opened the door quietly. The landing was dimly lit as usual. From Ranulph's bedroom he could hear the familiar sound of stertorous breathing. He closed his door and walked lightly along the length of the corridor toward the studio. The door was shut, as he had left it, but it opened quietly, and in the deepening twilight he felt for the light switch. The room flooded with artificial light, making the encroaching night outside seem blacker. On the stand was the new canvas, with the raging sea already painted and pointing excitingly forward to a disturbing picture. But it wasn't the new canvas that interested Declan.

He crossed the room to the corner where the older paintings were stacked. He bent down to go through them, but found that even the bright studio light didn't penetrate to this corner powerfully enough for him to get a good view on a mere flip through the stacked canvases. He stood up and began going through them one by one, holding them at arm's length, so as to take them in.

The ones at the outer end of the stack seemed to be recent ones: they *felt* new, smelled new, and were natural scenes, not unlike the two paintings Declan already knew. He decided these were paintings that had not yet been sent for sale, or perhaps ones that Ranulph adjudged failures even by the lowered standards applied to his current work. That latter judgment seemed to him justified when he went farther into the stack, and decided that the older pictures there seemed to his inexpert eye all unsatisfactory in some way.

Declan nearly gave up but, stifling his disappointment, he persisted. The pictures he was looking at were simply framed in a thin wooden band, but he saw that farther back there were more elaborate frames. He took up the first of these, however, without any great feeling of anticipation.

The picture hit him. It was like getting a sock on the

jaw from someone you'd just been having a decorous conversation with. He stood there paralyzed by a horrific
energy. The painting spilled over from the canvas onto the
frame, with red and black daubed roughly over the dark,
handsome wood. Red predominated on the canvas too,
but gradually Declan perceived other elements: two
touches of blue came to suggest eyes, strands of brown
crisscrossing down the picture from top to bottom suggested disheveled hair. He stood transfixed: this was a
face, but it was not a living face. It was a face that was
dead, and dead in a horrible way. It was, he felt sure,
recently dead: it was viewed as a sudden nightmare dis-
covery. It was a scream of—what?—surprised horror, or
gut-wrenching shock. And slowly, as he gazed on, the
frame became not just nominally but really part of the picture: the face was seen through an opening—quite what
sort of an opening, Declan was unable to decide. It
seemed more than just a hole or a gap. Some jagged lines
of bluish white low down in the picture suggested broken
glass. Looking, trying to let the picture tell him something, Declan became convinced he was looking at a face
through a window. A broken window. Of course, it suddenly came to him: a *car* window. A road accident—and
was this the face of the elder daughter of the family?

"And what exactly do you think you're doing, young
man?"

"Sure I felt I was frozen to the spot, Patrick," wrote Declan
next evening to his favorite brother, the one a year older
than himself, the one to whom he felt closest. "It wasn't
just the surprise—how the old woman had got up those

stairs without my hearing her, I'll never know, but I suppose I was so taken up with the picture I heard nothing—
it was the whole look of her, standing there with her back
as straight as a ramrod, and her voice too, the tone of it. It
was cold, threatening, like a judge's when he's going to
hand out a really tough sentence. Like Father Rafferty at
school, when you'd done something that really riled him.
All I could do was stammer out that I wanted to look at the
pictures because I was hoping there would be a really
good one, one he'd done when he was in his prime, so I
could see why he was considered such a great artist.

"That seemed to satisfy Melanie (that's what she tells
me to call her, though it's difficult, and doesn't seem right,
her being so old). Her whole body relaxed, but she said, 'I
think you've seen enough for today,' and waited while I
put the picture back in place and went out onto the landing. She turned off the light, then waited while I walked
back to my bedroom. I swear it was like those stories of
boarding school we used to read, with me as the boy who's
been up to something, and her as the matron!

"I felt upset, because they'd all been so nice to me up to
then. Making me comfortable, like, and I appreciated that
because I don't think it's really in their natures to make
people comfortable—or to be comfortable, come to that.
They're more prickly than companionable, if you take my
meaning. But Melanie and Martha had always been nice
to me, and said how well I was doing. 'I realize you won't
be here forever,' Melanie said once, 'but Martha and I
enjoy the rest while you *are* here.' And then to come down
so heavy just because I was taking a look at the great
man's pictures! He's an artist, for God's sake. Doesn't he
want people looking at his pictures?

"Sometimes I think they're mad as hatters, Patrick. Sometimes I catch him looking at me, and it's like he's sizing me up to make a picture out of me, though he says he doesn't paint portraits. I can't put it into words, but it's like I'm with people who are out on an entirely different wavelength from mine. And I'm on my own trying to get the hang of them. I miss having you to fight my battles for me, the way you always used to. I've never felt so alone in my life!"

8

STORM CLOUDS

Declan felt more than a little chastened next morning, during the painting session with Ranulph. He did not know how much of his visit of curiosity to the studio the night before had been reported to the painter. He hoped nothing at all, and certainly there was at first no observable difference in Byatt's behavior, which surely there would have been if he had known. He was quiet, and volunteered no confidences and no reprimand. The routine in the studio was the same as it had been every day since Declan had come to Ashworth. Declan got him to his chair, and then stood silent while the old man surveyed the canvas. He could see him contemplating the space that would become the sky, and he imagined him seeing it with his mind's eye: an angry, vengeful expanse of gray-and-black cloud flecked with white. But in the end Byatt settled on the cliff top as his next area of concern, and had Declan mix up a dark green mixture of shades, and began applying it, with black streaks, to the central area of the picture.

Yet there *was* a difference. Declan didn't notice it until he was squatting, back to the canvas, presenting the palette for his employer's use. Normally he could have been a dumbwaiter or a hat stand for all the visual notice that his employer took of him—he might talk to him, a phrase or two, or shout at him, insult him, even, but he never looked at him with the slightest interest beyond that of seeing that the palette was being held in the best position for his work. When he gave him the looks that Declan had reported to his brother was at other times, when he was helping Ranulph to dress, for example, or getting him into bed. That day, however, he twice contemplated Declan for some time—really looked at his face, as if he was trying to fix it in his mind's eye. Whatever he may have said about portraiture, Declan could not help wondering if he was being looked at with a view to a picture in the future. He felt he was being sized up not by one person judging another, but by a painter judging a subject. The experience made him uneasy.

The next day Ranulph expressed dissatisfaction with the green of the cliff top, and sat glumly in front of the picture for some time.

"I should have gone at the sky first."

Declan wondered whether to say he had expected him to, but thought he shouldn't venture into the practicalities of picture making. So he just said, "The sky should be really interesting." Byatt's response was something close to a harrumph.

Grays and blacks and blues were the chosen colors of the day, and Ranulph went at the top of the picture with a will that took the form of excitement, tension, and aggression, emotions that alternately seemed to take control of his frail body.

"Keep still, you bloody fool!" he bawled at Declan at one point. Declan, who had not moved, continued to do nothing.

At the end of the session the area around the cliff top had been painted: a lowering, changing, threatening sky, but flecked as Declan had imagined it with white. The area farther away and closer to the frame remained to be done. Declan wondered whether the sky would spill over onto the frame before the picture was finished. At one point Byatt muttered, "The cliff top will have to be done over," but at the end of the session Declan was gratified to see for the first time Byatt looking at the results of his morning's work with something approaching satisfaction. It was a revelation, the happiness, the savage happiness, on his face. Declan was still more surprised when the old painter said, "Tell Ivor Aston he can come and take a look."

Declan had in fact seldom spoken to Ivor Aston since the evening in the Grange.

"I'm sure he'll be happy to do that," he said. "Shall I ask his sister as well?"

Ranulph snorted.

"That silly bitch? Not on your life. She'd suggest I put a bunny rabbit in a sou'wester on the water's edge."

Declan burst out laughing, the first time he had done so in Byatt's presence. When he stopped he realized he was being looked at again, through narrowed eyelids.

The permission for Ivor Aston to see the picture, which was almost a summons to view it, was unprecedented, and Declan decided he should convey it as soon as possible to the chosen acolyte. Ranulph Byatt, after a snack for lunch, went into a sleep that Declan could see was born of exhaustion, and was going to last through the afternoon. When he saw Aston returning home along the lane from Stanbury, sketchbook in hand, he slipped out of Ashworth and met him at the gate.

"Mr. Aston—"

"Call me Ivor, dear boy."

Declan's quick glance took in the thin legs, and the baggy shorts and rakish straw hat that were the man's current gear, and decided he would rather not.

"Er, I have a message from Mr. Byatt. You know he's started a new painting?"

"So I'd heard."

"Well, he said to tell you that you could come and take a look at it."

"Really? *Really?*" Ivor Aston looked up at Declan with a surprise, a gratification, a conceit that Declan found very comic. "Now, that *is* unusual. That *is* an honor. Have you any idea why he should have asked me to look at this one?"

The man was oozing self-congratulation like a bullfrog who had received a testimonial to its bullfroggery. Declan would have rather liked to put him down, but couldn't think of any way of doing it.

"Well—I have an idea, but I don't know anything about painting. Perhaps it would be best if you judged for yourself."

"Yes, indeed. When should I come to—to *view*?"

"Maybe this afternoon, around teatime? He should be still asleep, and I shan't see him before then, so he won't have a chance to change his mind."

Ivor Aston's face fell.

"You think it might be a *whim*?"

"He has a great many whims, Mr. Aston. Best to be on the safe side."

"Yes, of course. . . . He hasn't asked Charmayne?"

"No, he hasn't." Ivor Aston's perkiness immediately returned. "I don't think you should mention it to her till after you've seen the picture."

"No, I shan't. But I shall certainly mention it after!"

They arranged to meet outside the farmhouse around four o'clock. Declan said that, to cover his back, he would tell Melanie. When he did so he had the impression she bridled.

"I don't know why Ranulph needs any other judgment to tell him he's doing good work again," she said.

She could have meant "any judgment other than his own," but Declan rather got the impression she meant "any judgment other than mine."

Ivor had, slightly comically, spruced himself up for his special viewing. When he came over from his cottage to the gate of Ashworth he was wearing his best (though still baggy) trousers, a collar and tie, and a jacket that had strange suggestions of early Beatles. He looked around nervously toward Charmayne's cottage, and urged Declan inside as quickly as possible.

"She's quite capable of coming over and making a scene, even of forcing her way in," he said in urgent but muted tones.

Once inside they tiptoed upstairs, registered the heavy breathing from Ranulph's bedroom with a conspiratorial wink, then silently made their way to the studio. Declan, leading the way, felt like some kind of impresario. Once there, in the room flooded with afternoon light, Ivor Aston looked at the picture on its easel and said, "Oh!"

He stood in front of it for several minutes, his affectation suddenly sloughed off. His face was intent, absorbed. He looked like a technician surveying some wonderful new piece of equipment. He subjected the painted sections to close scrutiny, then stood well back, as if trying to imagine the completed work.

"It's like a miracle," he said, his voice hushed. "A return to old form. Not his greatest periods, of course— that would be altogether too much to hope for at his age. But the energy! The eye for effect! The command!"

"His greatest period—would that be his red period?" Declan asked.

"One of them, one of them. Some would say that was the very greatest."

"There's a picture in the stack over there . . ."

Aston ignored his pointing hand and rushed into speech.

"Oh, I wouldn't want to pry. It would betray Ranulph's trust. This is sufficient joy for the moment."

Yet somehow Declan felt sure that Aston knew the picture. He pretended to be abashed.

"I just wondered if that was the red period."

"There are examples in all the best galleries," said Aston in rather a lordly voice. Declan persisted.

"And this—?"

"Oh, not in the same league. One couldn't expect it, with his physical condition, and at his time of life. But the power, the energy—I just can't imagine how he's recovered it. The effect is almost frightening."

And, looking at the picture, Declan could see what he meant.

Aston stayed for some minutes longer, still intent on the half-finished canvas. Then he said, "Mellors ought to be told he's not dealing in gallery fodder any longer, but real pictures. The man's got no visual sense, and probably wouldn't realize."

The switch to money talk surprised Declan a little, but the remark confirmed his impression that Arnold Mellors was an intermediary with the galleries that marketed late Byatts. The comment that he had no visual sense he dismissed as the routine spite and jealousy of a close but not united community.

After all this concentrated art worship, or hero worship, Declan felt the need for fresh air. He left the house with Ivor Aston, but at the gate he felt his hand on his arm, detaining him there.

"I hope Charmayne is watching," Aston hissed, ostensibly looking in any direction except his sister's cottage. "She'll be livid with rage." Unable to continue the pantomime any longer, he opened the gate, and the pair ambled in the direction of Aston's little cottage. To Declan's alarm the talk turned to personal matters. "Can you imagine what it was like, coming out—she'll have told you I've been inside—coming out and finding her here?"

"You mean you didn't know?"

"Good God, no! I'd arranged it all with Ranulph and Melanie from Strangeways. I'd known them both from before, of course—*worshiped* his work for years. I knew I could make a modest living from my own painting. It seemed ideal—idyllic, almost, though I knew Ranulph could be difficult. That's always been his reputation: difficult and demanding. And then to come out and find *her* already in residence!"

Declan was too young to avoid asking the obvious.

"You don't get on?"

Ivor Aston turned and faced him, utterly serious.

"Sometimes I feel I could murder her. That wouldn't be sensible, would it? I'd be the first to be suspected. Everyone around here knows how I feel about her. Mind you, she asks for it—by Jiminy she does! She attaches herself to me, especially if I'm likely to meet anyone, talk to anyone, have a drink anywhere. It's as if she's saying she's my warder, taking me everywhere in handcuffs. She's trying to convey the idea that I can't be trusted, that I'm a man of unbridled and disgusting passions, and if she wasn't around I'd let rip with them and do dreadful things to people. Do I strike you like that?"

"Er, no, no—of course not."

"Thank you, dear boy. I am *not*. I was put away for looking at pictures, and sharing them with other like-minded people. It was a *substitute* for doing! I know doing would be wrong, and I accept that. But if I asked you in now, within thirty seconds she'd be banging on the door."

"To protect my virtue?"

"To make people think your virtue was under threat. She doesn't give a damn about who does what or to whom. If Ranulph was in question he'd have carte blanche in her eyes to do whatever he liked with whoever he fancied doing it with or to. Down to the farm animals. That woman is evil, quite relentless. I have become her obsession, the mainstay of her existence. Her whole aim in life is to make mine a misery."

"Why don't you leave? Move somewhere else?"

"She'd follow. Anyway, why should I?" He puffed himself up very unattractively. "Why should I leave Ranulph? Being close to him is the greatest joy imaginable, and *I* organized it. I'm the only person here who is intellectually and creatively equipped to appreciate his genius. You can tell that, can't you, by today—by his wanting me to see the new picture? I'm not a great artist, but Ranulph's life would suffer if I were to leave, not just mine. *She's* the interloper. If anyone is to leave, it should be her. . . . I won't ask you in."

And he slipped through the front door of his cottage and shut it decisively. Turning, Declan saw that they were being observed, but on the instant of his seeing it Charmayne's head disappeared from the downstairs window of her cottage. Declan wandered down to the field, said hello to Hector the horse, looked in on the stables and wondered when they were going to get the old car that was garaged there repaired. It had gone wrong a week ago, and since then had been forgotten. Declan rather fancied learning to drive. He could become handyman-chauffeur—if he stayed that long.

On the way back to the farmhouse he heard voices from Ivor Aston's cottage, one male, one female. They were raised in anger. Sibling rivalry, he might have thought, if he'd been familiar with the term. Or just plain sibling antipathy. But Declan had no personal experience of either emotional state: in his family the children were closely united, in opposition to their father and in defense of their mother.

That evening Ranulph Byatt came down to dinner, but in an unusually good mood. That did not mean a sunny demeanor or jokes, but it did mean he was uncharacteristically quiet and directed no barbed remarks or brutal insults at anyone. Stephen not being there helped. He complimented Mrs. Max on the meal, which was no more than she deserved: her cooking was superb in the traditional English mode, being solid and satisfying if not particularly imaginative. It was a kind of cooking that Declan could relate to, being not too far from the sort of meals his mother might have cooked for him at home. Mrs. Max accepted the compliment with no pleasurable embarrassment, as only her right. Mrs. Max, Declan thought, was the most stable person in the Ashworth community. The reason, perhaps, was that she was the one least impressed by Ranulph Byatt's fame.

After dinner Melanie did an unusual thing. Instead of going back to the drawing room as she usually did, she followed Declan laboriously upstairs, and after a minute or two knocked on his door. When he called "Come in" she entered, leaning heavily on her stick, and went over and sat on his bed. Ah, ha! thought Declan. What's up? He went on strapping his guitar into its case.

"You've been a remarkable success, Declan," Melanie said, looking at him in a thoughtful way.

"Thank you, Melanie," he said, genuinely pleased.

"You only have to look at the new picture. The transformation is remarkable."

"Oh, I claim no credit for Mr. Byatt's picture," protested Declan, almost blushing. Melanie ignored him.

"You can't fake that kind of confidence, that commitment, that strength. You either have it or you don't. When Ranulph loses it the pictures—though perfectly competent, *technically* accomplished—become somehow listless, inert. They proclaim, 'I am competent,' but they also proclaim, 'I am no more than competent,' because everything in Ranulph tingles with the sense that he could do more. Do you understand me?"

"I think I do, Melanie."

"I think you do too, Declan. You're a remarkable boy."

Declan seized on the word as a diversion, and for once looked her straight in the eye, with new confidence.

"I'm a man, Melanie—in my own estimation, at least."

She considered this for a moment.

"You're quite right," she conceded, with a little bow of the head. "Forgive an old lady. A *young* man you are. . . . But the wonderful thing is, the power is returning. I can't tell you how that *warms* me. One puts up with so much. I don't need to tell you that Ranulph is a difficult man. Stephen exaggerates, in the bitterness of his mediocrity, but Ranulph *is* ruthless, selfish, totally inconsiderate— that I couldn't deny."

"He's never been too bad with me," said Declan. "Not after the first day or two."

"No, I think he *likes* you." She said it as if it was the most astonishing thing in the world. Declan, who was not conscious he had ever been disliked, decided that the remark was flattering rather than insulting. "We are very grateful that you . . . put up with him. You have a remarkably tolerant and equable nature." She paused, as she had several times in the conversation, as if she found the next stage of it difficult. "And, with all his faults, we have to recognize that he has genius. Artists are very different from the rest of us, Declan."

"I accept that, ma'am."

"Melanie. I'm sure you will have got some inkling of it from your weeks here, from being close to Ranulph as you have been. You mustn't wonder if he sometimes . . . surprises you."

"Surprises me? Sure, I'm not used to that kind of person. He surprises me all the time."

"I mean that Ranulph sometimes has fancies—*needs*— and he may ask you to do things that . . . surprise you. Maybe even shock you."

"I see," said Declan slowly. "Could you give me some idea of the kind of things you mean?"

Melanie waved her hand.

"Who can say? He has fancies. Ranulph is a genius, and we ordinary mortals could never predict his whims. I'm just letting you know he may have them, and I hope that you will be able to . . . go along with them."

Declan looked at her steadily.

"I'm a country boy, and haven't seen anything of the world yet, but I'll do my best to be broad-minded."

"That's it: be broad-minded. If you're that I'm sure you'll want to go along with anything Ranulph suggests."

"If it doesn't go against my religion, Melanie."

She looked nonplused. Then she frowned, in puzzlement or perhaps annoyance.

"I didn't know you were religious, Declan. Catholic, of

course. Personally, I've never found religion very helpful in making my decisions, but then, religion has never been very . . . vivid for me. I'm afraid I find such a remark from a young man rather odd." She got up and made slowly for the door. "I'm sure Ranulph wouldn't ask you to do anything that was *wrong*. But I hope your religion doesn't prevent you being tolerant, seeing things in perspective. That's all I was saying."

Declan let her go without further comment from him. He rather suspected that Melanie had been saying quite a lot more than she now pretended, but he had no idea what it was. He listened while she tapped with her stick along the landing and then down the stairs. When he thought she was safely in the drawing room he slung his guitar over his shoulder and went out onto the landing himself. His destination was a pub in Oxenhope where his ballads had found an enthusiastic audience. In the hall, however, he was detained. Martha darted out from the kitchen, where she was helping Mrs. Max with the washing up, and put her hand on his arm, her face its usual mixture of worry, uncertainty, and inner obstinacy.

"You had a long conversation with Mother."

"That's right."

"What did you talk about?"

"Mainly the fact that your father is doing good work again. She said she was very grateful, though it's nothing to do with me."

"Oh, we all think you've had a *wonderful* effect."

Declan shrugged and turned back toward the front door.

"Was that all you talked about?"

"She said your father sometimes had odd whims, but

that's not unusual with an old man, is it? She said she hoped I'd be able to go along with them, whatever they were."

"And will you?"

He turned back to her, looking directly into her upturned face.

"That depends on what they are, doesn't it? I'm not a man who's game for anything, you know. I wouldn't want anybody here to think that of me."

"I . . . I should hope not. I'm very glad to hear it, Declan."

And, red-faced, she turned and retreated to the kitchen.

9

TREMORS OF FEAR

Outside, summer was turning into a rather dreary autumn. In the studio the more dramatic weather on the canvas began to assume its final form: angry sky and violent sea being complemented by slatelike cliffs and a newly painted cliff top in which the green had become still darker, still less inviting. This was no lush oasis: nature in the picture was at its most minatory, a nature in which man could only feel a beleaguered outsider. It was as uncomfortable a landscape as one could imagine.

News of the painting, Declan found, spread quickly

through the Ashworth community. This was not surprising. Ivor Aston was cock-a-hoop at his privileged viewing, and he spoke of it at every opportunity. There was considerable jealousy. The community as a whole felt some sympathy for Ivor, burdened by a sister who represented a sort of ball and chain that he was constrained to take around with him wherever he went. On the other hand, no one actually liked him. Some managed pity, some professed wide tolerance, but he was in the community a man set apart, and this was not simply Charmayne's doing. He was perhaps best described as unappetizing.

And of course if his news of the picture aroused jealousy, that was precisely the emotion it was intended to arouse. Aston had no love whatsoever for any of his fellow acolytes. Where other communities might be described as united around a central figure, Ashworth was disunited around theirs.

Nevertheless, the excitement at Ranulph Byatt's renewed powers, though complicated by personalities and jealousies, also had its generous side. From some of the little community Declan did get a sense of genuine pleasure that, in the airy, light-filled studio at Ashworth, work was again being done that was on a high level. This was a pleasure that was both human—pleasure *for* Ranulph, that he should enjoy artistic fulfillment again after months or even years of journeyman's work—and also artistic and selfish—pleasure for themselves, that they should be close observers during a new and probably a last intensely creative phase.

"I wonder if you would like to try my rhubarb wine," Jenny Birdsell called to Declan early one evening as he returned with shopping from Oakworth. Declan was used to homemade wine, and by no means turned up his nose at it. He smiled back at her, knowing why he had been asked, and turned into her little garden. "Arnold is sampling it," Jenny went on. Declan nodded.

"I expect you can guess what we're talking about," said Jenny Birdsell brightly, her head birdlike to one side as she poured the purply pink liquid into a thick glass.

"The new picture," Declan said. They both nodded. "Nobody seems to be talking about anything else."

"Not surprising," said Arnold Mellors. "If this really is the beginning of a new period it will be immensely exciting for all of us. Certainly it will be a big challenge for me."

Declan sat down on a pinewood chair with strips of canvas across the seat and back. Mary Ann Birdsell had been a little unkind about her mother's taste in interior decorating, but not very: the room was certainly odd. There was a lot of pine, including the staircase, which was open and without banisters—slats for steps, with metal rods reaching to the floor, giving it a perilous appearance. It was against a wall that was painted a dark beige, and the same color bisected the adjacent wall diagonally from bottom left to top right, the rest of the wall and the other walls being painted a bright purple. Both colors tended to kill the pictures hung on them, but the paintings didn't have much in the way of vital spark to start with, being very dim watercolors of corners of moorlands and sections of dry stone walling, without an ounce of the Haworth moorlands' starkness and savagery. They could have been painted anywhere or nowhere.

"Why will it be a big challenge for you, sir?" Declan asked, though he thought he knew the answer.

Mellors, modest little man though he was, preened himself a little.

"I handle Ranulph's pictures for him. Quite informally, of course. His agent was a high-powered one who lost interest when—well, we can be brutally frank now, can't we?—when the pictures became comparatively tame and conventional. Ranulph was very angry, and said he'd have no more agents. I've learned the business by doing it to the best of my ability, going round to galleries and auction rooms. Now . . . well, I don't know what we shall do."

"Get a new agent?" suggested Jenny.

"I suppose that would be best, if we're looking to have a series of fine canvases. But if Ranulph doesn't want an agent, then I must say I would welcome the challenge of handling them myself, after having had to push hard for the less interesting pictures. Marketing is what we have to look at here. A special exhibition, that's what I have in mind: 'Ranulph Byatt—Recent Paintings.' I would enjoy the excitement."

"It *is* awfully exciting," said Jenny Birdsell, fussing around them both. "Do you think the Tate?"

"Not for what would be sure to be a smallish exhibition. Perhaps Manchester."

Jenny pouted.

"I'm not sure you're right when you say it could only be smallish. Ranulph is only seventy-eight. He may have plenty of working years ahead of him. Like Verdi or Ibsen. Autumnal masterpieces."

"I don't think from what Ivor has said that this new one is in the least autumnal," said Mellors, looking inquiringly at Declan. Declan nodded.

"It's very vigorous," he said. "Almost frightening. But

Byatt himself isn't vigorous. He works slowly most of the time, and he can't manage long each day—less time than he used to have on the more ordinary paintings. So I can't see him producing a whole stack of paintings in a hurry."

"No-o-o," said Jenny, though clearly reluctant to give up her notion of a sort of harvest festival period of Byatt activity. "But hasn't someone said . . . haven't you said to somebody, Declan, that he's using movements now when he's painting that you never realized his body still had?"

"Something like that."

"That's something I noticed quite often when I used to be a nurse. It could be, you know, that there's some kind of physical renewal in him, a sort of renaissance."

Heard only by Declan, so absorbed were the others by the topic, Mary Ann Birdsell had let herself in quietly through the front door, and had heard her mother.

"He's your messiah, and you're expecting a resurrection," she said matter-of-factly. "It's really blasphemous. But you'll be disappointed."

She shot a shy smile at Declan and ran upstairs.

"What have I done to deserve a Salvation Army daughter?" asked Jenny of her guests, looking from one to the other, not so much complaining as mildly puzzled. Her manner suggested that her daughter was little more than an irrelevant distraction in her life. "But then, I'm forgetting, you're religious, aren't you, Declan?"

"Within reason," muttered Declan, embarrassed that his convictions should be a matter for Ashworth gossip. "Not that sort of religion. And I don't make a song and dance about it."

"Well, *that's* an improvement on Mary Ann!"

"But there's things I'd never do." It came out in a rush, and Declan was very conscious of sounding naive.

"But of course there is!" said Arnold Mellors with a scoutmaster's heartiness that did not ring true. "That's how it should be. Religion shaping your life and keeping you on the straight and narrow."

"More wine, anybody?" asked Jenny brightly. And Declan, holding out his glass, was conscious that she had approved his keeping his religion under wraps, but had said nothing about his declaration that his beliefs limited his actions. He also had the impression, as the cloudy wine flowed into his glass, that Jenny and Arnold were for some reason *not* looking at him.

The conversation at Jenny Birdsell's was typical of many that took place in Ashworth as September set well in, and the first traces of brown appeared in the fields and the trees around the little community. The excitement that Jenny and Arnold expressed was no more than was felt by everyone there, and in all of them it was mingled with a strong sense of anticipation. A new golden age was approaching. Only Stephen was exempt from the excitement, and he was particularly contemptuous of the anticipation.

"They're getting so worked up it's positively orgasmic," he said with a sneer to Declan one day, poking his head out from under the old car in the stables, on which he was working, and looking up at Declan, who was standing beside the car, wishing he would ask him to help. "If the excitement gets through to the old man he'll have a heart attack, and where will the masterpieces be then?"

"Your grandfather is excited already," said Declan quietly. He always spoke respectfully of old people. "He knows he's doing good work again."

"Know a lot about painting, do you?" asked Stephen, and slid back under the ancient Volkswagen Golf.

"Nothing at all," said Declan. "I know a little bit about cars."

"Well, if I find I need the help of someone who knows a little bit about cars, I'll know who to call on," came Stephen's muffled voice.

Walking away Declan registered the waves of hostility that their brief conversation had revealed. When he analyzed the words, it would seem that the hostility was personally directed at himself. But when he looked at the situation, the *feeling* of the encounter, he felt that Stephen's frustration and aggression were directed first at his own little world of Ashworth, the family and the acolytes, and then at the world as a whole. He was a young man who had never found a place in either, and was beginning to fear he never would. That was how Declan saw the situation.

Over the succeeding week the canvas was brought toward completion with the addition of small touches and changes which Ranulph Byatt said no one would notice, but which represented the last stages in the struggle toward the ideal painting he had had from the beginning in his mind's eye. It was a bold, dramatic, forbidding work, imbued with an energy that none of them, only a month or two before, would have imagined possible. The dominant colors were grays and near blacks, in spite of the fact that the greens of the cliff top and the white of the foam also had prominent parts to play. Declan loved the picture. He felt he knew the weather, knew the sort of landscape depicted. There was an element of egotism in his love too: he felt this was a picture in which he had played a part.

His "part" was put before him in a less flattering light one day when Stephen emerged from an unused bedroom that served him as a darkroom. Stephen was a dabbler in photography, but an energetic and persevering one. Of the few specimens that Declan had seen, he had found the landscapes unremarkable—Stephen failed, as every amateur snap-taker failed, to take in the grim immensity of the moorlands surrounding Haworth—but one or two pictures of people, taken when they were unawares, had intrigued and amused him: a view of Jenny Birdsell's backside when she bent over weeding in her scrap of garden: a zoom lens view of his mother's face— anxious, pleading, middle-aged yet somehow unformed. Such pictures seemed to him in a way unfair, taking advantage as they did of their subjects, yet giving a more truthful view than a photograph taken when they were conscious of being snapped could have done.

"If I was on better terms with the old man," Stephen said, comparatively friendly, "I'd ask him if I could make a series of studies of him. As it is, this will have to do for posterity."

He handed Declan a photograph taken at the door to the studio. The definition was not sharp, but there was a vivid sense of situation: the photograph showed the back of Ranulph Byatt, leaning forward and vigorously attacking the foaming sea of his picture, the energy of the pose contradicting the decrepitude of the body. Declan was standing facing him, eyes down at the palette, looking for all the world like the dumbwaiter he sometimes imagined himself to be—the perfectly respectful, selfless, presence-less servant.

"Couldn't use a flash," said Stephen, a smile playing on his face as he watched Declan's reactions. "The old bugger would have registered it."

"Why did you take it?" asked Declan, handing it back and feeling somehow diminished. Stephen shrugged.

"Might come in useful. Someone's going to write a biography of him someday. Might as well make a penny or two out of him if I can." He grinned evilly. "Who knows? I might write the biography myself."

As he slipped the print back into the folder, Declan registered that there were other photographs, including one of his grandfather asleep in bed. He said nothing, but Stephen, as he turned down the stairs, said, "I might take some photographs at this viewing Melanie is planning. No one could object to that, could they?"

That was the first Declan had heard of the viewing. If he had been more sophisticated it might have struck him as a trifle absurd: a private viewing of an *exhibition,* in advance of the public, was one thing. But of a single picture? On the other hand Ranulph Byatt was very old, had had a long fallow period, and in the nature of things could not be expected to produce many more pictures of quality. And the people of Ashworth were all devotees. Weren't they?

The evening of the viewing was a Tuesday. Ranulph was given a meal of shepherd's pie and rhubarb crumble at six o'clock, and as expected it perked him up. His eyes—those terrible eyes—began to sparkle. Declan set him to rights, then walked him slowly along to the studio. It was quarter to seven, and the guests were expected at seven. Already Ranulph was showing that he intended to savor the occasion.

"I wonder what they'll make of it," he said, chuckling, as Declan eased him into his usual chair, the one he used for painting. "Not that any of them are capable of any appreciation worth a ha'pence. Even the child molester's opinion is something I wouldn't have given tuppence for twenty years ago."

"What about Mrs. Byatt's opinion?" Declan asked. He never called her Melanie to her husband.

"Oh, Melanie's my best critic," said Ranulph whole-heartedly. "Sounds a cliché, but it's true. If Melanie hadn't thought it good, we wouldn't be having this jamboree." He thought for a moment, then out of the blue added the only statement about himself that Declan could remember. "Melanie has been everything to me. Since I met her in 1947 I've never wanted another woman. I've *had* one or two who offered, but the wanting was all on their side. Without her none of the great pictures would have been painted. I'm well aware I'm considered an egotist. I don't deny it. And Melanie has been an egotist *for me.* Everything else in my life has been an irrelevance."

He stopped. Declan felt that anything he could say would seem an impertinence, or ridiculously weak.

Ranulph's chair had been moved away from the picture, and he flung the landscape a glance, just to assure himself it was there, and in a good light. Then he settled down to await the arrivals. "They'll all exclaim over it, like parrots!" he muttered, but it was clear he was looking forward to the occasion by the set of his body.

The animals went in two by two, but the Ashworth community arrived in ones and ones. Apart from Jenny

Birdsell and her daughter (and Mary Ann was certainly not likely to attend such a gathering) they were all solitaries, and proclaimed their solitude almost as if it were a proud gift. Melanie and Martha set out the finger buffet that Mrs. Max had prepared, then stood around in a hostessy manner, but apart. Stephen was standing near the easel with a camera slung over his shoulder, as if to say this was the only reason he was there at all, but he was finally persuaded to man the front door. ("I need Declan here with me," said Ranulph emphatically.)

Jenny was first, and exclaim over the picture she certainly did, and like a parrot too, just as Ranulph had predicted. Then there was Charmayne, then Arnold Mellors, then Colonel Chesney, and last—proclaiming by that gesture, and much to his sister's suppressed rage, that he had seen the painting and had no cause for eagerness—came Ivor Aston, both rakish and pathetic as usual. He gazed around him in a manner both triumphant and condescending: "You see, I told you it was good," the manner seemed to say. "Not that any of you is capable of real appreciation."

"Marvelous!" one of them would say after a period of awed inspection that varied from person to person, but was never less than a minute. "Wonderful!" came from another. "So vital, so powerful," said a third—Colonel Chesney, to be precise. "It's like a punch in the guts," said Charmayne daringly.

"After the sort of pictures you've been painting recently" was an addendum implied in what they all said, but it was never spoken. They were acolytes: they had not said it while the feebler pictures were being painted, so they would not say it now that those were being so magnificently transcended.

"It seems like a new beginning," said Arnold Mellors. *Snap!* went Stephen's camera, catching his expression as he looked toward Ranulph, a look of admiration, but with something supplicating about it, almost cringing.

"It is," harrumphed Ranulph, his voice rich with relish. "Have to get a new man to handle things."

Mellors behaved admirably, Declan thought. He was prepared for this. Physically, he did little more than swallow. A stiffening of the shoulders and back, however, told the watcher that the man had suffered a rebuff he had half expected.

"Then you expect . . . *more?*" he said, the voice very close to normal, the expression, snapped by Stephen, being that of a man who has just received a massive punch to the head. "You expect this new phase to last?"

"I do," said Ranulph, his voice loud with triumph. "To last, to develop, to mature." He turned his sunken face, like an old walnut, in Declan's direction and bared his teeth. "Thanks to this young man."

How much every person in the room, perhaps not even excepting Stephen, would have liked that to be said about them! It was an occasion for accepting blows as best they could.

"You owe him a lot," said Colonel Chesney.

"I do. And expect to owe him still more."

Declan wished he had Arnold Mellors's control over himself. When he saw the stained teeth bared once again, felt the sharp, glinting eyes fixed on his, he shivered uncontrollably, and hid his reaction by going over to

Byatt's chair and rearranging his overlarge cardigan around his withered frame. When he had put his employer to rights he moved away from the chair and stood silent. He was not allowed to remain in the shadows. Melanie came over to him, and Martha came nearer, listening.

"He's fond of you," Melanie said. Declan did not let his doubts show.

"I'm glad. It makes it easier—for him and for me."

"And it's so good for Martha and me to have a rest. Of course we both realize it can't last forever. A young man like you will stick it for only so long. It can't be what you want, being in the middle of nowhere as we are, and being so tied down to Ranulph and his needs. But when we take up our duties again, we'll be mightily refreshed."

"But of course not *yet*," said Jenny Birdsell, overhearing—or, rather, listening in. "Declan has a role to play in this wonderful renaissance."

Melanie's face tightened with displeasure, and as it did so Stephen's camera went *snap* again.

"Certainly Declan has a role to play in what your daughter unkindly calls Ranulph's *resurrection*," Melanie said in a cold voice. "Aren't religious people thoughtless?"

"I'm sorry Arnold told you that, Melanie," purred Jenny. "And you're certainly right about religious people. But I'm sure Declan is not thoughtless, and I'm sure he will want to do all he can to help Ranulph in this new, wonderful phase in his art."

"All I *can*," said Declan, trying to make his voice bland. But Melanie seemed to pick up at least part of his meaning.

"Do you mean your powers to help are limited?" she asked.

"I mean I can't force myself. . . . I mean, like I've said, there are things I wouldn't do."

"Ranulph lives by his own rules and codes," Melanie continued.

"That's fine, so long as he doesn't expect others to live by them too."

"I think you took me up rather too hastily when we talked before," Melanie swept on. Martha was watching and listening closely. "Of course we wouldn't want you to do anything seriously wrong. No question of that. But Ranulph has always been . . ." She paused, then let the rest of the sentence rush out, "excited by violence."

Declan left a pause, then nodded.

"I could guess that, from some of his pictures."

"Violence is everywhere these days, isn't it? Ranulph isn't alone—it's thrown into our living room all the time from the newspapers and the television screens, so lots of people must get their kicks from it."

Declan suddenly realized that, though the room had not gone silent, everyone in it had their eyes surreptitiously on him, and everyone was aware of the conversation that was going on. He said nothing. Melanie, who had seemed to be leading up to something, seemed also to become aware of that, and backtracked.

"That's all I meant. I wanted you to understand Ranulph's nature."

"I suppose I was bound to do that, in time."

"You're not quite the peasant boy we've all taken you for, are you, Declan?" said Melanie with malice in her voice. But then she softened it. "And I hope you will be able to . . . go along with him, so far as you can."

Without waiting for a reply she smiled in the direction

of Mrs. Max, who had come up with more refreshments and now stood observing the little party. Declan took a deep breath of relief, but found himself almost immediately surrounded.

"My boy," barked Colonel Chesney, "there are two heroes here tonight, and you are one of them."

Declan made modesty noises.

"You are," said Jenny Birdsell. "You have made it possible, revived Ranulph's will to do great work."

"Not great work *yet*," said Ivor Aston, with unattractive pedantry. "But who can doubt it is to come?"

"You must be *enor*mously proud," said Charmayne, coming over to stand, unwanted, beside her brother. "But the responsibility is awesome."

"I just do what I can in a practical way," said Declan.

"No, no—there must be more to it than that," said Jenny. "Your personality must *liberate* him, must concentrate all his powers, the ones that have been dormant. What a privilege for you! But it is a responsibility too, to see that those powers are never again allowed to fall fallow."

"You owe that to Ranulph," said Arnold Mellors. "You also owe it to yourself."

No, I don't, said something very powerful inside Declan. I'm just an Irish boy making his way around the world before deciding what to do with his life. I don't owe anything to anybody. And there's something here that I can't pin down. Something I don't like.

He looked around at the passionate eyes. He was getting tired of being looked at, at something being expected of him—something that nobody seemed willing to specify, that he could not begin to guess at, because he had not enough experience of the world, though he had *some*. And looking around at those faces, at Melanie and Martha watching from a distance, and conscious of Ranulph slumped in his chair but still obviously aware, Declan realized that he didn't feel only pressurized, badgered. Something in those eyes made him feel something else: uneasiness, apprehension, *fear*.

He shook himself.

"Come along, sir," he said in a lordly tone, going over to Ranulph. "You're tired. Time for bed."

PART III

The Investigation

IO

THE ARTIST AND
HIS WOMENFOLK

Charlie pushed open the gate and walked through it, shutting it carefully behind him. That much he knew about country practice, though he doubted whether he was shutting any farm animals in. He himself, though, was crossing a border, entering the confines of the dark tower. All the animals were human ones.

He shook himself, feeling he was being silly and fanciful. But he stopped for a moment, having a distinct sense of being watched—could it be eyes intending "to view the last of me, a living frame for one more picture," as Childe

Roland imagined? He grinned and shook himself again. There were no faces visible in the windows of any of the cottages as far as he could see. In any case, the big house was obviously his destination—the farmhouse, as it must once have been. He turned and made his way to its front door.

His ring produced no scuffles or muttered whisperings on the other side, merely, after a few seconds, a measured footstep, probably female, Charlie thought. When the door was opened it was by a worried-looking, middle-aged, slightly disorganized woman who seemed surprised to see a black man on her doorstep but not worried. The local bush telegraph, then, had not extended as far as the Ashworth community. They were somehow apart, socially as well as geographically.

"Yes?"

Charlie took out his ID and flashed it under her eyes, making sure that she had read it.

"I'm DC Peace of the West Yorkshire Criminal Investigation Department. I wanted to ask you a few questions about this man."

Yet again he fished out the picture. The woman frowned over it.

"You recognize him?"

"Well, it looks a little like Declan."

"That's the boy who worked here as a handyman?"

"Ah, you know? Why are you asking, then?" She handed it back to him as if to hasten the end of the questioning. "I wouldn't say it looked a lot like him, but that sort of picture—"

"Yes, they're always a bit generalized, aren't they? What was your handyman's full name?"

"Declan O'Hearn. He's Irish."

"And when did you last see him?"

"Oh . . ." She frowned. "He must have left about a week ago. I was away for the weekend in London and I wasn't back till Monday, and didn't hear of it till then."

"And did he just throw up the job, say good-bye, and leave?"

"No, it would have been a lot easier if he had—easier with Father, I mean. My father is Ranulph Byatt, the artist." She looked into Charlie's eyes, and he nodded with the air of being impressed. "He's been very upset since."

"So what happened when he left?"

"He just took off in the middle of the night, or early in the morning. Left a note and that was that."

"What did the note say?"

"I didn't see it, but Mother told me about it. It just said that he was leaving—he'd been paid the day before—and that he wanted to see a bit more of the country." She frowned again. "Why are you so interested in Declan? He was very naughty in the way he took off like that, and inconsiderate too, but he's the last person to be involved in anything criminal."

Charlie tried directness.

"A dead body has been discovered in the Haworth area. We think it might be him."

His instinct told him that her surprise and distress were genuine. His instinct had sometimes been wrong.

"Oh, no! I'm sure it's not Declan. I'm sure if he'd just left and gone to Haworth we would have heard. His note implied he was going a lot farther than that."

"Maybe he was on his way when—" He stopped when he saw the expression on her face. "Who saw the note?"

"My mother. Stephen too, I think."

"Do you mind if I come in and talk to them?"

"Oh, that wouldn't be very convenient. Just before dinner."

"Murder does tend to cause inconvenience."

He stood his ground, waiting, as if he had not had a refusal. But her mind had been diverted by his words.

"Murder. But you didn't say—"

"Death and police detectives do suggest murder to a lot of people."

"But I didn't—it could have been—" She stopped, and then swallowed. "But that makes it quite certain it's not Declan in that picture. The nicest boy you could imagine. No one could conceivably want to murder him."

"Murder is often a question of being in the wrong place at the wrong time. Now, I'd be obliged if you'd let me in to talk with your mother and father, and Stephen, whoever he is."

She had remained standing square in the doorway, but now she seemed to lose confidence, and stood uncertainly aside.

"Stephen is my son. He's at Oxford at the moment. . . . I do hope you don't need to talk to my father." She had led the way down the hall on a gesture from Charlie, and now she opened the sitting room door. "Mother, it's a policeman. It's about Declan. He thinks he may have been murdered."

"Quite impossible. I hope you've told him so."

The only person in the room was tall, strikingly handsome as fine-boned elderly people can be, and straight of back. Her voice had a distinctness of enunciation Charlie associated with a bygone era, as well as upper-class vowels, which spoke of the same time. She rose now with difficulty from her chair.

"Sit down and tell us the story, however improbable. Declan was a lovely boy, if a touch thoughtless. No one would want to murder him. Won't you join us in a sherry?"

"Thank you very much."

It was not Charlie's habit to drink with suspects, but he hoped they would be more unbuttoned in a social situation. Melanie moved painfully over to the sideboard, poured from a decanter into a large, modern sherry glass, then let Martha take it over to their guest. Charlie sipped his drink. It was very cold, and the sort of sherry he always thought tasted as if it had been made with grapefruit.

"Now, can you tell me all you know about Declan O'Hearn leaving here?"

He was looking at Melanie. She needed to make none of the elderly person's usual efforts to remember recent events.

"It was about a week ago. Friday night. Some time either in the night or the early morning he packed his knapsack and left. Let himself out by the front door and put his key through the letter box."

"I believe he left a note?"

"That's right. By the table in his bedroom."

"Can you tell me exactly what it said?"

She frowned.

"No, not exactly, but nearly so, I think. It was very short. 'I'm taking off to see a bit more of the world like you said. Sorry for any inconvenience caused.' That was pretty much it."

"I see. Do you still have it?"

"Good Lord, no. I just threw it out."

Charlie thought over the meager substance of the supposed note.

"What did he mean by saying 'like you said'? Had you told him it was time for him to go?"

Melanie shook her head vigorously.

"Oh, certainly *not!* Declan was a treasure, and so good with Ranulph. No, it was just that I'd said to him—several times, I think, but certainly at the viewing of the new picture a few days earlier—that I realized he wasn't in the job for life, and that he would want to move on before long."

"I see. He was Irish, your daughter said. Southern Irish?"

"That's right."

"Do you know where he was from?"

"Oh, dear, where was it?" Now she was exhibiting an elderly person's vagueness. "Was it County Clare? I have a feeling he mentioned a county but not a town—is that right, Martha?"

"That's right. I think it may have been County Clare."

At that point a head came around the door.

"Would you like dinner delayed a little, Melanie? Mr. Byatt has had his, and it will all keep quite well."

"Yes, if you could hold it for half an hour, could you, Mrs. Max?"

At that point, Charlie felt, it would have been natural for Melanie or Martha to ask Mrs. Max if she knew where Declan's home was. Declan and she were both, after all, domestic staff, who presumably had chances to talk to each other. But the question wasn't asked.

"Oh, Mrs.—Mrs. Max, is it?" he put in, as she was withdrawing her head. "I wonder, did you ever talk to Declan O'Hearn about his home?"

She came in and stood respectfully by the door.

"Oh, yes. He liked talking about Ireland. Not so much about his home or family, though he did mention a brother called Patrick and a sister called Mary."

"That's useful," said Charlie, though he thought that perhaps a Patrick and a Mary were not a great deal to go on, so far as Irish families were concerned. "Did he talk about his home village?" Mrs. Max nodded. "Do you remember where that is, precisely?"

"It's County Wicklow," she said, very positive. "Now, where was it? A little village . . . I think the name began with *D*. . . . It'll come back to me, I expect. I know that the nearest town is a place called Rathdrum. I must admit I'd never heard of it before he mentioned it."

"He never talked to you before he left here about his reasons for moving on?"

"Oh, no. Just disappeared into the night. Young people are like that these days. Keep their own counsel."

Then she withdrew. Charlie settled down in his chair and took another sip of his sherry.

"So, that should make things easier," he said, his eyes fixed on the two women. "We've narrowed it down quite nicely."

"I still do *not* believe it's Declan," pronounced Melanie. "Do you want me to come and see the body you've got? I'm quite willing. I'm not squeamish about dead bodies."

"No, that won't be necessary," said Charlie firmly. "We'll get family if possible. That's standard practice. It often makes it easier for them to accept what's happened. Now, tell me about O'Hearn's duties here."

They gave him a summary of the tasks Declan usually carried out: his personal attendance on Ranulph Byatt, his helping with his painting, his work around the house and garden, his occasional shopping and other excursions to the outside world.

"I even gave him a first driving lesson, once Stephen got the car going," said Martha with an undertone of resentment. "Stephen refused to, because he knew he'd be going to Oxford soon, so I did it. It's very ungrateful . . ."

"Had he given any sign he wasn't enjoying the job?"

"None at all," said Melanie. "And he was having such a good effect on Ranulph. He was starting to paint really fine pictures again."

"Though I don't *really* think that was down to Declan," put in Martha. "I'd noticed signs of an exciting new phase well before he came."

Charlie's antennae twitched.

"I'd like to talk to Mr. Byatt," he said. "Perhaps it would be best to do it now."

"Quite impossible," said Melanie. "He'll be ready for bed now."

"Really?" said Charlie, raising his eloquent eyebrows. "But I gather he's just had his dinner. I can't imagine he's likely to be ready for sleep yet."

"Ranulph is *old*," said Melanie. "He's seventy-eight. He's drifting out of life. There's really nothing he could tell you."

"And yet he's painting fine pictures," said Charlie, letting his skepticism show. "I'm afraid it's obvious he's had a great deal to do with O'Hearn, so I'm going to have to talk to him."

"Even if the murdered person turns out not to be Declan?" asked Martha. "Which I am sure will be the case."

"I am proceeding on the assumption that O'Hearn is the dead man, and, yes, I do have to talk with your father," said Charlie, getting up and standing before them, looking his most formidable. "I suggest you take me up to him now."

The gesture had its effect. Martha looked at her mother, then back at Charlie.

"Oh, very well, then." She led the way to the door. Charlie stood aside, then, as he was about to follow her, realized that Melanie too was struggling to her feet.

"Please don't bother to come up, Mrs. Byatt. I have to speak to him alone."

Melanie looked as if she might protest, then sank into the chair again. Charlie and Martha went up the stairs in silence, but at the top Martha turned, and in an urgent whisper said, "I hope you'll remember that my father is a *very* old man. His mind is not what it was. And he is an *artist*. A *great* artist. He doesn't think like ordinary men."

Charlie nodded to this in as neutral a way as possible. Policemen were used to dealing with people who didn't think like ordinary men and women. Frequently it ended with their being charged. Martha registered his reaction, marched along the landing, and opened a door.

"Father, this is a policeman, Constable . . . er . . . Peace. He's got the strange idea that Declan has been murdered. I've told him that it must be nonsense, but he insists on speaking to you."

She stood aside and let Charlie into the room. Then, exuding a miasma of disapproval, she closed the door behind her.

Ranulph Byatt had not been made ready for bed. He was sitting in an easy chair in trousers and shirt, with an old cardigan around his withered shoulders. He had no book or paper in his hands, and Charlie might have thought he had been dozing had there not been a brightness about the eyes that certainly did not speak of sleep. Although *brightness* was the wrong word. *Sharp* was better, or *piercing*, or, odd thought: *cruel*. They were not eyes that a prisoner in the dock would be happy to see in his judge. There was about the old body a tension too, an energy, which spoke somehow of the negative sides of energy—ruthlessness, unstoppable drive, maniacal egotism. Charlie felt that in his long life Byatt had seldom let any of the softer emotions get in the way of his wishes—which he probably confused with his art.

"Policeman, eh? What's my grandson been doing, then?"

"Is that Stephen? Nothing that I know of, sir."

"Did Martha say something about Declan?"

"Yes," said Charlie. He saw no reason to be other than businesslike. "I'm afraid we have reason to think he's been murdered."

"Nonsense!" said Byatt, his voice harsh with scorn. "He's just taken off. Wants to see more of the world."

"His taking off doesn't rule out the possibility of his having been murdered. We have a body."

There was a shrill, wheezy laugh from the chair.

"So do I. I have a body. Bloody useless thing it is too. Won't do a thing I want it to. Hardly even lets me paint. Have to go into all sorts of contortions to get what I want."

"A body was found in the boot of a car in the car park at the back of the Haworth Tandoori."

There was another wheezy laugh.

"The Haworth Tandoori! What nonsense! Can you imagine Emily and Anne Brontë tucking into a plate of chapatis?" The face suddenly became more serious, or more decorous. "But I'd be surprised if it's Declan. A nicer boy you couldn't hope to find—and I don't usually go for niceness. Nobody in the world could want to kill Declan."

Charlie reached into his pocket and drew out his picture.

"This is an artist's impression of the dead man."

Byatt took it from him, skepticism written on his face.

"Artist?" he roared. "That was no artist drew that. A navvy with elephantiasis in his fingers, more like. Any likeness to Declan is in having two eyes, one nose, and one mouth. Nothing more. You're on a wild-goose chase."

"How did you get on with O'Hearn?" asked Charlie, refusing to be deflected.

"Like a house on fire. Shouted at him now and then. Shout at everybody. But he was top-notch. Did all the things—dressing me and shaving me and all that sort of thing—as if he'd been born to it. Could have felt awkward about it, but he didn't. Then he stood quiet while I painted, mixed the paints to my direction—by the end he was a damned sight better at it than that fool Martha."

"So you must have been very upset when he left."

The old face twisted into something that may have been an expression of regret, but looked oddly like a grin.

"I was. It knocked the stuffing out of me."

"Did it seem ungrateful?"

"What had he got to be grateful for? You're talking like a Southern slave owner. The pay was poor, I wasn't the pleasantest person to work for, Stephen behaved like a boor to him, and the womenfolk are a collection of wet hens."

"That wasn't the impression I had of them."

"Hmmm. Well, not Melanie, of course."

"You say you shouted at him—"

"Now and again. Nothing serious."

"You hadn't had a row when he decided to leave?"

"No, we hadn't. We never had a row the whole time he was here. They've a long history of subservience, the Irish."

"And was that what Declan was, subservient?"

The old man considered.

"No, he wasn't. Forget I said that. You couldn't call the IRA subservient, could you? No, Declan was quiet, polite, efficient. If I was rude to him, he *endured* it. That's different. You always knew if he disapproved of what you said or did."

"Was there anything like *that* before he . . . left?"

"No, there wasn't. He just had a hankering to see the big world, and I'd have a lower opinion of him than I do if he was content to fritter away much of his life in a dump like this. Now, will you send Martha or Mrs. Max up to me, young man? It's time for my bed. I tell you, you're wasting your time. Know what I think? If you alert the police around the country you'll find Declan singing Irish ballads in the street somewhere where there's plenty of tourists with money. Good night, Constable."

Charlie Peace, going downstairs to fetch the great artist's "womenfolk," thought that the suggestion about alerting police all over the country to singing Irishmen was a good one, though he did not expect any results. By and large, looking at the whole interview, he had a definite sense of having been played with, of the old man having given a performance: for a lot of the time he had talked in clichés, and he had been acting a cliché too—the irascible old terror, with an implied heart of gold. The women of the house had been afraid that he, Charlie, would get a wrong impression from talking to Byatt. But in a very different way, that seemed to be exactly what Byatt had been trying to give him.

II

ONE OF THE ACOLYTES

After he had shut the front door of Ashworth, Charlie got himself through the little garden and out to the lane. There he took out his personal phone and got on to the West Yorkshire Police headquarters.

"Mike? I think we're getting somewhere. . . . Yes, identification. Our corpse is probably Declan O'Hearn, got that? He's a boy from the Irish Republic who worked over the summer as handyman and personal attendant to an artist called Ranulph Byatt—you know him? . . . What it is to work for a cultured cop. . . . I'm not knocking it, it will be very useful. . . . Oh, you just know the name. Well, I don't suppose there'll be any need for art crit. Anyway, there is a little hamlet—more of a community, really—centered round a farm called Ashworth, near Stanbury. This Declan O'Hearn took off, I'm being told, in the middle of the night, unexpectedly. . . . Could be true. He could have got no farther than Haworth. But I wouldn't bank on it. I'm told he came from a little village near Rathdrum, in County Wicklow—name uncertain, but may begin with a *D*. Comes from a large family, a brother Patrick, a sister Mary. . . . I know, but combined with the name Declan, and in a small village. . . . The priest may be more help than the policeman. I may talk to someone else here, then I've got to walk back to Haworth. . . . Yes, *walk*. . . . So I'll be, say, an hour or an hour and a half."

The call finished, Charlie slipped his mobile back into his pocket and looked around him. He felt like talking to someone else while he was in Ashworth—not least because he would be seen otherwise to walk away, and that might give the impression to the occupants of the farmhouse that he accepted their protestations that the body at the Tandoori could not be Declan. He felt a mite aggrieved about that. Did they take him for a fool? As if he had not seen bodies that no one could have imagined were asking to be murdered—blameless old men and women, no danger, no threat, not even any inconvenience to anybody. But murdered they had been, and sometimes raped as well. There was no such thing as a murderable person, or rather the category was so large as to be meaningless.

He was surprised to be spared the burden of random choice of the various cottages surrounding the farmhouse. While he was on his mobile a cottage door had opened, and now he was being beckoned from a gate by a well-set-up man in his sixties, someone who came from the same straight-backed school of deportment as Melanie Byatt. Charlie accepted that the choice had been made for him, and began in the man's direction.

"I say, I wonder if I may have a word?"

Charlie nodded, and followed him into his cottage. It was neat, conventional, everything beautifully in place except for that morning's post and *The Times*, still on a table beside an easy chair. There were only two small oil paintings on the wall, one of the inevitable moorland farm, the other of Stanbury's Main Street. If they were the ones that were worth hanging, the unhung ones had to be wretched.

"Corner!" barked the man at a black-and-white terrier-style mongrel. The dog crept to a corner where an old rug lay. He did not seem cowed or mistreated, yet his training seemed to have taken away his essential dogginess.

"It's about Declan," said the man, gesturing Charlie to a seat and sitting down himself in what was clearly the favorite chair. "I'm Chesney, by the way. Colonel Chesney. I hear you're investigating Declan's disappearance. It wasn't really a disappearance, you know. He just moved on, as he was bound to."

He talked in short, staccato bursts. Was that his usual conversational mode, or was he nervous? Charlie thought for a moment.

"I suppose Mrs. Byatt rang you while I was talking to her husband. Or her daughter?"

"Mrs. Mates. Yes, it was Mrs. Mates who rang."

"She rather misinformed you. We haven't police

resources to waste on a young man who's slung his hook. We're investigating a body found at the Haworth Tandoori."

Chesney cleared his throat.

"Ah, yes. Actually, she did mention that."

"But you preferred not to face up to the fact that the murder might be connected to Ashworth. Let's not beat about the bush: I've had all that from the people at the farm, Colonel Chesney. At the moment I'm acting on the probability that the body is that of Declan O'Hearn—right?"

Colonel Chesney coughed, a sharp, staccato bark.

"Oh, right. Yes, of course. You have your procedures—nobody knows better than I that procedures have to be followed. . . . Er, I wonder if they told you everything about Declan."

Charlie wanted to smile.

"I doubt it, Colonel. We had quite a short conversation. What is it that you think I ought to know?"

Charlie's bluntness seemed to disconcert the colonel, who had planned a more roundabout strategy, a sort of pincer movement. Charlie guessed he was in any case no strategist: the clipped military manner seemed to conceal a muddled mind, directed by nothing more definite than a desire to be of service to the people at the farmhouse.

"Ah, well, you see," he began, already stumbling. He tried to pull things together. "Now, the point is this: the ladies at the farm know what there is to know about Declan while he was with them. But I know for a fact that he used to get around in the evenings after dinner. Did the rounds of the pubs in the area. Sometimes sang, if they had a piano and a player, or if he knew he'd be welcome he'd take his guitar. That's what he was doing when he saw the advertisement for handyman here: playing the guitar and singing folk songs and suchlike in the street in Haworth."

"I know. What exactly are you suggesting, sir?"

"Well, it's obvious he could have a side to his life that the ladies at the farmhouse, dear souls, know nothing about. You get me? He could have got in with any sort of crowd."

"I know the pubs in the area can get pretty rough at weekends," said Charlie, keeping his tone ironical and light. "But I've never heard they're hotbeds of crime."

"Well, of course, not normally, no. But at this time of year they're absolutely swarming with all sorts of people. He could have met up with just anyone, and got drawn into something. To take just one example: the IRA."

"I'll look into it, sir," said Charlie, adding to himself: *if all else fails.* "About O'Hearn during his time here: was it your impression he was an easily led young man?"

Chesney blew out his cheeks.

"He was only about twenty, Constable. I mean—"

"What *do* you mean, sir?"

"At that age one can be led into anything."

"So if someone suggested something dubious, whether here, or in one of the pubs around Haworth . . ."

"Well, I mean—no, I wouldn't go so far. I don't want you to get the wrong impression of the lad." Chesney was conscious of having got himself into an awful muddle, and in particular of having been unfair to a young man he had genuinely liked. Defensiveness about the community had been struggling with honesty. "He was a nice lad, make no mistake. And he had his religion. I respect that.

Haven't got a great deal myself. 'Thought for the Day' on Radio Four is about my limit. But I respect those who have. . . . Spot! Back in your corner! . . . And he wasn't one of those Catholics who think they can do whatever they like and confess it on Saturday and make everything all right. No, Declan was a boy who really had standards."

"Really? What makes you say that?"

"I heard him say there were things he wouldn't do—said it out, just like that, very serious. Not the sort of remark you'd often hear from one of today's young people. And it was all of a piece with the boy generally. He was very quiet, but he was . . . I think 'upright' is the best word."

Charlie kept his voice casual.

"That's interesting, sir. Did you hear in what connection he said that there were things he wouldn't do?"

His voice wasn't casual enough. Chesney spluttered.

"Ah, well, I can't quite . . . I think it was the viewing—Ranulph's new picture, you know."

"Was this a public viewing, sir?"

"Oh, no, just us, the people here. But we were all there, even Stephen. He was taking pictures. Even he realized it was something of an event, Ranulph painting first-rate pictures again."

"Can you remember who Declan was talking to?"

"No. No, I can't—just general, I expect. I mean, philosophical: what would you do, what would you draw the line at, that kind of thing, you know."

"Ah," said Charlie. "You know, I rather doubt that."

Chesney jumped. "Eh?"

"You get me over here to suggest that O'Hearn could have got in with any sort of criminal crowd in the pubs around Haworth. You're presumably trying to direct my attention away from the people here at Ashworth."

"I say, nothing of the sort—"

"You then, out of all honesty—and I respect you for that—you have to admit that Declan was a young man with a strong moral sense. And you base this on a conversation that you overheard. Abstract philosophical arguments don't tell one anything much about people's moral character. I suspect someone put a suggestion to O'Hearn, or seemed to be leading up to a certain suggestion, and he reacted in a perhaps immature but straightforward way: 'There are some things I would never do.' Am I right?"

Chesney became obstinate.

"I just heard the words. In a babble of conversation. Impressed me with the lad's honesty. That's all."

"Hmmm."

"Just trying to help," said Chesney lamely.

Charlie thought it was time to store this fascinating piece of information in his memory bank and pass on. To relieve Chesney's embarrassment he asked, "How did this—what should I call it?—this community come to be established?"

Chesney breathed a sigh of relief.

"Well, it's just happened that admirers of Ranulph Byatt—admirers of his work—have had the chance to take these cottages around the farm."

"Rent them?"

"That's right. They were derelict when Ranulph inherited the whole place—farm, cottages, estate. Some of them he had put into a shipshape state, and then let them. Others, like myself, took them on and only began paying rent—reduced rent—when they were in good order. Great opportunity. A challenge. I like a challenge."

Charlie nodded his acceptance of this unexceptionable sentiment.

"But how did you come to hear of them?"

Chesney looked down into his lap.

"Bit embarrassing, really, at my age. I wrote him a fan letter. Can't describe it as anything else. Went to a big retrospective of his work at the Hayward, and I was just bowled over: the power, the passion. I said in the letter that I dabbled, was quite frank about having no talent at all, said I was about to leave the army, and, well, things developed from there."

"I see. The community was already in existence then?"

"Yes. The Birdsells were well installed, and Charmayne Churton had just moved here—waiting for Ivor. You know these people?"

"I haven't had the pleasure," said Charlie urbanely.

"Pleasure wouldn't be my word for it. She was waiting for Ivor to be released when she came here. He'd organized a cottage for himself, and she got wind of it. He was in jail—so far as I can understand that was for possessing and circulating child pornography of a particularly revolting kind. I suppose I'm old-fashioned, but an offense like that strikes me as beyond the pale."

"You don't have to be old-fashioned to feel that, sir."

Chesney gave a brisk nod, dismissing his emotion as somehow unsoldierly.

"No, well . . . The trouble is, it ought to be admirable for Charmayne to come and live with or live near her brother, to help his rehabilitation, keep him on the straight and narrow, but somehow—I can't explain—"

"Try, sir."

"Somehow she seems even worse than him."

Charlie frowned, finding his inarticulateness bewildering.

"I see. There must be something—something about her, or something she has done—that makes you say that."

"She seems to gloat. Tells everyone what Ivor went to jail for. It's as if his offense has given her a reason for living. You know, she's the last person he wants around him—you could see his horror when he came out and found her here. Now he can hardly take a step but she's there beside him."

Charlie thought it sounded like a very odd relationship indeed.

"So then this man Ivor came out of jail. Has there been anyone else join the community since?"

"Arnold Mellors. Nice enough chap, and capable, but not very inspiring. I suppose none of us is very inspiring, though."

That was a thought that had occurred to Charlie during his account, but he found it difficult to express tactfully.

"So—how shall I put this?—Ranulph Byatt didn't use these cottages to get fellow artists around him?"

"Oh, no, we're rank amateurs, and not particularly good amateurs at that. Ivor Aston is the best: he sells the odd picture to tourists, usually through one of the shops on Haworth Main Street. Charmayne sells occasionally to greeting card people. But we are none of us serious artists."

"So what is the purpose, the point, of the community?"

"Well . . . I suppose . . . really we're all tremendous

admirers of Ranulph's work. That seems to be enough. It's the only thing that keeps us together."

Charlie stepped delicately into these difficult waters.

"You said 'none of us is very inspiring.' Would you say that Ranulph Byatt wouldn't want to have people around him who were, particularly good artists, or very strong personalities? That he likes being the focal point of admiration—the big fish surrounded by minnows?"

"That's unkind," spluttered Chesney, though on whose behalf Charlie was unclear. "It's a cruel way of putting things. Best not said. It's Melanie decided these things quite as much as Ranulph, you know. And nobody could describe her as a minnow. Remember, first-rate painters don't grow on trees. Not many would want to shut themselves away in a little cottage miles from anywhere. Ranulph just wants to have like-minded people around him, people who share his ideals."

"Right! I see," said Charlie, who thought his earlier assessment of the situation had not been so wide of the mark. "Now, what about Mrs. Max?"

"Mrs. Max? Oh, she was around when I arrived here." He looked a bit embarrassed. "Tell you the truth, I was afraid the whole setup was going to be a gaggle of women. Not so good with the ladies, me. Not that she's a silly body—not at all. She's got the best head of anyone around here, apart from Melanie."

"I really meant, what's her place here in the community?"

"Well, she cooks at the farm, every meal except breakfast. Does as much cleaning as she can fit into the hours."

"She has no artistic aspirations?"

"Good Lord, no. She's just a local who was glad enough

of a cottage and a job when her husband took up with another woman. She had a lad when she came here, though he took off for the bright lights a year or two ago."

"And her relationship with Ranulph Byatt?"

"Relationship?" Chesney's tone implied that she was a servant and had no business having any kind of relationship with her employers. "She likes it when he's a bit more active, comes down to dinner, and so on. The womenfolk get in her hair, and she doesn't like Stephen, who used to treat her son like dirt. Beyond that . . ."

Charlie got up to go.

"Thanks for talking to me. I'm beginning to get the picture, I think."

"But, Constable, there really isn't any picture to get," said Chesney, getting up too and looking him straight in the eye, which aroused all Charlie's suspicions. "I mean, not from your point of view, not from the point of view of a murder inquiry."

"Now I, on the contrary, am starting to feel there are a great number of pictures, of a great many kinds," said Charlie with relish. "I'll be surprised if we don't meet again, sir."

Chesney's face showed that he far from looked forward to the prospect. In fact, he seemed to have a sense that he had got himself further into the very thing he had been intent on getting himself out of.

Back at the police headquarters in Leeds after a long walk and a drive through late rush-hour traffic, Charlie found Mike Oddie with a small pile of stuff on Ranulph Byatt.

"Nothing of interest from our point of view," he said,

looking up from it. "Only time he's come to our notice was a pretty sad business: elder daughter and her husband killed in a motorway crash on their wedding day. That was back in 1980. It was about that time he inherited Ashworth, but they didn't move up till 1982. So nothing much in our records. I've had a look at his entry for *Who's Who*. It just charts growing fame—at least in the art world, not popular fame—over the last fifty years or so. Went to art school just before and then just after the war (he'd been in the desert campaign, then through Italy), and then the entry charts a series of exhibitions at increasingly prestigious galleries. Married in 1951, and been married to her ever since. Hobbies, sailing and rock climbing."

"Not much chance of him indulging in them these days," commented Charlie. "He's not quite bedridden, but he's only a stage or two away from it."

"Not a likely murderer, then."

"Not a possible one, unless we were talking about poison or something like that. Otherwise I might have guessed he had the temperament for it."

"Meaning?"

"Ruthless, egotistical, amoral."

They were interrupted by a young man who came over and handed Oddie a sheet of paper. It was Michaelson, one of the pathologists most used by the West Yorkshire Police—young, intense, withdrawn. Charlie was struck by the unusualness of a pathologist delivering a preliminary report himself and standing by for questions. There must be something—

"Christ!" said Oddie.

"What is it?" asked Charlie, bending down to read.

"Will you tell him?" said Oddie, turning to the patholo-gist.

"It's a mite unusual," said Michaelson, with a sort of reluctance rare in someone usually cold and scientific. "The boy's hands were secured, not by a rope, but proba-bly some kind of handcuffs, possibly of leather. His feet seem to have been roughly tied with something plastic, maybe a clothesline. And then he was garroted."

"He was *what*?" demanded Charlie.

"A sort of halter—I think of metal, maybe brass—was put around his neck, and then a screw was turned to tighten it. He was slowly strangled."

12

BOYS TOGETHER

They faxed the Gardaí in Rathdrum that night, and had a reply on their desks when they got back to West Yorkshire Police headquarters in the morning.

There was a family that answered the description they had sent in a village called Donclody. The father, now dead, had been a violent man, both outside and inside his family circle, not otherwise criminal but brutal and stupid. The eldest boy, Patrick, was a tearaway with minor convictions, but nothing was known against the second son, Declan, or against anyone else in the immediate fam-

ROBERT BARNARD

ily. The message helpfully added the name and telephone number of the Donclody parish priest. Charlie wondered cynically if they were in the habit of unloading awkward jobs on to the nearest available priest, in this case Father Baillie.

He sounded an elderly, compassionate man when they got him on the line after early morning Mass.

"The O'Hearns? Oh, yes, Patrick is the eldest, then Declan, and Mary is the third. Mrs. O'Hearn's done a fine job, on the whole, and against the odds, from all I hear. . . . No, I've only been here two years. . . . Well, I wouldn't want to be speaking ill of the dead, but the father by all accounts was a bit of a drunken brute, God rest his soul."

Mike Oddie began to explain the situation, but was soon interrupted.

"Not Declan! You're not saying Declan has been murdered. Oh, but it'll break the poor mother's heart! I tell you, you couldn't have wished to find a nicer boy. And he had a brain too, a good, sharp brain, but with it all he was as willing and helpful as you could find in a year of looking. Oh, dear, oh, dear."

"We've no certain identification as yet," admitted Oddie. "We're hoping the mother might come over—"

"Oh, dear, is that necessary? The poor woman will be suffering so sorely at the loss."

"We do find it is helpful to the survivors, as well as to us," said Oddie. It was special pleading but it struck home.

"I can see that," admitted Father Baillie. "Sometimes they have fantasies that it was never him at all, I suppose. You want me to talk to poor Eileen, don't you?"

"We'd be very grateful. And if you could persuade her to come over as soon as possible."

"That might be difficult. I'm guessing that Rathdrum is as far as she's been in her life. And she'll certainly never have flown or been on water."

"Persuade her, please. It's not only identification we need, but background too. Things such as, is there anything that we need to look into over there or can we concentrate on the young lad's life since he came to this area?"

"I can see that. I promise I'll do my best. If she wants me to I'll take her to the airport myself and do all that's necessary. Is it Manchester she should fly to?"

"Manchester or Leeds/Bradford. If you'll just phone and let us know we'll pick her up ourselves."

Meanwhile there were things to be done, with most of the acolytes at Ashworth remaining to be interviewed, and the people at the farmhouse still largely unpressured about their story. But before they could get going Mike Oddie was handed a note about a phone message that had come in before they clocked in for the morning. News traveled fast in any small community, and in Haworth it traveled with the speed of light. Everyone by now knew that Ashworth was in the frame for a murder investigation. The message was from a Haworth garage, one situated in the bottom part of the town, not far from the railway station. It said that on Monday morning the Ashworth car had been in the garage's tiny forecourt when the proprietor arrived to open up. There was a phone call from Stephen Mates at Ashworth around 8:15, saying it had broken down the night before, and would they put it in going order again. They were not the Byatts' regular garage, if indeed they had one.

"What say we split up?" Oddie said. "I'll look in on the garage, see if there's anything else they can tell us about the car—for instance, the interior, though it's not something garages especially notice. You go on to Ashworth, and I'll follow when I'm through in Haworth. Just keep it informal and delicately probing for the moment, at least until we have a positive identification. Who do you fancy taking first?"

"I'd like a word with Mrs. Max. She's the only outsider in the place, and she may, with luck, have an outsider's skepticism, unless loyalty gets in the way."

"Who should I take, if I've time to do one on my own?"

"Try Arnold Mellors, in the cottage built on to the farmhouse," said Charlie, after thought. "Then we'll take the others together—Ivor Aston and his sister, and Jenny Birdsell and her daughter."

"Meaning you fancy those four?"

"As suspects? Well, especially the Aston pair. But I'm really thinking they may be more open with information, especially if we play one off against the other. It may need the pair of us to get the best out of them."

It was the first time Charlie had driven down the rutted track to Ashworth. Even driving slowly and carefully it made for a bone-shaking trip. As he opened the gate, drove through it, then closed it again, Charlie wondered about the Byatts' car. Presumably it was in the stables, just visible at the end of the field; presumably it would be by now as clean as a whistle—though with modern techniques that could well be more apparent than real, and Forensics might well come up with one of their infinitesimal traces. Anyway, the time to bring Forensics in was when the body had been identified.

He left the car just inside the gate, parked over a ditch. He got out and looked around him. Which cottage would be Mrs. Max's? He guessed that most of Ranulph Byatt's disciples had a little bit of money behind them when they moved here, but that Mrs. Max would have had none. He chose the smallest of the cottages, one that was really a sort of end bit to Colonel Chesney's, and he struck lucky.

"Oh, are you back?" she said, bluntly but not unfriendly, as she opened the door. "I was just on my way up to the house."

"Can it wait a bit, say, half an hour?"

"I suppose so."

"Who is it, Mum?" came a man's shout from the back of the tiny cottage.

"Just the police."

A young man came forward and appeared at the door. He was slight but wiry, and had a pinched but intelligent-looking face. He put his arm around his mother's shoulders, and Charlie felt that this was a pair he could do business with.

"Can I come in?"

"Of course. Where's your manners, Mum? We want to give you all the help we can."

But Mrs. Max had not stood aside.

"I'm not going to be disloyal, Joe."

"You don't have to be, Mum. But I don't owe anybody here any loyalty."

"They gave us a home," said Mrs. Max, finally moving her homely shape aside and letting Charlie into a minute sitting room, furnished with pieces too big for it—pieces that had probably come from her former, marital home. Charlie threaded his way between them and sat down in a fat armchair. He found that he had to tuck in his legs if he were not to make foot contact with the mother and son on the sofa opposite him. Charlie had already decided that the boy was likely to be his best or possibly his only source of unbiased information, and he turned to him first.

"Right. Now, you are—"

"Joe. Joe Paisley."

"Ah." He turned back to the mother. "So you are really Mrs. Paisley?"

"Jeanette Paisley, by rights. My husband was one of two brothers well known in the Haworth area—mostly for the wrong reasons, I'm sorry to say. They called us, their wives, Mrs. Martin and Mrs. Max, and it's stuck."

"I see. And you came here when?"

"Oh, when Joe was a little lad. Nineteen eighty-two, it was, when the Byatts moved here from Stamford."

"I take it they needed domestic help, and you needed somewhere to live?"

"Pretty much, though I had family in Haworth, and they *wanted* domestic help rather than needed it, to my mind, with two women in the house. Melanie was perfectly able-bodied at the time, and Ranulph's arthritis was in the very early stages. Martha could cope perfectly well if she got herself organized. But it suited me to get a bit away from the Haworth and Stanbury gossip."

"I see. . . . The night that Declan O'Hearn took off, last Friday night, you didn't hear anything, weren't wakened by any activity?"

"I was not."

"Nor maybe Saturday or Sunday night?"

"No, I always sleep through."

"Nothing wakes Mum," said her son. "I often had to wake her in the morning if they needed her earlier than usual at the farm. Now she has an alarm clock."

"I see," said Charlie, nodding. "And how did you hear about Declan's . . . moving on?"

"They just said, last Saturday morning, that he'd taken off during the night and left a note."

"You didn't read the note?"

"No, I didn't." She thought. "But I saw Melanie screw it up and throw it into the fire."

"What she said was the note."

She thought, then nodded.

"Well, yes. She said how disappointed she was in Declan."

"As if Ashworth was some kind of worthy cause," said her son, "like the Peace Corps or something, that young people ought to serve in for next to nothing."

"Did they try that on with you?" asked Charlie, turning back to Joe, registering the strength of feeling in the voice.

"They were working round to that," he replied with relish. "Making remarks like 'A strong lad like you will always be useful at Ashworth,' or 'Ranulph's always happiest with someone he knows.' Work at Ashworth? I should 'eck as like!"

"Don't believe everything Joe says about the people at the farm," said his mother, her lips tightened. "He's got his own views. They never jelled, like."

"Wouldn't want to jell wi' people like that," said her son. "And it's not just them."

"You mean," probed Charlie, "that you don't jell with the people in the cottages either?"

"Gives me the creeps," said Joe, with a touch of youthful self-righteousness. "The whole setup does. All this worship of Ranulph bloody Byatt. You can admire somebody's painting wi'out giving up your whole life to him."

"And you think that's what they've done?"

"I'm bloody sure it is. Body, soul—"

"Conscience?"

Joe blinked at him.

"Well, yes. I wouldn't have put it like that, but, yes, they have."

Charlie decided to show his hand a little.

"I mention that because I believe O'Hearn was heard to say that there were 'things he wouldn't do.'"

"Good for him." Joe thought for a moment. "Not that it did the poor bugger any good."

"Maybe the reverse. Maybe it was the reason he was killed."

"You mean they put something to him, and it was so horrible or maybe so criminal that when he refused to do it they had to kill him?"

"It's a possibility."

Joe Paisley pondered for a second or two.

"I've wanted Mum to get away from here for ages."

"Don't be silly, Joe," his mother said forcefully. "What the policeman was just saying was nothing but speculation."

"That may be, but his thoughts are going the same way as my thoughts always have. Get shot of them, Mum." He turned to Charlie. "I've got a flat in Bolton. There's room for both of us."

"Get away with you!" said Mrs. Max vehemently. "No

young man wants his mother permanently encamped with him! And what happens when you get a girlfriend? *She's* going to be delighted to have me there the whole time, isn't she?"

"Let's get this clear," said Charlie, breaking in. "Why did you want your mother to get away from Ashworth?"

"Isn't it obvious?"

"Well, if you ignore what's happened in the last week, no, it's not. I've met Colonel Chesney, and he seems perfectly normal, and he describes Arnold Mellors as if he's, if anything, terribly dull. The women at the house, on the surface, seem pleasant enough. The old lady, Melanie, isn't what I'm used to, but she was friendly and helpful in her rather regal way. I just wonder why you've been trying to get your mother to leave 'for ages.'"

"Silly fancies, that's all it was," said Mrs. Max. Her son sat there thinking. He was one of those people who don't speak till they have their thoughts in order.

"First of all, we were always going to be outsiders here. Most of the people in the cottages are not *artistic* people, to my way of thinking: they're arty-farty people. But either way round, we were never going to be in with a crowd like that. Now she's on her own here, Mum's very isolated. She doesn't realize it, but she is. She needs to be in a place where she has her friends, things to go to, that kind of thing."

His mother was scornful.

"People to gossip with, you mean. That's all you think women are good for when they get older. I've been talked about too much to want to do it to other people."

Her son ignored her.

"Then there's the sort of people he gathers around him. They don't just admire him: they're devoted to him, they're his creatures. They're emotional bloody cripples, if you ask me. You may say they sound dull and ordinary, but he fills their lives, gives them a reason for existing. You can't say that's healthy and normal."

"Agreed, if it's true. But your mum has escaped the influence."

"She has. And Stephen and Mary Ann, you could say, though Stephen is *obsessed* with his grandfather, even if he isn't a member of the fan club."

"I'm not getting an altogether pleasant picture of Stephen," said Charlie. Joe's mouth curled.

"Stephen Mates is a prat. He's really quite ordinary, but he has to feel superior to people, and the only way he can do that is by setting himself up as the young master, the heir to the estate. Estate! What crap!"

"His grandfather said he behaved like a boor to Declan O'Hearn."

"I can believe it. Why should he make an exception of O'Hearn? That's how he behaved to me all the time we were growing up here. Except when he wanted something."

That last remark puzzled Charlie.

"What sort of thing would he want from you?"

"He was often at a loose end. Not much to do around here if nobody likes you. I'd be tinkering with a car— that's my job; I'm a car mechanic, and I've always been good wi' engines—and he'd come over and want to know what I was doing, how a car engine worked, how I knew what was wrong and what I had to do to fix it. Well, you could go so far with him and no farther: you could teach him how an engine worked, but you couldn't teach him how to put it right when it was broken."

"Interesting. . . . I don't feel you've got to the heart yet of why you're unhappy about your mother staying at Ashworth."

"No. Oh, well, the *heart* is Ranulph Byatt, isn't it?"

"I suppose so. Though these days he seems sort of marginal because of his physical state."

Joe Paisley shook his head vigorously.

"He won't be marginal, whatever his physical shape. I should have said that the heart of Ashworth is not Ranulph but Ranulph and Melanie. Always a partnership. I'm not up in this place at the moment, but as long as he's got Melanie to help him, his physical state won't get in his way."

"Get in his way as far as what is concerned?"

"Get in the way of doing exactly what he wants. He is the most selfish man I've ever come across. He has to have what he wants, do what he wants, when he wants, come hell or high water."

"Aren't we all a bit like that?"

Joe shook his head again.

"A *bit* like. He is *completely* like that. No one gets in his way. Totally selfish means totally ruthless. That's why I was interested in this boy saying there were limits to what he could do. Poor bloody lad. . . . If you want to know why I worry about my mum it's because she's in a community centered around Ranulph Byatt, and Ranulph Byatt is *evil*. Pure evil."

"Don't take any notice of him," said his mother, turning to look urgently at Charlie. "Ranulph and I have always got on well, though I'll give you he's sometimes naughty, likes winding people up. But he's an individual, his own man. More than you can say for his daughter or his grandson, to my way of thinking."

"Stephen interests me," said Charlie. "He may not have escaped his grandfather's shadow, but in other respects he seems to be his own man."

"Trouble is, the man in question is a shit," said Joe.

"Very much out for himself, would you say?"

"Totally."

"We're talking murder here, as you will have heard. Is Stephen capable of killing to further his own interests?"

Joe thought, then shook his head reluctantly.

"Wouldn't have thought the arrogant prat would have it in him."

It was a testimonial of sorts.

"Youngsters can be very sharp, judging each other," said Oddie when he joined Charlie at Ashworth and was told of Joe Paisley's view of Stephen. "On the other hand, they *are* a young person's views, and in any case Stephen may have grown more dangerous and decisive in the years since Joe left Ashworth."

Charlie nodded agreement.

"What did you learn at the garage?"

"It was Stephen Mates who rang about the car, and Stephen Mates who went to collect it."

"He'd got a bit of expertise in car repairing from Joe Paisley," contributed Charlie. "Not enough, apparently."

"You told me that Martha Mates talked about giving Declan a driving lesson once Stephen got the car going," said Oddie thoughtfully. "I think the sequence of events is clear: the car was broken down for some time, but Stephen knew enough about engines to get it going. On the night of Sunday the twentieth he drove it into Haworth, with the body in it, but it broke down on the flat bit between the two steep hills—between the station and Bridge House. He disposed of the body in a clapped-out old car in the car park of the Tandoori, and managed to push his car along to the garage. Now, the pathologist gives the whole weekend, from Friday night to Sunday night, as the likely time the boy was killed. Leaving us with a question."

Charlie saw the point at once.

"If Declan disappeared on Friday night, and the body was shifted on Sunday night, what happened in the intervening forty-eight hours?"

"And was the body alive or dead while it was happening?" added Oddie.

13

MATER DOLOROSA

The question was still hanging in the air when the phone rang, and all possibility of more interviewing was at an end.

Mrs. O'Hearn had been surprisingly easily persuaded—or possibly bounced—into flying to England. She was due in at Manchester at 2:25. After some discussion it was agreed that Charlie should collect her, and try for some informal discussion about family background on the drive back over the Pennines to Leeds. If the poor woman was up to it, of course.

Charlie didn't like waiting at airport exits carrying a placard. He'd only done it once before, and it made him feel like a low-grade courier. This time the causes of his unease were less personal and social: he was meeting a newly bereaved mother, and one who had just gone through the experience of flying for the first time. He could well imagine that her jumble of emotions, fear fighting with grief, would be difficult and embarrassing to cope with, and would need the utmost care in handling.

One further point struck him: from what little he knew about Ireland, he guessed that he would be the first black person Eileen O'Hearn would ever have had a conversation with. That presaged badly. All things considered, the going seemed likely to be sticky.

The plane was already ten minutes late. Looking around him Charlie concluded that Mrs. O'Hearn could have been told that she was being met by a black man and there would have been no possibility of confusion. The voices around him were all North Country or Irish, and the faces all white. It was at that point that the sleeve of his jacket was tugged, and he looked down at a red-eyed, fearful face, but one with an indomitable, straight mouth.

"Is it me you're meeting? Eileen O'Hearn? They told me your name and I've forgotten it entirely. I've made a terrible fool of myself on the airplane. We'd no sooner started moving and going toward the—the runway, do they call it?—than I had a terrible fit of panic and cried out to them to let me off, I couldn't face it, and I don't know what else, and people were looking at me and smiling, and there was this kind hostess—such a sweet-looking girl, she was—who came and sat beside me and held my hand and told me to close my eyes, and we talked and before I really knew it we were in the air and in no time we were down again and they were getting me off before all the rest. I wish I'd taken her name so I could send her something—one of my best sponges, maybe, and some ginger nuts. Sure, I hate making a fool of myself in public. I've always hated people laughing at me, or pitying me, and that's what they were doing on that plane. And it's a fool I was, because what if the plane did go down? What's that when you've just lost a son, and a son as good to me as Declan was, and a good man too—everyone will tell you the same. But there, I have to think of the others, like Father Baillie said. The truth is I always favored Declan, because of his lovely nature. But it's the young ones I have to live for now, God give me strength."

This, and more like it, got them to the car park and the car that Charlie was to drive them in to Leeds. As he bent down to open the passenger door Eileen O'Hearn's face told him that she was registering for the first time the fact that he was black: she had seen her name on the placard, which he had been holding to his chest at about her eye level, and she had not looked upward but in her sorrow and nervousness had started chattering on at once. Well, it had certainly got them over any awkwardness. He let her in, went around to the driver's seat, and set off.

"It sounds like you've got a big family," he said. "You'll have to explain that to me. I'm an only child, and there's just me and my mother."

"Oh, dear, your father's dead, is he? That's sad for a young chap like you are if he was a good one." Charlie didn't explain about his father, who was not so much dead as unidentified. "The three eldest were Patrick, Declan, and Mary. Just a year or so between each o' them." She smiled shyly. "Then my husband got a job in America, so there's a gap. Mary's twenty this year. Then there's Anne, who's sixteen, Stephen, who's fourteen, and John Paul, who's ten. That's a larger family than people have these days, even in Ireland. But it's sad for an only child like you, isn't it? You learn about being with people by being with your own brothers and sisters."

"I suppose I have always been a loner," admitted Charlie, "at least at work. I prefer to go at things on my own."

"How could you not be, with no people around you to bring you out of yourself."

"But you say that it was Declan who was always your favorite of your children?"

"It's a dreadful mother you'll probably be thinking I am, to favor one over the rest like that. But Declan was such a nice-natured boy—no, I'll not say that. They're all very nice-natured children, even Patrick. . . . Well, Patrick has got too much of his father in him, but it's not his fault, that, and when he and Declan were together, which they always were as much as they could be, Declan would be holding him back from wrongdoing, thank the Lord."

"They were very close?"

"They were. That's how it happens in large families, they sort of divide off. People called them the O'Hearn twins, and they were like twins, though their natures were so very different."

"You said Patrick was like his father," hinted Charlie delicately.

"I'd not want to speak ill of the dead," said Mrs. O'Hearn, but it seemed more of a formality than anything deeply felt, for she went on: "But I'd not want to tell lies about him either, for fear you didn't understand about

Declan. My Jack was a big man with a bit of a temper, and he could be very rough with the children, or . . . or with anyone who got in his way when he was in the drink. And sometimes when he wasn't too."

"And Patrick takes after him?"

"Too much. Too ready with his fists an' all. I've had to stand up to him since his father's death, make it clear that I'm not going to be my own son's punching bag. But Declan could always manage him. It looked as if it was Patrick in charge, but that wasn't the case at all. His father always wanted to 'make a man of him,' but since Jack died I haven't stood any nonsense from Patrick."

"And Declan, anyway, went in entirely the opposite direction, did he?"

"Oh, he did. A lovely boy." She brought out a little scrap of handkerchief with lace edging and dabbed at her eyes. "I don't know how I can talk about him without crying, but you're a good listener. . . . I wondered whether he would be a priest, but it wasn't to be. There's hardly a soul has the vocation these days, is there? How's the Church to survive? Oh, Declan was always kind, and took endless trouble with the little ones, and stood up to his father when he was big enough—and that was brave, you'd say, if you could have seen the size of his fists."

"How did your husband die?"

She turned to him, her eyes sharp now.

"What are you implying? There was nothing like that!"

Charlie backed off at once.

"I wasn't implying anything, Mrs. O'Hearn. We have to get the whole picture. And since by your own account your husband was a violent man, I wondered how he died."

"I'm sorry. It's with you saying Declan was murdered.

I *can't* believe it, not Declan, not a sweet boy like that. . . . Jack was killed when scaffolding collapsed on a new building he was putting up in Rathdrum. There was few to mourn him. Even his brothers and sisters—and one or two of them are a bit too much like him to my way of thinking—even they could hardly weep for him. And I had to stop the children saying they were glad."

"Did he leave you well off financially?"

"He did *not*. It all went over the bar. It's been a struggle, but we've managed."

"It sounds as if your family has been a happier one since he died."

"It has. Life has been much better, I'd not deny it. There have been difficulties, no question, but there's been no *fear*. Declan has been a rock, but of course he's young—I *can't* talk about him as if he's dead—and being a young man he wanted to see a bit of the world before he settled down. If only he'd stayed in Donclody, maybe found work in Rathdrum. Finding work is a bit easier these days in Ireland, so they tell me. . . . If he had he'd still be with us!"

She raised her handkerchief again and wept silently into it. Charlie was silent for a few minutes, as they drove through bleak Pennine landscapes. This, since the Moors murders, was landscape that was associated in the popular mind with sadistic killings. It was something that everyone tried to put out of their minds but nobody could.

"Will you tell me about Declan's decision to travel a bit?" he asked at last. Mrs. O'Hearn put her handkerchief away.

"In a way I'd expected it. It's what most young Irish people do when they're twenty or so—the young girls maybe get jobs with children, and the boys make their ways around doing casual jobs. In the past it's been either America or Britain, but now it's often Europe. Anyway, Jack didn't leave many contacts in America, not ones you'd want a young man to take up. The way Jack got through to people in America was breaking their noses in bars. So it was to England Declan came—not that he had any contacts here, not family contacts, but it would be easier to get home if he ran out of money. He was hoping to go to Europe later on, but that would depend on his making a bit of money."

"When did he leave home?"

"End of July it was. The last time I saw him. If I'd known . . . But there, I didn't have any fears for him, not more than normal. I've never known any young person from our area come to any harm, apart from those that were always heading full-speed for the rocks wherever they happened to be."

"So, how did he leave? Train?"

"No, a friend took him to Dublin by car. Then he got a boat to Liverpool."

"Do you know what happened to him after that? Did he write?"

"Oh, yes. Postcards first. One from Dublin, one from Liverpool, which he liked, but said it was desperately poor. Then cards from Manchester and Leeds."

"Was he singing in these places?"

"Yes. And he did some washing up in cafés and restaurants, even a bit of waiting at table in the places where the singing didn't bring in much money."

"Did he tell you about the job at Ashworth?"

"Is that the place near Haworth? Yes, he did. Just a

short letter saying he'd got a job looking after an old painter. Said he might stay a month or two, or maybe longer if he liked it. Said helping the old chap paint was interesting."

"And that was the last you heard?"

"I had a postcard saying he was still enjoying himself. Patrick had a letter telling him more about the artist and the setup at the place—Ashworth, you say? Pat went and looked up the artist in the library in Rathdrum, and he said he was quite well known. I think Declan regarded it as an honor working for the man."

"And that was the last you heard?"

"That was the last."

As they neared Leeds, Charlie said, "I have one more question, a very important one. Will you think about this before you answer?" She nodded, looking faintly scared. "Is there anything you know of, in Declan's life in Ireland, maybe something in which he himself was entirely guilt-less, that could mean that someone there could have a grudge against him?"

She paid him the compliment of thinking hard for some moments before she shook her head.

"No, there's nothing, nothing at all. Everyone loved Declan, and that's the truth, and he didn't get involved with anything that wasn't straightforward."

"He couldn't have got himself caught up in anything political?"

"Political? Is it terrorism you're meaning? That's quite impossible. Declan hated the bombers and killers, despised them, hated what they do to the minds of the young people who get caught up with them. Called it brainwashing. I tell you there's not a chance. Declan's whole life was spent in Donclody and Rathdrum. There's no IRA cells in places like that. That kind of scum flourishes in the big towns."

"And are you quite sure there was nothing in the letters and cards he wrote you that might give a clue as to why someone on this side of the water might have it in for him?"

Again she thought hard and long.

"There wasn't. They were just short, do you see, and not very informative—the sort of letters a boy writes to his mother. I didn't get the impression he felt at home with those people he took the job with, didn't feel he understood their sort, but that's about all. There may have been more in the ones he wrote to Patrick, because, like I said, they're of an age, and very close."

"But Patrick didn't tell you anything about them?"

"No, he didn't. And wouldn't. Patrick's still at the 'wild boy' stage, when all the adults he knows are enemies. Things between him and Declan would stay between the two of them. I doubt he'd even have told Mary."

They drew up outside the Millgarth Police headquarters in Leeds. Mrs. O'Hearn looked up at it as if it were the cause of all her grief. Charlie said nothing because he could think of nothing, and got out of the car, ushered her out, and led her inside.

"Mike in?" he asked the sergeant, and, getting a nod, led her through to CID. Oddie saw them and got up from his desk. He was his usual concerned self, but his whole body seemed to say that he could no more think of words of encouragement or comfort than Charlie could.

"Would you like a cup of tea?" was all that came to his mind, and it sounded very lame.

"No, thank you. Not yet. I'd like to get it over with, please. Talking to Mr.—Peace, is it? That's a nice name— Mr. Peace here made me almost forget, and so did the airplane; I was that terrified. But losing Declan is the worst thing that could happen to me, to all of us, and I'd like to get it over with, say my prayers, and try to make sense of it, such a terrible thing."

Oddie nodded to Charlie, who took her arm, and silently they led her in the direction of the mortuary. They knew that everything that could be done had been to restore the boy's face to normality, rid it of the hideous scream of anguish and apoplexy that had disfigured it when it had been found. The walk seemed endless. Mrs. O'Hearn said nothing, except that at one point Charlie thought he heard her murmur, "It's worse than flying."

Eventually Mike Oddie pushed open a door, and they were in the mortuary, with its terrible chill, and its smell of chemicals and death.

"The Haworth body," said Mike to the mortuary attendant, who had it ready as instructed, not in the hideous impersonality of a drawer, but covered with a sheet on a table. As she approached it, Mrs. O'Hearn seemed to be saying a prayer, her eyes closed. Then she opened them and nodded that she was ready. The attendant drew the sheet back slowly, and she gazed at the dead face. After a second or two her eyes widened.

"Praise be to God. It's Patrick," she said.

14
ART CRITIC

"It's incredible!" said Mike Oddie the next morning, throwing himself into a chair in the big CID office. "Hello, square one: I didn't expect to be back on you so soon."

"We are not back on square one," insisted Charlie, parking his backside on the neighboring desk.

They had phoned the Irish Club in Leeds, nice and full on a Sunday evening, and had got in touch with a homely woman who would put Eileen O'Hearn up for the night and listen to her self-lacerating monologues. The reaction after her words of relief had been extreme: she was a wicked woman, she lamented, to be glad that one son was dead rather than another, a wicked woman to question God's will; she was justly punished for taking against a son who followed in his father's footsteps by losing him entirely. And so on, and so on. It was all totally understandable, but difficult to take when they wanted to settle down and reorientate entirely their ideas on the case. In the end they had hit on a way of making the woman feel as at home as she would ever be outside Ireland, with the chance of sorting out her emotions and calming her mind. But they had been glad to put her into a car, to be driven by a fresh-faced police constable to her temporary accommodations. A good night's sleep, however, had not sorted out Oddie's ideas for him.

"Square one is where we are," he insisted. "We have a body which has nothing whatsoever to connect it with Ashworth or with the people there."

"His brother Declan connects him, and the letter or letters he wrote him while he was there."

"He'd already left the place. The two could have arranged to meet in the Haworth area. They could have been sleeping rough on the moors. Come to that, Declan could have murdered him."

"You're thrashing around. That last possibility is almost inconceivable from everything we know."

"OK, OK. But what we know comes from a doting mother. More likely, I'd agree, is that Patrick got into some kind of quarrel or brawl."

"How many brawls have you come across which ended with someone being garroted?" Charlie inquired.

"You're getting to be a real smarty-pants," complained

Oddie. "All right: let's hear your guesses—because guesses are what we are reduced to."

Charlie had been stewing over the implications of the turnabout in the case in intervals of troubled sleep. But what he had were a mass of deductions and conjectures that needed time before they could be ordered into a string of causes and consequences.

"Patrick takes off for the wider world outside Donclody, and naturally the first person he makes contact with in mainland Britain is his brother," said Charlie, talking slowly as he thought through the implications of his conjectures. "Or—more guesswork—he gets a letter from his brother which makes him uneasy about what's happening at Ashworth, and he comes over to see for himself. Their mother gave the impression that Patrick thought he was the leader and protector, the one in control, as the eldest always does, but that in fact it was Declan who was the one who generally reined in his brother, calmed him down, limited his impetuosity. That suggests that Patrick may have come over to offer protection to his brother, and found that the brother had already made his own decisions, had packed his bags and left."

"Just as the Ashworth people said."

"Just as they said."

"Nice. As a conjecture I like it. But not a scrap of evidence."

"I bet if the body was in that car, Forensics will find traces. And if the living Patrick was in that house, or any of the Ashworth cottages, they'll find traces there too."

"And if they do the question will arise: why were they all so silent on the subject of Declan's brother? They'll hardly be able to shrug and say they didn't think it relevant."

"No. . . . You don't think he can have gone there without revealing he was Declan's brother, do you?"

"No," said Oddie confidently. "The fact that he was so like him was what made people put us on to the wrong track from the first. Look, we're getting ourselves boxed into a house of cards based entirely on guesswork. We should be asking ourselves what we should do in the new situation—apart from letting Forensics loose on Ashworth, and their work will take days, and then weeks before we have a definite report. What do we do in the meantime?"

Charlie took refuge in his subordinate position.

"You're boss, Boss."

"Meaning you've run out of ideas."

Charlie grinned.

"Not far off the mark. I've got one or two, but I'm not sure how you'll take them."

"Try me."

"Right. In spite of what you say, to me everything about this murder takes us to Ashworth. And at Ashworth everything centers on Ranulph Byatt. Yet we know practically nothing about him—not his background, his career, tastes, reputation—nothing."

"And?"

"I'd like to find out," said Charlie simply. Oddie nodded.

"Makes sense. How?"

Charlie improvised.

"I've got one or two contacts at the City Art Gallery.

They had a problem last year with a persistent vandal when they put on that lavatory seat sculpture exhibition. They should have realized lavatories attract vandals like honey attracts flies. I could try them—they might be able to recommend some books, or maybe an expert."

Mike nodded slowly, having no better ideas, and Charlie went away to get started. It was one of the younger staff members at the gallery who, when Charlie rang, came up trumps.

"I've read about the murder and the Ashworth connection," she said when they had got over the usual courtesies. "Set me wondering about Ranulph Byatt."

"Good. With what result?"

"It's rather an old-fashioned setup there, or seems to be on the surface: the artistic community with shared ideals, and so on. Puts you in mind of Eric Gill and Ditchling."* It didn't put Charlie in mind of anything of the sort, but he gave an intelligent grunt to show that he was keeping up. "But when you get down to it it's not an artistic community at all. Everyone except Byatt is a rank amateur, mostly of a fairly dreary kind. It's more of a glorified fan club, or one of those cult villages the Americans seem to go in for."

"Is Byatt important enough in your view to warrant that kind of admiration society?"

"In a word, yes. At his best he's a wonderful painter."

"Is there a lot written about him, stuff that I could look up?"

There was silence at the other end of the line.

*Eric Gill (1882–1940) English carver, engraver, writer who founded an ideal community at Ditchling.

"Hmmm. Not a lot, now you come to mention it. I could get the people in the art library to look up what there is, but I don't think it will amount to much beyond newspaper reviews and articles. It's a bit surprising, since it's generally agreed he's a major artist. I suppose the fact that he's shut himself away in that little hamlet miles from anywhere hasn't helped, or the fact that he's surrounded himself with tenth-raters who probably write even worse than they paint and couldn't begin to do justice to him if they went into print. That's probably what has scared other possible writers and critics off. There was someone who meditated a book on him, but it didn't get anywhere, I don't think, because the last I heard he was working on the umpteenth book on Francis Bacon."

"You know this chap?"

"Oh, yes, or I've met him. Funny little man who used to work at Cartwright Hall, in Bradford. Retired last year. I can get you his telephone number, if you're interested."

"I am, very."

The man in question was called Bertie Briscott, and he turned out to be very ready to talk about Ranulph Byatt.

"Look, I live not far from Cartwright Hall," he said in a thin voice that seemed to verge on a giggle even when he was saying nothing remotely funny. "We've got a Byatt there that might be a fruitful starting point."

"I don't need an art lecture," said Charlie hurriedly.

"If you're a policeman I expect that's exactly what you do need," he countered, and went off into paroxysms of chuckles. "But that wasn't the point of my suggestion at all. Now, then, you find the picture and you'll find me. We can go out into the park and have our talk."

Cartwright Hall and its park are together one of the

jewels of Bradford (not, its critics would contend, a notably jewel-bedecked city). Pity about the pictures inside, thought Charlie, as he strolled through gallery after gallery on his way to the contemporary stuff: embarrassing neoclassical kitsch from the late-Victorian era, celebrations of imperial victories from the same period, muddy British landscapes from the interwar years, and feeble portraits of local notables by local nonentities. Either the Bradford wool kings had bequeathed only their turkeys to the local gallery, or they'd never bought anything worth looking at in the first place.

Once in the room devoted to the second half of the twentieth century, Charlie stood for a moment to look around him. He didn't know what drew him to one particular picture, but he decided when he thought about it later that it was its violence. He went up close and saw that this violence—the impression it gave of having been painted in one bout of fury—had even spilled over onto the frame, making it part of the whole ferocious statement. The effect was of seeing something through a window—a smashed window that left glass everywhere. What it was he was seeing through the frame he could by no means pin down, but he thought there was broken glass, perhaps a hand, and certainly blood—blotches of red were everywhere, disfiguring the hand, the glass, something that could be some kind of seat, indeed everything that might after contemplation assume the shape of an object.

Underneath the caption read: "Ranulph Byatt (1920–): ACCIDENT."

"Very sharp," came a voice at his elbow. "Cleverly identified, and without hesitation."

Charlie turned and looked down into an elderly face

with something pixielike in its expression, a good deal of self-love, and a single brown tooth pointing outward, the sole remnant, at least to the eye, of a rabbity set that could never have been one of the face's better features.

"Mr. Briscott?"

"Bertie. Call me Bertie." The man smiled ingratiatingly. He was clutching a very old hold-all and when he looked around the room he gave the impression that he owned the place. "Are you ready to come along and have our little chat? I've brought along my packet of sandwiches—'sarnies,' people call them these days, don't they? So amusing." He chortled through his nose. "I always used to enjoy my *sarnies* in the park on fine days when I worked here. Would you like to pick up a bun or something from the cafeteria?"

"I think I can last out," said Charlie. Together they strolled back through the detritus of Britain's artistic heritage.

"So what did you think of the picture?" Bertie Briscott asked as they emerged into the sunlight.

"Very impressive, very powerful," Charlie ventured, but nervously. There was an irritating little snigger in reply, as if any fool could see that.

"But what did you *see* in it, what did you get out of it?" the unappetizing little man persisted.

"Violence, fury, rage?" said Charlie in a slightly miffed voice.

"Yes, yes. All of those things." Bertie Briscott selected his favorite seat and they sat down looking over toward a large old school. Briscott undid the greaseproof paper around his sandwich packet, revealing a stack of open sandwiches. The top one was egg mayonnaise. Charlie thought the tooth could probably cope with that. He preferred to look away while it did so.

"That's one of the best paintings of his red period," said Bertie Briscott, his voice muffled by eating. Charlie had the impossible impression that crumbs were spraying out of his nose. "One of a series of related paintings that really made his name. People talk as if that series came completely out of the blue, a total surprise. That's people who don't really know his output." Charlie looked back, and saw a catlike expression of self-satisfaction on the man's face. "Before that he'd had a substantial reputation as a landscape painter in the British tradition—good, solid, painterly works. But there had also been other pictures in a more fractured, tormented, uncertain style— pictures that suggested he was struggling with something in himself he barely understood."

"Abstracts?" asked Charlie, looking away again from the open mouth full of sandwich, through which could be glimpsed in a ring four or five isolated brown stumps, a sort of odontological Stonehenge.

"I'm not sure the term has much value," Bertie Briscott said judiciously. "They had titles—'Girl Weeping,' or 'Child on Swing'—but one couldn't readily relate the title to the picture itself. Not uncommon, of course. And then came the red period, and the man's name was made."

"When was this?"

"Early in the eighties. He was born in 1920, so you can see he wasn't young."

"Was there anything that sparked this new phase?"

Bertie Briscott leaned back in his seat, and even rested his sandwich pack on his lap: this was the part he had been looking forward to telling.

"Oh, yes. There's not much doubt about that. Of course it wasn't general knowledge at the time, but over the years the facts have emerged." He looked down, and Charlie had to wait while he selected a sandwich topped with thick roast pork. "It was the death of his daughter Catriona in a car accident. It was the day of her wedding, and she and her husband were killed together."

"Ahhh." Charlie breathed out. Bertie Briscott appeared delighted to have made such an effect, and Charlie had to watch, fascinated, while a large piece of pork sandwich, apparently unchewed, made its way down the man's throat like a rodent swallowed by a snake. "And did he actually . . . *see?*"

"Yes, he did. Apparently the pair left the reception, at Stamford, where they then lived, and drove off for their honeymoon in Scotland. Soon afterward Byatt and his wife drove off up to Yorkshire for their first look at Ashworth, which they had just been left by an admirer. They passed the accident on the motorway, recognized their new son-in-law's car, and stopped. Yes, they saw everything."

"And were you going to deal with this in your book about Byatt?"

"Oh, yes. There was no objection to that."

"But there was objection to something else?"

Bertie Briscott gave a nervous little giggle, screwed up the empty sandwich packet, and stuffed it into his hold-all. He seemed to be considering the question.

"It's very difficult to say, really," he said at last. "Cooperation had in any case been spasmodic. I hadn't been granted an interview. If I wrote to him I might or might not get a reply, but in any case there was nothing that could be described as an exchange of letters, or regular answers to my questions. Then at one point when the biographical part was getting toward the present day, I had a note that just said: 'I don't see any point in talking about recent stuff. Too close. Leave that to the historians.' He never doubted that art historians would be interested in him, you notice. Anyway, after that—nothing."

"You wrote to him?"

"Oh, yes. Gently disagreeing with him. Then further questions. But I never got a reply."

"Was that why you gave up the book?"

"To be honest, not entirely." He discovered a stray crust that had dropped onto the seat, and he popped it in his mouth on the principle of "waste not, want not." "I wanted to earn an honest penny to buy a few home comforts in my retirement. I wasn't writing for fun, or to increase the sum of human knowledge. Byatt had several bursts of splendid creativity after his red period masterpieces, but frankly, in the last few years it's been downhill all the way. The grapevine has it that he has suffered a bad decline physically."

"He certainly is crippled with arthritis, or something similar."

The little man swiveled around in his seat.

"Oh, you have been allowed to meet him? Talk to him? You are honored—or very persistent. I suppose policemen have ways of insisting. Anyway, because of the poor quality of the recent stuff, public interest in him at the moment is frankly not high. The publisher I had lined up began to have doubts. I began to have doubts myself. An extra publication on your CV is not much use to you when you are retired. I thought about it and decided that Fran-

cis Bacon was much more likely to turn an honest penny
for me."

"I'm afraid I thought Francis Bacon was a writer."

"He was. Also a modern British painter. Specializing
in painting popes."

"Popes?" said Charlie, surprised. "You wouldn't get
much work painting popes, would you? The present one
seems to have been around forever."

Bertie Briscott burst into a paroxysm of nasal chuckling.

"Not living popes, *dead* ones. *One* dead pope in particular. He was quite obsessive on the subject." A thought
struck him and he went suddenly silent. Charlie let him
think on, looking over the rolling green lawns of
Cartwright Hall. "Not unlike Ranulph Byatt and his car
accident, now one comes to think of it. Though Bacon's
obsession lasted longer. . . . You don't think I could *team*
them, do you? Put them in tandem and write a book link-
ing them?" Charlie did not think the question was
addressed to him, so he saw no reason to reply. "I wonder,
do you think as a result of this murder there might be
increased interest in Ranulph Byatt?"

His face was tilted toward Charlie, the tone beseech-
ing. In other words, Charlie thought, is Byatt likely to be
hauled away in handcuffs? He always found that official
jargon was immensely useful in such circumstances.

"Our investigations are at an early stage," he replied
robotically. "We're not yet sure of the precise connection
between the dead man and Byatt's circle."

The bromide acted as a rebuke, and Bertie Briscott
looked chastened.

"Oh, really? I thought . . . I wondered, you know,

whether it would be of any help to you to have a copy of my manuscript, so far as it went."

It was in the nature of a peace offering, and Charlie accepted it as such.

"That would be very useful indeed, depending, of course, on whether there is a connection with Ashworth in this case."

"Of course." Briscott dived into the hold-all. "I took the liberty of making a photocopy on the Hall's machine before you came. You know, this has been a most interesting conversation. The idea of there being a connection between Bacon and Byatt hadn't occurred to me before our talk. But I wonder—the sadomasochistic vision in both their oeuvres. That could be a very strong sel—a very strong line of argument, drawing comparisons between the two. Otherwise the sexual line of comparison between them doesn't seem very strong, with Byatt being heterosexual and apparently largely monogamous. You would say that he and his wife were devoted, wouldn't you?"

"Apparently so," agreed Charlie.

"That's the accepted view, that she's been his muse, his helpmeet, his manager, the linchpin of his life, and that by and large he's been unusually faithful, for an artist. Whereas Bacon, of course . . . just any bloke he could manage to pick up. You wouldn't say the community at Ashworth were a sort of seraglio for Byatt, then?"

"I didn't get that impression."

"No-o-o. Pity. From the point of view of selling the book, of course. Well, if there's nothing else you want to know, I mustn't hold you up."

Charlie watched the self-important little man trotting in the direction of the hall, and wondered if he was ever going to write anything good enough or market satisfying enough to net himself a nest egg of reasonable proportion from any publisher. Somehow he suspected that the bottom would have dropped out of the Francis Bacon market before he had a manuscript to hawk. He stood up and got on the phone to Mike.

"What next, Mike? I've done all I could here."

"Well, I've just had a list from the police at Keighley of all the people at Ashworth, and a bit about their records. Not much there, apart from this Ivor Aston, who you know about. I think we could look a bit further into that. Mrs. Mates's husband took off in 1983, but no one ever thought there were suspicious circumstances. I think it's inevitably Ashworth next, if only to test your ideas."

"Thanks for that. Can I meet you there?"

"Yes, say in forty minutes' time, and we'll meet up by the gate."

"With all eyes on us."

"No bad thing. See you there."

Charlie took the back road, through Thornton and the little villages around Haworth. As he drove through Haworth itself he wondered if there was anything more to be done there with the new information they now had, but he decided not: if Patrick had been there, done anything to make an impression there, it would surely have come out in his painstaking questioning up and down Main Street—particularly as it would have been fresh in people's minds. He was willing to bet that Patrick had not gone near Haworth. In fact he could have taken the train from Manchester to Colne, then hitched a lift across the moors, getting put off at Stanbury before reaching Haworth.

He parked the car on the edge of a ditch just outside the Ashworth gate, and leaned on it, waiting for Mike to arrive. This time nobody came out anxious to share confidences with him. It was probably fancifulness, but this time he sensed apprehension: they were back, he imagined people thinking, and this time they might have new evidence. Well, they had that, and with a vengeance, and Charlie hoped he was right that this new evidence pinned the case unquestionably on the Ashworth community, rather than diverting suspicion elsewhere.

Ten minutes later Oddie drew up behind him, got out of the car, and joined him at the gate.

"Where do we start?" Charlie asked.

"At the top. The Forensics boys and girls are going to be here in an hour's time. It's the farmhouse and stables they'll need to start with. We'll have to prepare the people there, and give them the news of whose murder it is we're investigating now."

"As a surprise?"

"Most definitely as a surprise. That we're onto it, though whether it will be a surprise the boy is Patrick is another matter."

"I'll leave it to you."

"You have a watching brief. Definitely watching." Charlie nodded. Silent watching was something Charlie was good at.

Oddie swung open the gate and they walked purposefully up to the front door of the old farmhouse and rang the bell. The door was opened by Mrs. Max.

"Oh, it's you again."

"I'm afraid it is," said Charlie. "This is Superintendent Oddie. He's in charge of the case. Is everybody in?"

"Oh, yes. Not Master Stephen, of course—he's at Oxford as you know."

"I'd like to see everyone," said Oddie, "but I can dispense with Mr. Byatt if that's not convenient."

"He's asleep. He always has a long sleep in the afternoon. That'll be Mrs. Byatt and her daughter, then."

"And yourself, Mrs. Max, too, please," put in Charlie. She looked at him hard.

"I'll take you through."

She led the way down the hall to the sitting room door and opened it.

"It's the police again, Melanie."

Ranulph Byatt's wife and daughter were at tea, with a little plate of cakes and biscuits and a good large pot with a cozy over it. Both looked up, not particularly welcoming.

"Mrs. Byatt? I'm Superintendent Oddie. DC Peace you know. I have some news for you."

"I see," said Melanie, inclining her head. "That will be all, Mrs. Max."

"I'd like her to stay and hear the news," said Oddie. Melanie frowned but eventually nodded. She gestured them to chairs, but Mrs. Max remained standing by the door, as if to emphasize that she might be on Christian name terms with the ladies of the house, but she was not on sitting-down terms with them.

"What is your news?" Martha Mates asked eagerly.

Oddie looked at them benignly.

"I know that you have always believed that Declan O'Hearn left here of his own volition on the Friday before last. My news is that, to the best of our knowledge, that is probably true. Again, to the best of our knowledge, the boy is still alive."

"Thank God," said Mrs. Max.

"I told your constable here all along that he was making a serious mistake," said Melanie magisterially. "A *serious* mistake."

"You were quite right. It was a mistaken identification. What I would like to ask you now is what contact you have had with Declan's brother Patrick, whose body it actually was."

Because she had stayed by the door Charlie was unable to catch the initial reaction of Mrs. Max to the news. When he looked her way, her brow was furrowed. Melanie's reaction from the moment the words came out of Oddie's mouth was stone-faced: no emotion of any kind was visible there. But Martha's had been an instant dropping of the mouth in surprise, and Charlie could have sworn it was genuine, that this was the first she had heard of the presence of Declan's brother Patrick in the area. He had a sudden vision, in the form of a picture, of Martha as a babe in the wood—a lost and bemused child in a particularly threatening and impenetrable forest.

15

CRACKS IN THE SURFACE

As soon as he had revealed the identity of the corpse, Mike Oddie announced that a forensic team would be arriving shortly, and that he would like to question informally all three women separately. Melanie was still insistently playing, or overplaying, her role as the iron lady.

"I see no reason why forensic scientists or anyone else should pay any attention to this house," she said, her voice acquiring the boom of the born tyrant. "The dead young man had no connection whatever with the place, or with anyone in it."

"Then that is what they will find, isn't it?" countered Oddie, unfailingly courteous and quiet. "They will be investigating all the Ashworth cottages, not just this farmhouse. We believe the first thing Patrick O'Hearn would have done when he came to Britain was make contact with his brother."

"Why should he do that? Why shouldn't he bum—that is the word, isn't it?—his way round the country, as others do?"

"Because he and Declan were unusually close," said Oddie, and then chanced his arm by turning a guess into a fact. "And because he'd been made uneasy by some of the things his brother had said about this place in letters."

Melanie opened her mouth to continue the argument, then shut it again.

"If I might use your dining room, which I saw on the way in, to ask you all a few questions?" Oddie suggested, still quiet but now authoritative. Melanie nodded grimly. "And if you would stay here while we start with Mrs. Mates, and if you, Mrs. Max, would go about your business in the kitchen?"

Mrs. Max seemed relieved to escape; she was, Oddie guessed, a woman who had always preferred men's company to women's. Melanie appeared upset at being left on her own while her daughter was being questioned, but gave no clue as to why that should worry her. Charlie felt confirmed in his guess that Martha was the outsider of the family—the one who knew least, and was dangerous for that reason, since she had not been party to a coordination of stories.

Once in the dining room Oddie gestured Martha Mates to one side of the long table, while he himself sat opposite her. He told Charlie to leave the door open and to stand in the doorway, thus giving himself a good view of the hallway and of any movement in it, but also of Martha herself.

Martha was clearly nervous, and was making little or no effort to hide it. Perhaps she knew herself well enough to realize that she couldn't. She was not wringing her hands, but her fingers were engaged in agonized couplings, and her face was the battleground for occasional spasms, which gave her an aspect both twisted and slightly wild.

"I wasn't here, you know," she began, before Oddie was properly seated. "Not on the weekend Declan left."

"I know that," said Oddie. "Let me ask the questions I want you to answer. Where exactly were you?"

"I . . . I went to see a private detective on the Saturday. He's trying to trace my husband. I stayed with an old school friend: Hattie Wilmslow, Twenty-four Barton Street, Bellingham, SE6. We went to morning service in Saint Paul's on the Sunday." Her drab face lit up. "It was absolutely lovely. The services in Stanbury church are short these days, and of course they're very simple, but one does like something *more* sometimes, doesn't one? After that we did tourist things—went to Windsor in the afternoon, had a lovely meal at a good local Chinese in the evening."

"You were together the whole time?"

"Practically. Except on the Saturday morning when I went to the detective's office, of course."

"You say you're trying to trace your husband. Is this so you can obtain a divorce?"

"Oh, *no!*" Her eyes widened, adding to the wild expression. "That would hardly be worth the trouble, unless *he* wanted it. No, it seemed to me so unfair that my father is having to pay all Stephen's college fees and living expenses. I suddenly realized that Morgan may very well be able to contribute his share if he's still alive, and after all, why shouldn't he? The days are past when fathers can just walk away from their responsibilities, which is exactly what Morgan did. I just feel he should be found and made to pay up!"

She stopped, breathless and excited. Oddie would have liked to stop the interview and talk over impressions of what they had just heard with Charlie. Oddie's feeling was that the lady protested too much, that she was voluble not to explain but to hide—from herself as much as from them. But his instinct was to go on to other matters and to ambush her later on the subject of her husband.

"So when did you get back to Ashworth on—when was it?—Monday?" he asked.

"Yes, Monday." She quieted down a little, and thought back. "Let me see: Hattie and I had a nice, chatty breakfast together, and then I went for the train. That left King's Cross at about eleven, so it will have got to Leeds around half past one, but it was late, so I had a bit of a wait, twenty minutes or so, for a train to Keighley, then I got a taxi back here."

"So you'd be back here by about three?"

"About then."

"And when you arrived back you learned that Declan had left the previous Friday."

"That's right."

"Nobody mentioned his brother Patrick having been here?"

"No, of *course* they didn't," she said, firing up, "because

he hadn't. Not all that much happens here, Superintendent, especially now Dad is bedridden, so any visitor is a
subject of conversation. When I got back we just talked
about Declan, and how naughty it was of him to leave in
the night without giving us notice so we could make other
arrangements."

Oddie nodded gravely, suppressing any skepticism.

"Was your son still here then?"

"No, Stephen had just left for Oxford. The car had broken down again, but when the garage said it was something quite minor wrong, he packed a bag, walked to
Haworth, then drove it to Keighley. If I'd known it was in
a car park there I needn't have taken a taxi—but I suppose
I would, because I didn't have the key. I had to go to
Keighley to fetch it the next day."

She was at her best, or most relaxed, when prattling on
about trivialities. Oddie had a notion that all her life she
had seized on the banal to avoid facing up to reality, and
for this reason she was usually dismissed as a silly
woman.

"What happened when your husband left you?" he
asked. At once the fingers started knotting into each other
again.

"What happened? Well, he just left."

"Did you have a row, agree to separate after a long
period of not getting on, or what? You've obviously lost
touch."

She swallowed, as if what was in her throat was an
unpalatable fact she wanted to get rid of.

"He just left while I was away from home. That was
typical of Morgan—he hated facing up to things. The mar-
riage hadn't been going too well, but he wasn't even will-

ing to talk about why. Stephen had been a difficult baby, and was by then a very noisy child. Morgan got very irritated about *that*, but I don't know . . ."

"If that was the reason he left?"

"No. I've never understood that, really. Maybe it was everything building up. . . ."

"How did it happen?"

"I was away with Stephen in Manchester, seeing a specialist about his asthma, and having three days of tests. It *worked* too, because over the years he's had less and less trouble with it, until now he never thinks about it. When I got back here Morgan had gone, told Dad and Mum that he was fed up and needed more space. That was typical of Morgan."

"What did he do?"

"Do?"

"For a living."

"Oh, well, that's difficult to say, really," she said with a perplexed frown, as if Morgan Mates was a man she had barely known. "He did a bit of journalism, a bit of cartooning—*Punch* took several of his drawings. He was an insurance salesman for a while. I had a bit of money: my grandmother, Mother's mother, had left money to both her granddaughters, and I got Catriona's share as well when she died. We managed."

It seemed to Oddie and Charlie that if one were to make a guess about what had happened to Morgan Mates after leaving Ashworth, it would be more likely that he would be on the streets than that he would be able to contribute to his son's Oxford fees.

"Did you live here at Ashworth while you were married?" Oddie asked.

"Yes. At Stamford we lived with my parents, but here we had the cottage that Arnold Mellors is in now. Morgan was just starting to decorate it when he . . . left me."

At the doorway, looking alternately down the hallway (where the only event had been Melanie opening the sitting room door, regarding him, then retreating back into the room) and at the questioning in progress at the table, Charlie had been bursting to ask a question. At this point he could hold it back no more.

"Mrs. Mates, do you suspect that your husband is dead?"

She jumped.

"No, of course not! Why?" She paused. "Well, of course it's a possibility. It's a long time since he left me."

"How long?"

"Fourteen years. Nineteen eighty-three it was. Stephen was five at the time."

"It occurred to me that your hiring a private detective might really be a way of finding out whether he is alive or dead."

"I told you why I'm hiring him," she said, an obstinate expression settling on her face, but her fingers telling another story. "If the detective found out he was dead, that would be the end of it, but it's not the reason I'm using him. I expect Morgan has stumbled from one job to another, or is sponging off one person or another."

Charlie wanted to ask one more question, and it came out before he had weighed the wisdom or folly of asking it.

"Are you quite sure your husband was alive when he left Ashworth? Isn't what you're really afraid of that he was dead by the time you and Stephen got back from Manchester?"

The chin shot up.

"*No*, of *course* that's not what I think. I was told all about his leaving, and his things were gone." The fingers suddenly stopped feverishly interlocking with each other and went up to her face. "Why are you asking me about Morgan? And such silly questions!"

Suddenly, as if making a decision, she went tense, then got up and without looking at either of them almost ran out of the room. They heard her stumbling up the stairs.

"I'm not sure that was wise," admitted Charlie at once.

"It's done now. Time will show. You notice how she jumped. She assumed that's what you meant when you asked that first question, that he'd been murdered, and then realized she'd half fallen into a trap, and said in effect 'of course he could have died in the meanwhile.' Do you really think her husband was killed here?"

"I think she has that suspicion at the back of her mind," said Charlie cautiously. "I wouldn't go further than that. You weren't happy with her explanation of why she was going to a private detective, were you?"

"No, of course not."

"I thought it had to be a question of finding out whether he was alive or dead. And I instinctively felt she was desperate to discover that he is *alive*."

"To still doubts?"

"Exactly. But whether it was wise to ask that now, with no evidence of any sort . . ."

"Anyway, I don't think we'll ask Mrs. Byatt about that. We've no reason, as you say, to think that Mates's disappearance was anything other than a discontented husband taking off—though you're probably right that she, at the back of her mind, was suspicious. It will be interesting, if we can find out, to know whether the daughter brings up our question with her mother, or whether she lets the suspicion fester, as it presumably has up to now."

It mattered very little, in fact, what they brought up with Melanie Byatt. On almost every subject she stonewalled the question completely. In her manner, somewhere between the Roman matriarch Volumnia and Lady Bracknell, she sat straight, rarely deigned to look either of them in the eye, and answered where possible in monosyllables. By and large she treated them like the under-gardeners which, her manner suggested, would naturally have been part of her establishment in an earlier age.

Since she denied ever having seen Declan's brother Patrick, denied he had come to Ashworth, said she could not even remember whether she had ever heard him mentioned and had to be reminded that Mrs. Max had mentioned him on Charlie's first visit, it was not long before Oddie, from the drying up of possible questions, was forced on to another subject.

"Your grandson Stephen left Ashworth on Monday?"

"Yes."

"Why did he do that?"

"He decided to go up to Oxford early."

"That was a sudden decision, wasn't it?" She shrugged. "Was there anything that triggered it?"

For once she looked in Charlie's direction.

"Mr. Peace," she said, her voice oozing condescension, "tell your superior that young people do unpredictable things."

"Yes, they do," agreed Charlie easily. "But often they

seem unpredictable to older people, but seem logical and well thought out to the young person himself. Monday was—what—September the twenty-first."

"Something like that."

"The Oxford term doesn't start till well into October. Could you make an effort to get into Stephen's mind, guess at what reason he could have had for going up so early?"

There was a long silence. Was she meditating on whether to reply, or what to reply, or trying to think up a convincing reason that would satisfy them? Eventually she said, still as if offering a few pence to a beggar, "Stephen is not a very intelligent young man. Sad but true, and something he tries to hide from himself. He went to a very good private school near York, but he never prospered there. He finally got into Brasenose because his father had had an undistinguished career there back in the sixties, and because Ranulph offered the college a very good picture for their hall. I suspect Stephen realized that if he was to make anything of his chance he either had to get into a good set, or he had to work hard to get a reasonable degree. He has never yet shone socially, so the second alternative was the only one open to him. He's gone up to get a lot of reading done so he can steal a march on the other freshmen."

So if you're so confident of his reasons, Oddie felt like asking, why didn't you tell us that from the start? Instead he said, "So that's what he told you on Monday before he set off?"

"Not in so many words," Melanie said carefully. "We were making practical arrangements about where he'd leave the car in Keighley, and who would pick it up."

"And financial arrangements too?"

"Oh, Stephen had enough money for the fares and the first few days. He was going to set up a bank account in Oxford, and then we would forward the necessary funds."

"We? His grandfather, you mean?"

"Of course."

"Mr. Byatt is presumably very fond of his only grandchild."

"Naturally."

It was the only thing she could say, granted the line she was taking, but it was said after a brief pause, and with firmly set lips.

Mrs. Max, when they talked to her, was much more accommodating, but the real disappointment was that weekends were her time off.

"Saturdays I always come in for the mornings," she said, "and I serve them a light lunch and leave them the wherewithal for their evening meal—either a cold one or something in the oven they can just switch on. Sundays Martha usually cooks a roast or a pie or something—she can cook if she wants to."

"Martha was away last weekend," said Oddie.

"Oh, they'll have managed. It's not part of my job to worry about what they do when I'm not here. They'll probably have rung one of the Chinese or Indian places in Haworth that deliver."

"Melanie can't cook?"

"Won't, if she can help it."

"So after midday on Saturday you were free until Monday morning?"

"That's right."

"What did you do?"

"In the afternoon I pottered around in my little bit of garden, clearing up dead stuff, and in the evening I read my magazine and then watched *Casualty* on television."

"And Sunday?"

"Sundays I like to cook for myself—things I wouldn't serve at the house because *some*one would turn up their nose: tripe, liver, kidneys, that sort of thing. In the afternoon last weekend I went to my sister's—she lives between Oakworth and Keighley, and I walked there."

"Did you see anything unusual, or hear anything from the house on your way there or back?"

"No, I didn't. I was driven back to Stanbury about seven, and just walked down the lane. Frankly, it's not likely I would, is it? If anything was done, it wouldn't be done by a window, would it? I don't think anything was done at all."

"You said, I believe, that on Saturday you saw Mrs. Byatt throw Declan's note in the fire. What about Monday? Was anything more said about his leaving Ashworth then?"

"Nothing beyond how inconvenient it was."

"His brother Patrick wasn't mentioned?"

"He was *not*," she said without hesitation. "And surely he would have been if he'd called there."

"What about Stephen, and his decision to go up to Oxford early: what did you hear about that?"

"Not a great deal. Quite early on, while I was washing up breakfast things, I'd heard him phoning the garage from the hall. He phoned again about an hour later, and I heard him tell Melanie it was 'no big deal' what was wrong with the car. Then there were several huddles around the place, and the next I knew he was striding out with a big knapsack on his back, and Melanie told me he'd gone to

Oxford for a bit to get down to work. Another of his fancies, I thought. Your constable will have told you he's not a favorite here. He's changeable, goes hell for leather in one direction, then changes tack—particularly when he has a hangover."

"He had a hangover?"

"Well, he looked very tired, anyway. He wasn't back that late the night before, so I don't know that it was the drink."

"You heard him come back on Sunday night?"

"Oh, yes. It was about ten o'clock or so."

"What do you mean, you heard him? What sort of noise was he making?"

"The *car*. I heard the car. I should know the noises it makes. I'd seen him drive out about half past seven, and I heard him drive back as I was going to bed about half past ten."

"I see. Could he have gone out again later?"

"Easily. I hear nothing after I've dropped off, like my son told your young constable there. Someone must have, mustn't they, if the car landed up in Haworth that night."

"Of course. When he drove out at seven-thirty, did he have anyone with him in the car?"

"No one. He was alone. Unless someone was hiding."

"Or unless someone was a corpse in the boot," said Charlie to Oddie when they were alone in the dining room. But neither of them was happy with that idea.

"Then why didn't he dispose of it?" asked Oddie. "It was dark long before ten-thirty, when he returned."

"The most likely reason," said Charlie slowly, "is that when he went out there was no corpse to dispose of, and when he came back there was."

Oddie considered this.

"Or there was soon after. Because either Stephen Mates did the garroting after he came back, or it was done while he was away. And if it was the latter, who on earth did it? Because looking at Mrs. Byatt, I can't see her hands having enough strength. And from what you've told me about her husband, he needs help painting, let alone turning the screw on that horrible implement."

"That leaves us with one of the disciples," said Charlie. "Or with all of them together."

16

SEE NO EVIL

They were interrupted by the sound of cars. Charlie registered with a start how much his ear had accustomed itself to a car-free environment. No wonder the ears of the Ashworth people took note of the comings and goings of their one vehicle. The arrival of Forensics meant four cars left higgledy-piggledy in the lanes around the farmhouse. Mike got up to let in the six- or seven-strong team, then came back into the dining room.

"They know what they're looking for," he said. "What

say we let them get on with it? I think it's time we talked to the disciples."

"Shall we do them together, or divide them up?"

"Together, I think. You know these people better than I do."

"I've only really talked to Colonel Chesney."

"By reputation, anyway. You may pick up things I would miss if I was on my own—discrepancies, contradictions. You can have a watching brief."

"'Forgive me, Lord, I have sinned.'"

"It's nothing to do with what you asked Mrs. Mates. We've yet to learn that that was counterproductive. Don't go all sensitive just because I ask you to button your lip."

"I'm all girlish uncertainty," said Charlie. "You know that."

They emerged from the house, which was filled with the subdued bustle of the forensics people going about their finicky business, and in the weak, late-afternoon sun, they looked about them.

"Where do we start, Boss?"

"With the one who's done time, I think," said Oddie, after a thought. "It's where we normally would. I don't see why we should make a difference, even if he is middle class and artistic as hell."

Ivor Aston had had ample time to adopt the manner that seemed to him the best form of counterattack. He greeted them in a friendly, courteous way, sat them down, and offered them tea or coffee, which they refused. All in all he seemed to be presenting a surface of normality for their inspection. Here I am, he seemed to be saying, your friendly neighborhood child pornographer.

"Do you want to discuss my record first," he said easily, "or recent events at the farmhouse?"

"I think we'll discuss recent matters first," said Oddie, equally easy.

"Right you are. I hear it was Declan's brother who was the actual victim. I had no idea he had one."

"Can we stick to the question-and-answer approach?" said Oddie, smiling more kindly than he felt. "It usually works rather well. We're working now on the assumption that Declan O'Hearn did indeed leave Ashworth voluntarily on the night of Friday-Saturday last week. Have you any idea why he left?"

Aston shrugged.

"None at all. Just the itchy feet of the young, I would imagine. My impression was that he'd rather enjoyed helping Ranulph paint, been rather proud of being part of a new creative surge. I had a fair bit of chitchat with him when Ranulph invited me to a special private viewing of his new canvas, and that was the feeling I got. But in the long run that's not going to weigh against seeing the world, mixing with people of his own age, having a few girls, maybe experimenting with drugs."

"Doing what all young people do, eh?"

"That's right."

"You say you didn't know that Declan had a brother. Did you see any young man around Ashworth that weekend?"

"No."

"Didn't suspect that the Byatt household might have found a replacement for Declan?"

"No. And I very much doubt they did."

Oddie nodded neutrally.

"What were you doing on that Saturday, sir?"

"I went sketching over toward Hardcastle Crags. It's a favorite spot of mine. I walked over the moors and spent the day there. I have my sketchbook to prove it."

"Someone who remembers you would be useful, sir."

Ivor Aston thought—or gave the appearance of thinking. Because surely he had got it all thought out before they came?

"I stopped on the way for a pint and a sandwich at the Horse and Whippet. They'll remember me there. I'm well known—and well shunned—in this area."

Oddie nodded, still neutral.

"I see. Talk to anyone while you were sketching, sir?"

"No. The odd walker was around, but I didn't talk to any of them. I began back about half-four, so as to be home by nightfall. I had another pint at the Grange—the same applies as at the Horse and Whippet: at the Grange they serve me through clenched teeth, if you can imagine that, thanks to my sister."

"And when you got back to Ashworth itself, you didn't notice anything unusual?"

"Nothing at all."

"Nor saw anybody you wouldn't normally see?"

"No."

"Well, the fact that you were walking may make it easier to check your alibi than if you had driven. What about Sunday?"

"I went to church in Haworth. They have a new rector—very good, he is. Then I came back here, cooked a simple meal, then read and relaxed for the rest of the day."

"And you noticed nothing unusual around the place?"

"Nothing. I was in rather than out, working up one of my sketches to a watercolor."

"I see." Oddie decided to go off on a new tack. "You mentioned your sister. I gather there seems to be some idea around the place that she enjoys telling everybody about your record and what you were inside for. Is that what you think, sir?"

"It's certainly one of her very small tally of conversational topics."

"Why should that be, sir?"

"You'd have to ask her that."

"You don't seem averse to mentioning the topic yourself."

Ivor Aston grimaced.

"I don't have much choice, do I? If she hadn't wormed her way into Ashworth I don't suppose I'd ever bring the question up, unless someone here became a good friend, which no one *has*. As it is, the best way is to talk about it openly."

"You are ashamed of your past, then, sir?"

"*No*," he said with sudden force. "I am certainly not ashamed. I wouldn't have talked about it because I know what the popular attitude is—and the people here are nothing if not commonplace in their reactions. But don't imagine it's an attitude I share. I have certain tastes, and they were born in me. How can I be ashamed of things I had no choice about?"

"You weren't imprisoned for having tastes," countered Oddie quietly.

"In effect I was. I get my kicks from looking at a certain sort of picture, and I shared them with other like-minded men."

"The pictures and printed material you circulated," Oddie pressed on, having done his homework before he left police headquarters, "covered a range of . . . interests, tastes, involving children; some of them were quite revolting, some of them extremely sadistic."

"They were *acted*, Superintendent, *posed*. They fed the fantasies of people with those tastes. Pornography like that saves them, us, from acting out our fantasies in reality."

"Oh? And do they never *stimulate* people to act them out in reality?"

Ivor Aston sighed.

"This is an old and well-trodden argument, as I'm sure you know. All right, I won't generalize, I'll speak for myself: as far as I was concerned, this was fantasy stuff I was circulating. In any case, what happened as a consequence was not my responsibility."

"Nor how the photographs were obtained, nor the effects on the children who 'acted' them out?"

"No. Children are remarkably resilient."

"Hmmm. What made you decide to come here, sir, on your release?"

Ivor Aston sat back in his chair, relaxing his tense pose.

"I'd always admired Ranulph Byatt. I am a modest but a real artist myself—the only artist here, in fact, apart from Byatt, and the only one he can communicate with."

"And you told him about your prison sentence and what it was for?"

"Of course."

"And his reaction?"

"In his letter of reply he never mentioned it, and he never has since. Don't confuse Byatt with the mediocrities who have gathered around him."

"You say you've 'always' admired him, sir. How long would that be?"

"Well"—he smiled—"not my whole lifetime, I must admit. I went to an exhibition, a traveling one, at the Leeds City Art Gallery, oh, around 1985."

"And what was it you admired about these paintings?"

"Oh, their power, the imaginative sweep, the completeness of the artistic vision."

"I see. Would you say that was what attracted most of the disciples here?"

"You'd have to ask them. They wouldn't choose *me* as their spokesman, would they?" His face twisted into a sneer. "I'm the loner, the one out on a limb. And that suits me fine, just fine."

"Fire away," said Charmayne Churton. She was sitting in the one downstairs room of her bijou cottage, filling an old armchair, with her legs just too far apart for anyone's comfort but her own. For some reason, whether social, sexual, or personal, she had dabbed an unusual amount of makeup on her face, but she reminded Charlie of nothing so much as a battleship decked out for a fleet inspection.

"Could you tell us about your movements last weekend?" Oddie asked her.

"Saturday I was in Manchester practically all day: shopping in the afternoon, Cliff Richard in *Heathcliff* in the evening. Wonderful show. Got the train back to Halifax, then took a taxi back here."

"When did you hear about Declan O'Hearn leaving?"

She had her pat answer.

"Someone told me on Sunday morning, when I was

pottering around the place. Surprised me. I'd rather liked the lad, and I'd've thought he'd have had more staying power."

"Did you notice anything unusual about the place on Sunday—any*thing* or any*one*?"

"Nothing at all. Should I have?"

Oddie's face was impassive. If she had heard about Patrick O'Hearn, this was something she was not letting on.

"How did you come to settle in this place?"

"Well, of course I'd always admired Ranulph Byatt. I'm speaking as an amateur, a dauber and a dabbler," she simpered, "but I'd been struck by the imaginative nature of his work, its tremendous variety, its sheer *punch*. So when I heard that Ivor was planning to come here when he got out—of Strangeways, that is—I thought: That's for me. I've got a bit of money from our parents: they left everything to me after . . . you know. So I came over to see if there was a vacant cottage, and, bingo!"

"You're fond of your brother?"

She paused before she replied, wondering, Charlie thought, whether to lie or to sugarcoat the truth.

"Not really. We've never had much in common. But I thought I should do what I can."

"In what way? You don't live together or anything."

She snorted.

"God forbid. I mean rehabilitation, getting back into the community, that kind of thing."

"But you've never made any secret, I believe, of his prison sentence?"

"No. Should I? If you're going to rehabilitate yourself, you shouldn't do it on the basis of a lie."

It should have sounded good, but it didn't, coming from her.

"It's a point of view," said Oddie noncommittally.

She leaned her prow forward and pushed her stern back.

"If you had young kiddies, would you want a man like that living near you? People are waking up to the dangers these days. They've a right to know. People like that never change."

So much for rehabilitation and getting back into the community.

"Does your brother have any convictions for offenses against children?" asked Oddie, very conscious of having changed his position too.

"He peddled child pornography. Isn't that an offense against children? As far as I'm concerned, that tells you where his tastes lie, and tells you what a danger he will always be."

"Maybe."

"There's no 'maybe' about it. As long as there's breath in my body I'll make sure people know what kind of a man he is." She groped into the recesses of her mind and produced an old-fashioned phrase to cloak her motivation: "I'd be failing in my duty if I didn't."

Both men watching her had the strongest sense not just of pleasure and satisfaction—that, they had expected from what Colonel Chesney had told Charlie—but of a life that had been adrift, rudderless, but which had suddenly found a purpose: the persecution of her brother and an unfailing, never-ending means of accomplishing it. To Charlie they seemed locked in a perverse bond, and he wondered whether there was any great moral difference between the persecutor and the pornographer. He also wondered whether there was anything in their childhood, their background, that would account for it. He was willing to bet that Ivor Aston's first sexual experiments had been with his younger sister. That, surely, must have been the origin of the perverse bond. He felt sad that he could summon up no sympathy for the victim.

"Now, then, what is it you want to know?" asked Arnold Mellors, rubbing his hands.

They had already run through his activities of the past weekend, established that he was at home virtually all of the time, but had seen no strangers in the area and noticed nothing out of the ordinary at the house. Kipling's monkeys, Oddie decided, had nothing on the Ashworth community.

"You say you spent a lot of time on the phone, sir."

"That and consulting the *Directory of Art*. I was looking for an agent for Ranulph's new pictures. Of course I could only ring those who looked as if they were working from home, it being a Saturday."

"Byatt is thinking of changing his agent?"

Mellors's face fell a fraction.

"Well, acquiring one again. I've been doing the donkey work for him these past few years. Frankly his . . . his genius has been in remission. Mostly rather tame, ordinary pictures, and prices had to be modest accordingly. There was nothing much an agent could do for him. I was announcing that he was starting a new and remarkable phase, and sizing up possible agents to act for him. Just trying to be useful."

"What personal qualities were you looking for?"

"A willingness to subdue their own personality to Ranulph's. An ability to take orders, to take abuse."

"To be subservient, at least apparently?"

"Yes, I think that would be fair."

"You have no illusions about him?"

"I have no illusions about his *greatness*," corrected Mellors. "So I take all the rest as part of the package."

"This new phase, how long has it lasted?"

Mellors shuffled his feet a little.

"Oh, only a few weeks so far. You think it ridiculous to talk of a new phase on that basis, but, you see, we know Ranulph. When he is gripped by his de—when inspiration strikes, it lasts: picture after picture tumbles out. Of course, in his condition we don't expect the feverish production of his red period, but a series of remarkable pictures *is* very much in the cards. In fact, I would say it's a certainty."

"And Byatt is concerned that they fetch the best possible price?"

"Of course. Is there anything wrong with that?"

"No, no."

Mellors rubbed his hands, gripped by the enticing prospects.

"What would be ideal would be a much-talked-about exhibition, as much publicity as Ranulph could stand in his current state of health, and then the pictures released on to the market, probably gradually. But, of course, that will be up to his agent."

Wistfulness came into his voice with the last sentence. Oddie decided to press him.

"You found an agent for him?"

"Oh, that will be Ranulph's choice. I talked to several, and selected three or four possibilities. I'm just trying to be useful."

"You seem to have enjoyed acting as Byatt's agent."

"Oh, I did, I did. Even if I never handled first-rate stuff."

"I find this community here rather puzzling," said Oddie, in confessional mode. "I expected to find a community of artists, kindred creative spirits to Byatt, and that's apparently its local reputation. But it's not, is it?"

"No-o-o."

"What exactly brings you together, motivates you?"

Arnold Mellors pondered.

"Well, of course we've all been interested in art, in different ways. And when we discovered Ranulph's work we realized he was *the* great modern British artist, as far as we were concerned. When a cottage became vacant I was over the moon. It's a privilege to live near him—we all feel that: to watch him making art, whether on a lower level or, as now, the finest, most creative level."

"Hmmm. You're saying it's a sort of residential cheer group, a very superior fan club."

Mellors's face expressed distaste.

"All right: mock us. I'd prefer to say we are a circle of appreciation."

But Oddie felt that neither of them had really got to the heart of the matter.

"What was I doing last weekend?" asked Jenny Birdsell. "Oh, gracious! If you asked me what I was doing yesterday

I probably couldn't give you a clear statement. But last weekend! Impossible! Do you remember, Mary Ann?"

"I wasn't here," said Mary Ann, looking up from a book with bright pictures of men in white bathrobes in the Holy Land. "I was working in the bookshop in the morning and bearing witness in Keighley market in the afternoon."

"Oh, dear, I suppose you *would* have been." She shot her a look, uncaught by her daughter, that was baleful to the point of dislike. "I *wish* you would do the normal things that other girls do—you know, like bringing home boyfriends instead of elderly men in peaked caps who bang drums and hand out hymn sheets. Oh, well—where was I?"

"Saturday," prompted Oddie. "Let's start with last Saturday."

"If only I *could*. I just can't remember. Unless I visited old Mrs. Young in Stanbury. In fact, I think I probably did."

"My mother tends people's bodies," said her daughter in her clear, fresh voice. "Bodies are within her scope, souls way outside it."

"I don't *tend* them. It's so long since I was a nurse I'm way out of date with medicines and techniques. But I do know enough to be able to bring them a bit of ease and comfort, and, of course, some of them never get a visitor from one week to the next. Do away with me if I ever get to that stage!"

"When was this visit? Morning or afternoon?"

"Oh, afternoon, I should think."

"And what did you do for the rest of the day?"

"Pottered in the garden, I would imagine. Or pottered in the kitchen and around the house."

"You noticed nothing unusual around here either then, or when you went to and from Stanbury?"

"Good heavens, no. I'm afraid I'm not the noticing type. Though I would register people. And really, I think you are on the wildest of wild-goose chases if you're connecting this young man—who I gather is *not* Declan, as you originally thought—with Ranulph and the people at the house. Anyway, I saw nothing and nobody out of the ordinary."

"What about Sunday?"

"Well, Mary Ann is always occupied with the Army's church service in Keighley in the morning, but I try to make sure she has a good traditional Sunday dinner afterward." She made it sound like a poultice on a wound. "I *think* I went out painting in the afternoon—probably Pennistone Hill, I think. I'm so vague. Anyway, if that *was* Sunday I came home as the light was fading, and I was *exhausted* as I often am after that sort of activity, and I went to bed with a book. I *think* I heard Mary Ann come in about nine, but that was all I did. After that I was out to the world."

"I see," said Oddie. He turned to Mary Ann. "And you?"

"In the afternoon I rested and played records. We have a small CD section in the shop, and I borrow them sometimes. Then I went to Bible discussion class in Stanbury in the evening."

"You didn't see or hear anything unusual during the day, or later when you got back from Stanbury?"

"Not what you'd call unusual. I heard Stephen come home just as I was going to bed."

"Good," said Oddie, glad of the confirmation. "Do you remember when this was?"

"It would be about ten, I think. I generally get home from Bible study around nine, but I had a cup of Ovaltine and listened to the radio after that."

"Are you sure it was Stephen you heard?"

"I know the car. It wheezes and coughs."

"A car is not a person."

"Only Stephen and his mother drive it. And his mother was away that weekend."

Oddie thought. He turned back to her mother.

"You didn't hear him arrive home?"

"I hoped you wouldn't ask me that. Now Mary Ann has mentioned it I have a slight feeling that I heard the car, and then footsteps, but you really *mustn't* rely on anything I say, because it could have been the night before or the night afterward."

"The night afterward Stephen had left," Oddie said. He turned back to Mary Ann. "As I said before, the car is not a person. Did you hear footsteps too?"

"Yes. Yes, I did. Man's footsteps. But now Mother's mentioned it I heard them later too. When I'd gone off to sleep. I'm sure I half woke up and heard someone going back to the stables."

"Were they the same footsteps as you heard earlier?"

"Yes, I think so. Stephen's footsteps. But it's just an impression, nothing more. And I wouldn't want to stand up in court and *say* it was Stephen. After all, can you identify someone's footsteps, particularly when they're just walking down an earth lane?"

"When I lived in Bournemouth, in the nurses' home,"

said Mrs. Birdsell, "we used to lie in bed and identify the footsteps of nurses coming home or going on shift, and we were right eighty percent of the time. But of course they were women. Men aren't at all as individual. Their shoes are very similar, for one thing. Even earlier, I wouldn't dream of saying the footsteps I heard coming home *were* Stephen's."

No, no, thought Charlie, who had listened in uncongenial silence, but he did wonder what precisely was Jenny Birdsell's game. Because he couldn't accept that she was vague to the point of imbecility, which was obviously her match plan at the start of the interview. Yet as soon as her daughter had mentioned hearing Stephen's footsteps— obviously the first she'd heard of the matter, since apparently they did not communicate—she'd felt obliged to go along with it and give it what identification she could consistent with the pose of vagueness she'd assumed.

Which didn't alter the fact that both Mary Ann and Mrs. Max had heard Stephen that night, and Mary Ann had thought she had heard him later on after she'd gone to sleep. Charlie thought it was about time someone had a talk with Stephen.

17

AFTER THE FACT

They paused outside the gate of Mrs. Birdsell's cottage but then, since her garden was as bijou as her cottage, looked at each other and moved farther away.

"Only Colonel Chesney to go," said Oddie.

"I've talked to him," said Charlie, "but not about what he may have seen last weekend."

"Do you know, I'm beginning to discern a pattern," said Mike. "And I have a strong suspicion that Colonel Chesney will have seen nothing last weekend."

"Good detection," said Charlie, "sound reasoning."

They were interrupted by a bleep on Oddie's phone.

"From Mrs. O'Hearn?" he said, after identifying himself. "To tell you the truth I wasn't expecting to get much sense out of her yet, poor woman. . . . I see. . . . A painting? Well, we can't know till we've looked into it, can we?"

As Oddie tucked his phone back into his pocket, Charlie asked, "What was all that about?"

"Mrs. O'Hearn has talked with her other children, back home in Donclody. I don't know how relevant this is, seeing the victim was Patrick, not Declan, but apparently Patrick got a letter from Declan only a few days before he took off for England. Still fairly happy about being part of the Byatt household, and happy about helping the old man paint. But there was a proviso this time, a nagging doubt. He'd seen a painting that made him unhappy. Said all the usual things about not knowing anything about art, but he said he was worried about the mind behind it."

"That's all?"

"Yes. I'd like to talk to the O'Hearn children—still more, see the letter, if it was kept."

"As the next best thing we can look at the pictures," said Charlie. "It's probably one he saw in the house, and there's a chance it may still be around."

"If he was sensible he wouldn't have voiced his worries," agreed Oddie.

"He's still around, remember."

"Of course. We ought to be talking to him before long if our description was halfway accurate. It was Patrick that was killed, and he hardly had time enough here to start making an issue of pictures. I see Patrick as a very different kettle of fish from his brother. If he arrived here he may have been in an aggressive mood, and he died because he picked a quarrel."

"He was *garroted*," said Charlie, for at least the second time. Mike nodded in agreement.

"OK, OK. Let's forget Chesney and have a look at the pictures."

The ground floor of the farmhouse was a hive of activity, and when they started upstairs they realized that the first floor was too. As they reached the landing they were stopped short by a bellow from Ranulph Byatt's bedroom.

"Who's that, then? *More* of you? How many do you need?"

Charlie raised his eyebrows at Mike and went to the door.

"Hello, Mr. Byatt. Do you remember me?"

He was rewarded by a sulfurous glare.

"Don't talk to me as if I were an idiot. I'm old, not retarded. Of course I remember you. Do you think you don't stick out?"

"This is Superintendent Oddie, who's leading the investigation."

"Ah. Well, I hope you know whose death you're investigating this time."

"The body was found to be that of Patrick O'Hearn," said Oddie. "Declan's brother."

"Hmmm. Well, he never was here. Your people, who are *infesting* this place, won't find any traces of him."

"Well, if we find that's so we'll relieve you of our presence. Because modern forensic science is so accurate and meticulous that if he has been here he'll leave a trace for our boffins to identify. We don't need threads caught on nails these days, Mr. Byatt."

For a moment his eyes showed disconcertment. Then he growled, "Well, they won't find traces here, unless they plant them themselves."

In the corridor Oddie sighed.

"If only coppers who plant evidence on suspects realized what a legacy they leave for other coppers investigating other cases. . . . Hello—what have you got there?"

A fresh-faced, young constable had come up, one of the forensic team, holding in his plastic-gloved hand a wodge of black-and-white photographs. He put his finger to his lips, and moved some way away from the door of Byatt's bedroom, over to an ancient and dusty trunk. He spread the photographs across the top, and said in a low voice, "Thought you'd like to see them—not for evidence, just for background, like."

Oddie and Charlie bent close. The pictures showed the Ashworth people at some kind of party. In several of them a painting on a easel appeared.

"The viewing of the new painting," said Charlie. "Ivor Aston had a private one, but there was a general one as well."

They looked at the faces. The intention of the photographer had clearly been satirical. He had aimed to catch the expressions and body attitudes of a group of devotees—of fawners and flatterers, anyway. But the devotion did seem genuine, even if exaggerated. Jenny Birdsell gaped, Ivor Aston was smug in his previous knowledge of the picture, Arnold Mellors was judicious but openly admiring.

"We found them in the young man's darkroom," said the boffin. "Stephen Mates, his name is. I thought they might be of interest."

There were three photographs of a group that included Declan O'Hearn. They picked out Jenny Birdsell, still looking breathless and yet watchful. In the background they made out Martha, looking suspicious yet uncertain. In the foreground was Melanie, talking to Declan. All three pictures had been taken from different vantage points, seemingly within a few seconds of one another. Melanie in one was looking at Declan out of the corner of her eye. Testing him, Charlie guessed. Probing. Declan's attitude was courteous, self-deprecating. Then in the third picture his face had changed. A shutter had come down. It was not so much blank as defensive.

"A suggestion has been made," said Charlie.

"A suggestion? Something specific?"

"I don't think so. I think Melanie was circling round a subject, and when she got close Declan told her flatly that there were things he wouldn't do."

"Right. I wonder if there were things that Declan wouldn't do but that his brother might do. I rather think there might have been. Now, where are these paintings?"

They found the studio without difficulty, and Charlie switched on the lights. There was no picture on the easel, which intrigued him. Perhaps Arnold Mellors had already taken charge of the new one. His eyes roamed around the spacious double room, and eventually lighted on a stack of framed pictures leaning against the wall in a dusty corner.

"Let's have a look at those," said Oddie, whose eyes had followed Charlie's. "If Declan's duties were mainly here, helping with the process of painting, then those seem the most likely ones."

Slowly, in the less-than-perfect light, Charlie displayed

the paintings one after another. Landscape after land-scape—accomplished, not unattractive, but lacking in energy, not very much superior to the sort of thing that any technically well-equipped painter could produce.

"I see what that Mellors man meant," said Oddie, "when he talked about genius in remission."

The picture, when it was finally reached, well down in the pile, jumped out at them. It seized attention by the ferocity of its attack. It seemed not just from another period, but from another world. Charlie noted its place, then took it over and put it on the easel, so as to scan it in the best possible light.

"It must be from the same phase as the one I saw in Bradford," he said. "The red period."

The red predominated in the lower right side of the picture, but gradually the men took in other aspects—the outflow of the picture onto the frame, the bluish white of splintered glass, the gradually emerging dead face. It was like a tormented shriek, and yet the energy of the painting gave it something of the quality of a triumphant war cry.

"Remember that motorway crash?" asked Oddie. "The only reason the Byatts got on our computer? That's what this picture puts me in mind of."

"Funny no one's mentioned the accident," said Char-lie. Then he added, after thinking, "If it was the basis of this picture, of the one in Bradford, maybe of others in the red period—maybe *all* the pictures in that period—then it *is* funny no one at Ashworth has mentioned it."

Oddie looked dissatisfied.

"Sometimes people don't mention things because they're *known*," he said. "For all we know it may be a cliché of art criticism: 'Inspired by the horrible death of his daughter and her bridegroom in a smash on the M1 after their wedding, the paintings of the red period . . .' and so on."

"Could be," said Charlie. "I'll read the typescript of the book I got from the little gnome in Bradford. That should tell me. I can still see this picture coming as a big shock to young Declan."

"*That's* true."

"Because there's a sort of . . . *relish* of the horror of it. I wonder if he knew about the motorway smash. Either way, after those landscapes this picture must have come as a shock."

Leaving the picture on the easel, Charlie strolled over to the collection of pictures stacked face out to the room. The red period picture had been nearly, but not quite, at the end of the stack—five more pictures to go, in fact. He began leafing through them: landscape, landscape, a chalk picture of Melanie, landscape, and then—

The last picture of all. Charlie saw at once it would have to be taken out and looked at closely. Even in dim light its power, the hideous punch it packed, almost unnerved him. He took it from the stack and brought it over to the light. Together, and in silence, they looked at it.

The subject matter of the picture was unusually clear, presented in realistic terms though with a degree of distortion. At the forefront was a face—empurpled, screaming or gagging, enlarged for impact, while behind it the small body was arching in an agony of pain and terror. It was clearly a picture of someone in their last throes, and in the most desperate torment. It was done without mercy—even, both men sensed, with a species of perverted pleasure.

"Who'd want a picture like that on their wall?" said Charlie.

"Not even the painter, apparently," agreed Oddie, "considering the fact that he keeps it from the general gaze."

"I think it's time I read up about Byatt's other significant 'periods,'" said Charlie. "I would think this must be part of one of them."

"You do that. Tonight. And I think it's time someone went to have a talk with Stephen Mates. You."

"Me? Alone?"

"I think it would be best. Young men together."

Charlie grimaced.

"He doesn't sound the sort I'd get along with. He sounds a snotty git, anxious to impress you with his own superiority."

"Well, you've got enough evidence to kick the stuffing out of him. Get him frightened, and find out how much he knows."

As he drove down to Oxford next day two subjects were warring in Charlie's mind: how to deal with a touchy and difficult young man, and the manuscript he had read the previous evening about the later paintings of Ranulph Byatt.

"The pictures that comprise his purple phase," Briscott had written, "seem to have been painted late in 1984 and early in 1985, though they were not released on to the market until two years later. The pictures of this intensely concentrated phase are more abstract than the classic 'red period' paintings, with the horror more thoroughly assimilated. Here and there one may think one can discern a bulging eye, an empurpled tongue, even perhaps the outlines of a human form. But in general what impresses the viewer is the energy of execution, and how this energy conveys violence and terror even while it assumes no recognizable form or meaning."

Did it make sense? Charlie would not have been able to put that sense into his own words, but after having seen the pictures in Byatt's studio it did. That last picture in the stack, he felt sure, was the realistic picture from which all the later, more abstract versions sprang.

What was worrying was that there was at least one other "phase" of remarkable pictures mentioned in the Briscott book, though he had fallen asleep before he had reached the details.

The dreaming spires may have looked like the New Jerusalem from a distance, but in among them, in the dust, noise, and fumes of the Oxford traffic system, they were more like a medieval Detroit. Charlie made it, with five wrong turns, to police headquarters in the city and there left his car. He made a courtesy call on the duty sergeant, picked up a map, and set off for Brasenose on foot.

The porter in the lodge at Brasenose was hunched over a computer, picking his nose. He was dismissive.

"Is that the bloke who turned up out of the blue one evening last week?" He pressed some keys on his computer. "Yeah, that's him. Said he'd come up early, and demanded a room cool as you like, as if we were a hotel. I said, 'Look, mate, the college is full of toffee and sweet-meat manufacturers'—their annual convention, it was, and we were bursting at the seams. I said, 'This college can't afford to be empty during long vacation, or any other vacation, come to that.' I sent him off with a flea in his ear, but I gave him a printout of landladies who are willing to take young gentlemen—so-called—in the vacs."

"Has he been back," Charlie asked, as the man was turning away, "or told you he's got rooms?"

The man turned back reluctantly.

"I've seen him go through on the way to the library. Looked a bit at a loose end." He sat down and pressed some more keys on his computer. "Yeah, he must have told the night porter. He's got a room at Thirty-one, Meadow Lane. Grotty, but close by. It'll be three weeks before he can have his room here."

The porter sent him off on the first stage of his journey, and he consulted his map for the later ones. The lodgings were about ten minutes' walk away, a peeling Victorian terrace house with all the charm of a detention center. The only good thing about the landlady Charlie could think of to say was that she probably made no difference in her manner on account of his color: it was clear she was horrible to everyone.

"No, 'e's not in," she said, standing as if barring the way of an invading army. "I don't encourage them to stay in. 'You didn't come up early in order to sit in your room reading,' I says. 'You get out and study in one of them liberies. 'Nuff of them around,' I says. I'd never be able to call me 'ome me own if I let 'em stop in all day. Oh, Gawd, there 'e is."

Slouching along the road, scuffing his feet, was a tall,

saturnine young man in a deep green shirt and light slacks, both of which looked expensive. The expression on his face showed he was neither confident nor happy. He stopped at the gate.

"Mr. Mates?"

"Yes?" The manner said "So what?" or "What's it to you?" As with the landlady it was a manner that seemed habitual rather than racist. Charlie flashed his ID at him.

"DC Peace, West Yorkshire Police. Could we talk somewhere?"

Stephen swallowed. The landlady looked implacable.

"Best not here," he said. "You can see why. We could walk. Or go to a pub."

"Not a pub. Is there any park nearby, or place where we could sit down?"

"Magdalen hasn't got a conference on at the moment. I suppose we could go there."

As they walked toward the bridge Stephen said, "How did you find me?"

"No great feat of detection. I asked the Brasenose porter. Why? You're not in hiding, are you?"

"*No.*" He swallowed again. "Though it's sometimes seemed like I'm in exile. There's no one up at all. Nothing but conferences and conventions. Not a soul worth talking to."

"Tough," said Charlie, his word being accepted at face value. "I believe you're getting your reading done early."

"Oh, yes, there's that. But I had hoped to make a few contacts as well." They turned into Magdalen, and Charlie found they had to pay for the privilege of entry. Stephen Mates gazed at the sky, and with a sigh Charlie felt in his pocket. "Now, this is a college!" breathed Stephen.

"Brasenose not up to scratch?" inquired Charlie, keeping his voice neutral. This time Stephen shot him a glance.

"Above my level," he admitted. "Well above. I only got in because my father was there."

"Useful," said Charlie.

"Even then it was touch-and-go. I've been to introduce myself to the principal, who was up when Dad was up. He says his main interests were practical jokes and fast cars. He obviously wasn't impressed at all. I think it was Grandfather who tipped the scales: his money, his picture, and his name."

The bitterness in his voice was unmistakable. By now they were in the largest quad, New Buildings lawn, which was almost deserted. Just what Charlie had hoped for. He nodded at a park bench, and they sat down, one at each end.

"You've been in touch with Ashworth?" Charlie asked.

"I spoke to Mother a couple of days ago. She was away when I left. She said you were investigating Declan's disappearance—if he *has* disappeared."

Charlie let that ride.

"You were in the house at the time. Did you hear him take off during the night?"

"No."

The boy veered between confidentiality and truculence. He had had a week to decide on his attitude, but he hadn't picked one. It didn't seem to Charlie that he was a fast learner. He also seemed strangely unformed, as a fifteen- or sixteen-year-old will often be, but as a nineteen-year-old should not be. Charlie guessed it sprang from growing up in a household with two dominant personalities in it. He hoped it meant that the young man might still choose a fruitful rather than a self-destructive path for his life.

"What about the other arrivals at the farmhouse that weekend?"

"Other arrivals? There weren't any other arrivals."

"There was one, at any rate. The boy whose body you disposed of in the car park behind the Haworth Tandoori."

"I didn't! You can't prove anything like that!"

The voice was raised, but a note of panic could not be disguised.

"Oh, but we can," said Charlie, hoping he was right. "Our forensic team is probably going over the car and the stable at this moment. If the body was in the boot, traces will be in the boot. And with your mother away, you were the only one who drove."

"That's not true. Plenty of people at Ashworth can drive. They just don't because Granddad disapproves of cars. Isn't that a joke, when he's the only one who's got one?"

"You were heard coming home, then going out again." Charlie decided to come clean with what he suspected to have been the order of events. "I don't think you had anything to do with the murder, Stephen. But I do think you agreed to dispose of the body." He waited, and a flicker appeared in the boy's eyes. "If you're going to keep out of jail, which I don't promise, and if you're ever going to make anything of yourself at Oxford, you're going to need all the goodwill from the police you can muster. Do you want time to think about it? I can take a turn around the quad if it would help you make up your mind."

After a second Stephen shook his head.

"No. I don't need time."

"Right, then. Let's get back to my earlier question. When did Declan's brother arrive at Ashworth?"

Stephen's dark eyes were set into reminiscence.

"It was the Saturday afternoon. We'd had lunch, and Mrs. Max had gone. I was upstairs in my little darkroom, doing some developing. I heard the doorbell, laid down the print I was working on to dry, then went out onto the landing. By then, though, Melanie had got to the front door, so I didn't bother to go down."

"So you didn't meet or see him then?"

"No, it was later, a lot later. I went out, walked to Stanbury to get some cigarettes at the pub. On the way out I heard Melanie and a man laughing and talking in the drawing room. By the time I got back they were upstairs with Ranulph, still laughing and talking. The voice sounded like Declan's—same brogue, same quality—and I thought he was back, so I went into Granddad's bedroom."

He paused.

"You weren't welcome?"

"The talking and the laughter stopped. Then Melanie introduced me, explained who I was and who the visitor was. I made some small talk to him for a minute or two, said I was sorry he'd missed his brother, that sort of thing. Then I sensed they wanted me to be off. I went along to my bedroom, opened and shut the door, but I stayed on the landing, listening."

"Why?"

"I don't know. . . . I felt they were up to something."

"And did you hear anything that told you what it was?"

"No. Not really." Stephen screwed up his face. "But

they were being so nice to him. Even Granddad. They were *making up* to him. Do you understand?"

Charlie nodded encouragingly.

"I think so. Were they being so nice it seemed they were trying to entrap him, hold him there?"

"Something like that. But nothing you could pin down. The only thing I really remember was Granddad saying, 'Declan was a nice boy, a lovely lad. A bit straitlaced, though. You're a young man who's seen a bit more of the world.' Granddad never soft-soaps people as a rule. But it was mainly their friendliness, their welcoming him. Granddad's not like that, nor Melanie, by nature."

"How much more of Patrick did you see?"

Stephen shook his head.

"Hardly anything. I saw him taking a tray up to Granddad's room, saw him and Melanie talking in the kitchen."

"You didn't talk to him again?"

"No. I was out, mostly."

"Why?"

"*Why?* Well, I was going to pubs. I drove to Hebden Bridge—"

"You're not telling me *why* you were out so much," Charlie pressed him. "Did you not want to be at home?"

After a moment's hesitation, Stephen nodded.

"I suppose not. It felt all *wrong,* somehow."

"Did you ever have suspicions about your father's disappearance?"

"*What?* My father's?" He had almost jumped when the surprise question was sprung on him. There was shock in his voice and eyes, but there was something else too: was it surprise at its being brought out into the open for the first time? Was the mere question a revelation of things in his mind he had never acknowledged. "I never had suspicions. I just wondered—wondered what happened to him. I thought it odd, his going out of our lives so entirely."

"Do you think your mother has suspicions? Is that why she's using a private detective?"

"I never thought of that!" He seemed dumbstruck. Charlie felt sorry for him. He was really not very bright, even about his own situation. "I suppose you could be right. Do you mean she wants confirmation that he left her, but she really fears he was . . . *mur*dered?"

"Yes."

"Poor woman. My poor, bloody mother. And everybody there looks down on her, thinks her next thing to an idiot." He shook his head. "God, what a household! I've always said it. That, at any rate, isn't something I've just woken up to."

It was like a silly boast. It was pathetic. Again he seemed to Charlie more boy than man.

"What happened on the Sunday night?"

"I got back from a pub in Cullingworth. I wasn't drunk. I'd just been spinning out the time, hoping they'd be in bed when I got back. But they weren't. They were waiting for me."

"In what way? Who was?"

"Ranulph and Melanie. In Ranulph's bedroom."

"Anybody else?"

"No."

"And no body?"

"No. All that came out of the blue."

"How did they break it to you?"

"Oh, indirectly. There was something they wanted me

to do. I might find it shocking. But there'd been an accident. Nobody would understand."

Charlie's eyebrows shot up.

"Not a very original story. How did you react?"

"I thought if they wanted me to do something nasty, perhaps illegal, they were going to pay for it." He looked at Charlie. "I didn't know what it was then!"

His tone was anguished. He was trying to convey that he did have a conscience, hidden somewhere. Perhaps it was true.

"When did they tell you it was a body?"

"As . . . negotiations went on. Eventually, if we were going to agree on a price, I had to know what it was. I was appalled."

"Why did you agree?"

He looked down like a guilty dog.

"Melanie appealed to me. Said Granddad's life couldn't end like that, shut up in jail. . . . All right, I admit it: I suppose I thought if that was what they wanted me to do, I could screw a lot of money out of them."

"Did they tell you what happened?"

"No! I didn't want to know. Was it very nasty?"

"You don't want to know. Keep it like that. Where was the body, then?"

"It was already in the boot of the car. I didn't see it till the car broke down in Haworth."

"Really? So someone had taken it to the stable, then. They must have been waiting to put it in when you got home."

"Someone must have. Melanie just said, 'You'll find it in the boot.' They had Mother's keys, of course."

"This was when you agreed on a price?"

"All fees paid, and five thousand pounds down." He said

it almost with self-loathing. Perhaps he was redeemable. Charlie was lost in thought.

"So someone killed him, then humped him down to the paddock, then into the car. Who could manage that?"

"A lot of people. He wasn't a big chap. Wiry, thin, quite short."

"I suppose you speak with experience."

Stephen shuddered.

"It was horrible beyond belief. The car broke down on the straight between Bridge House and Haworth station. I got it into the little station forecourt and sat there, out of my mind with worry what to do. I'd been aiming to drive over to Bingley Moor and dump him there—as far away from Stanbury as I thought the car would go."

"You say 'him.' Did you know who it was?"

"Somehow I did. I suppose it was the buildup, all the niceness to him. 'Come into my parlor'—that sort of feeling. But they'd not said and I'd not asked. Anyway, there I was, stuck in Haworth. I got out of the car and started looking around. I knew the area well, but having a body to dispose of gives any place a whole new perspective. There are steps up to the car park from almost opposite the station. I got to the top and was just wondering whether this was a good place to leave him when the lights went off in the Tandoori and two of the waiters came out. They went toward a car together and they were talking in English. One asked the other whether he'd got to a garage yet, and the other said, 'No, I don't know whether it's worthwhile. I think it's a write-off.' They drove off, and that left one old car in the car park. I went over and checked and the lock on the boot was broken. It seemed as good a place as any."

"It was, in a way: it wasn't discovered for days."

"I thought it might stay there till it began stinking. I went back to my car and waited till the traffic had dwindled to virtually nothing. Then I opened the boot and got the body out. . . . I don't want to talk about that. I tried not to look. Anyway, I got it up the steps and into the boot, then I banged the lid down and ran. I thought it would draw attention to the car, and us, if I left it in the forecourt, so I managed to turn it round and push it with the driver's door open back along the straight to the garage."

"You did well, in the circumstances. It was the circumstances that you did badly in."

"I know."

"Then you walked home, I suppose. What sort of reception did you get?"

"The house was in darkness. But as I walked along the landing Melanie's door opened—gave me a hell of a fright, though I should have expected it. She just asked me if I'd got rid of the body, and I said yes and went on to my room. It was the truth too!" he added, as if what he was being accused of was untruthfulness.

"And the next day you left for here."

"Can you imagine how much I wanted to get away? If the car hadn't been fixed I would have walked. I had a bit of money myself, and I got out of Melanie any cash there was in the house, with the promise that the balance would be sent by check when I had opened a bank account here. Melanie has always handled the household's money, at any rate since Granddad became so feeble. Then I got the hell out of there. For some reason I didn't want to face Mother."

"Why not?"

His brow furrowed.

"I don't know. I had some feeling that she's always been somehow out of it, kept apart from all that, whatever it was. Innocent, if you like. And I didn't want to see her, knowing what I knew . . . having done what I had done. God, what a mess I've made of my life. What's going to happen to me?"

"I don't know," said Charlie, with a real sense of pity. "You've helped yourself a lot, telling me all this without too much pressure and before Forensics comes up with physical evidence. But you're going to need all the brownie points you can muster with the college authorities, I would guess."

"God, yes. Is it worth it? I came here to get away from Ashworth and my life there, and all I get is the same kind of loneliness."

Charlie felt very old, giving him advice.

"You'll make friends. But do you want the sort of friends who'll make up to you for all the wrong reasons? Because you're a famous painter's grandson? Because you're involved in a notorious murder case in which you got rid of the body? Any sort of fast or snob set here is not likely to welcome you on any other grounds, are they? Think about it. Wouldn't you be better off getting your head down, getting into your reading and finding your friends among people who need to do the same?"

Stephen brooded. "Maybe. . . . Yes, I suppose that's true. I'll never find anybody who's cocked things up in quite the monumental way I've done."

"I don't know. Don't wallow in self-accusations. If you cocked things up you had a lot of help doing it. You might ask yourself what kind of people would ask a young man, just setting out in the world, to get rid of the body of a murder victim."

Stephen nodded.

"The sort of people who provided the body in the first place, I suppose."

Charlie stood up.

"I think that about sums it up. If you're in trouble, they're in much more. Come on: let's go back to your lodgings and pack. I'm afraid you're going to have to come back to Yorkshire."

18

THE HELPING HAND

"Did you believe him?" asked Oddie the next day as they sat in Oddie's office in Leeds Police HQ with Stephen Mates in custody in one of the cells.

"Yes, by and large, I did," said Charlie, who had thought over the interview a lot the night before. "Of course, there may have been a degree of slanting—letting himself off the hook, exaggerating his own horror and reluctance. Wouldn't you, in the circumstances? But on the facts, and the sequence of events, I believed him. And what he said is borne out by Mary Ann Birdsell's memories, hazy though they may be."

"Not to mention her mother's even hazier ones. Though we may ignore those, in my view."

"Absolutely. We treat with skepticism everything said by any of the Ashworth disciples."

"Because on any assessment," said Oddie somberly, remembering his talk with the medical experts, "garroting a victim would need the sort of strength in the hands neither Byatt nor his wife remotely has at this stage of their lives."

Charlie nodded.

"And according to Stephen Mates's story, someone took the body down to the stable area, then put the body in the boot, while Melanie and Byatt himself negotiated terms for its disposal."

"It might be worth investigating which of the Ashworth disciples has a driving license."

"But it was Stephen who drove the body and dumped it," protested Charlie.

"Precisely. Why didn't the person who had done the murder also drive the car and dump the body?"

"Right. I should have thought of that. . . . You know, if it hadn't been Stephen, they would have tried to persuade one of the other drivers there to do it, and probably succeeded."

"Why do you say that?"

"Because I see all of the Ashworth mob as in it, in some way. Not directly, not participating or watching, but *knowing*. Realizing that Ranulph is an artist turned on by violence, by cruelty, and knowing that things have occurred in the past that stimulated his creative urges to heights he couldn't otherwise have reached. And they all keep quiet about it, probably don't even discuss it among themselves, because they're not close to each other. But each one *knows,* is aware, or at the very least suspects."

"I wonder if you're right," said Oddie reflectively. "You know them better than I do. If you are, it will be the devil's own job to prove—and another one to frame any charge based on it."

"Probably out of the question. I wonder if Declan O'Hearn suspected the same thing, and that helped him to his decision to get the hell out of there."

"I *wish* he'd been picked up," said Oddie. "Until we find him, there's always the nagging doubt in the back of our minds as to whether he's alive or not."

"I think he is. We have enough bodies. What we need now is a lot more facts."

"Here's one," said Oddie. "Stephen Mates was treated for asthma and related illnesses at the Royal Salford Hospital in late September 1984. They specialize in diseases of the lungs."

"And while the boy and his mother were away, the father disappeared," mused Charlie. "And in the succeeding months there was a second sharp upsurge in creativity on the part of Ranulph Byatt. By the way—this is a very long shot—what sort of detail is there on the motorway accident that killed Catriona Byatt and her husband?"

"A fair bit. It was a very nasty accident. I've got a computer printout somewhere here." Oddie rummaged in the mass of paper that regularly blotted out the plasticized wood of his desk when he was on a difficult case. "Here."

Charlie took it and read.

"Hmmm. A fast car overtook them and cut in, causing them to brake sharply and be hit from behind by an old Land Rover, the driver of which was severely injured. . . . Interesting. I must get something checked."

"Before you go," yelled Oddie to his departing back, "what about that other 'period' in Byatt's painting?"

"Ah, yes," said Charlie, turning back, "I read up about that last night when I got home. Not as interesting as the earlier ones—not to art critics, I mean. No predominant color this time: some critics call it his 'black' or 'gray' period, but apparently that's stretching a point. Briscott quotes one or two critics from influential newspapers and periodicals. One mentions feet, shoed feet, looking as if they were suspended just an inch or two over a floor."

"But the pictures are not admired?"

"I didn't say that, but not so admired as the earlier ones. Apparently most of them are very abstract, at a time when abstraction is rather going out of fashion."

"I see. And when were these painted?"

"More slowly, not so much in a burst of energy as both of the earlier 'period' paintings were. The arthritis taking hold, presumably. But most of them came in the years ninety and ninety-one."

"We don't, to put it bluntly, have anyone who disappeared around 1990, do we?"

"Not that I've heard of."

"We could ask the Keighley Police."

"Sure. Except that the Keighley Police would never have heard of Patrick O'Hearn, or Declan either, and they don't seem to have been informed of the disappearance of Morgan Mates either." Charlie paused. "There was one thing I wondered . . ."

"Spit it out."

"Most of these people seem to have done up their cottages from a semiderelict condition. But Arnold Mellors talked about his cottage becoming vacant. That's rather different, isn't it?"

"It is. It's a long shot, but a possibility. What do you think our best move would be, psychologically?"

Charlie meditated for a moment or two.

"Take Melanie Byatt in for questioning. Remove her from their midst. We've ample evidence against her for the disposal of the body. Taking Byatt himself might be an extreme step, what with his fame and his state of health. But we can insulate him. Then all the disciples are on their own."

"I was thinking along those lines." Oddie paused. "I'm far from feeling tenderly disposed toward Byatt, and I wouldn't think twice before taking him in, but maybe you're right. Go off and do your checking, and then we'll bring in the matriarch. I'll ring Keighley, see if they have a suitable cell. You can take her there to cool her heels, and then come back to Ashworth and we can do some questioning and thinking."

When, a little over an hour later, they drove once again down the rutted track to Ashworth, a few questions had been answered in their minds, but many more remained unclear. This, Charlie felt sure, would turn out to be the crunch day. They left their car ostentatiously outside the farmhouse and rang on the doorbell. It was Martha Mates who opened it. Her face showed the frankest of apprehensions.

"Oh, it's you. I thought you'd be back. Stephen rang last night and said your constable was asking about Morgan."

The Corpse at the Haworth Tandoori

"I know he rang. I was with him."

"Morgan was his father, but my husband. Why were you asking Stephen, not me, about him? Why were you asking about him at all?"

"I think you can guess why, Mrs. Mates," said Charlie. "Today we're needing to speak with your mother."

"My mother?"

They ignored her as people seemed to do in her circle, and she bumbled after them as they proceeded down the hallway and into the sitting room. No apprehension or uncertainty disfigured the face of Melanie Byatt as she sat, straight-backed, in a tall chair, gripping her cane.

"Yes?"

"Mrs. Byatt," Oddie began, looking at her unflinchingly. "I must ask you to come with us for questioning in connection with the murder of Patrick O'Hearn, and—"

"But you can't! Mother, tell them they can't!" Faced with an implacable stare, Martha turned to the policemen. "How dare you! My mother is an old woman. Can't you see how weak she is? She is in no state to—"

But Melanie Byatt was struggling up, and she now began walking to the door, paying no more attention to her daughter than if she were a buzzing fly. At the sitting room door she paused, not to look back in any sort of retrospection, but to get her breath. Then she walked magisterially down the hall and out the front door. Outside the gate a second police car had arrived, containing two uniformed policemen from Leeds, who Oddie had arranged would follow them. Over by Charmayne Churton's cottage a little knot of Ashworth residents was gathering, a ripple of whispering rising from it. They did not look threatening—a chorus rather than a rescue posse.

Melanie ignored them all. Charlie led her to the second car and helped her into the backseat. Then he went around and got in beside her, and signaled to the uniformed driver to start.

"Keighley Police station," he said.

The car backed up, then drove toward the gate, through it, and up to Stanbury. On the whole of the quarter-hour trip to Keighley, Melanie said nothing, but stared straight ahead. Charlie thought that questioning her was going to be about as informative as Prime Minister's Question Time in the House of Commons, and a lot more silent.

In the farmhouse Oddie had stationed the other uniformed constable outside Ranulph Byatt's bedroom. When the artist started roaring questions and abuse, Martha pleaded to be allowed to talk with him. Reluctantly Oddie agreed, but insisted that the constable stay in the room throughout.

"Five minutes, that's all I can allow," he said. "Then I'll expect you down in the sitting room."

In the meantime he went downstairs and through to the kitchen. The morning's events had not stopped Mrs. Max in her preparations for lunch. But she paused in her activities to regard him balefully.

"I don't know what things are coming to," she said, "when a sick old woman is bothered and badgered and driven away like a criminal by grown men who should know their manners better."

"Mrs. Max, I'm investigating three possible murders," said Oddie. The woman's jaw dropped. "Someone's age or

fragility is not going to stop me asking questions and trying to get at the truth. Do you understand me?"

Mrs. Max, after a moment, nodded.

"And that includes Ranulph Byatt himself. Now, how
long has Byatt been crippled with arthritis?"

"Oh, Lord . . . Well, it came on gradually, like it usually
does. Of course it was regarded as a great tragedy here,
because of the paintings. There was no sign of it at the
time of what they called the 'red period' paintings. These
silly labels. . . . On the other hand he *was* having difficulty
when he painted those last pictures which the critics really
liked. Six or seven years ago, that would be. They had to
develop ways to keep him painting. He'd have been in a
terrible state otherwise—if he couldn't paint, I mean.
Martha took over the mixing of the colors, and was always
on duty during his painting session. We had to get a new,
higher chair for him. Everything was done that could be.
He has so little power left in his hands, you see."

"Yes, I see."

"It's tragic to see him at times."

"What about Mrs. Byatt?"

She couldn't answer for few moments.

"Oh, I'm not sure. It was slower in her case, and of
course we didn't pay so much attention, weren't so worried, because it wasn't as if she did very much with her
hands. I'd say she was already sometimes in pain when I
came here fifteen years ago, but it's been very gradual, and
she's coped accordingly."

Through the window over the kitchen sink Mike saw
the Ashworth acolytes still clustered around Charmayne
Churton's front gate, still talking. From time to time

they glanced apprehensively in the direction of the farm-house.

"Thank you, Mrs. Max," he said, and left the kitchen.

As he walked down the hall he satisfied himself that Martha Mates had, obediently if reluctantly, put herself in the sitting room, where she seemed to be having difficulty finding anything to do. As he let himself out through the front door, Charlie and the other uniformed constable drove up and parked behind him.

"Stay with me," he said to Charlie. He turned to the uniformed man. "Will you go and take guard duty outside the sitting room? It's where the daughter is."

They were being watched. Any policeman is watched, either directly or out of the corners of eyes. Oddie and Charlie were both inured to it. As they sauntered up to the group it showed signs of spontaneously breaking up. Oddie held up his hand.

"Don't go. I can see you're all worried. Mrs. Byatt is simply helping us with our inquiries—I'm sure you've heard that phrase often enough on television, but it's a perfectly good one, and the truth. That's what she's doing. I'd like to ask you to do the same. Will you?"

They all after a second or two nodded, like solemn schoolchildren.

"I'd like to know how this little community formed itself. Who was the first of you to come here?"

"Oh, I was!" It was Jenny Birdsell speaking, trilling enthusiastically. "When I came there were just the Byatts here, and Mrs. Max and Joe."

"And that would be?"

"Well, Mary Ann was three. I'm not good on dates, but she's now eighteen, so you can work it out."

"When you say the Byatts were here, does that include the Mateses?"

"Oh, yes. Martha, Morgan, and little Stephen. He was a lovely little boy then. Such a shame . . ."

"Right. Who was next?"

"I was," said Charmayne Churton, with something like a simper. "Ivor had his cottage reserved for him, but he was unavoidably detained." She leered at Oddie. "So I came here and got his cottage ready, *not* that I got any thanks for it. And then Walter came, just a month or two later."

"That's me," said Colonel Chesney. "There were several cottages became available at that time, because Ranulph had several of them done up at once—roofed, electricity installed, just the most basic things. The rest we did ourselves, or had done for us by professional people if we hadn't the skills."

"That was with the proceeds of the 'purple period' paintings," said Ivor Aston.

"I see," said Oddie. "When exactly was this?"

"I came out in 1990," said Aston, deliberately unembarrassed, as a snub to his sister. "Was I next? No, Mellors was already here, weren't you? I was in fact the last."

"That's right," said Mellors. "I came in June 1990, a month or two before Ivor."

"But yours was not one of the newly refurbished cottages?"

"No. It had been done up for some time, and someone had been in it before me."

"Who was that, sir?"

Mellors seemed puzzled by the question.

"Bloke called—what was it now?—Jake. Jake Felgott. A Yank."

"And he left?"

"Found it didn't suit him. So I got his cottage."

"Some of you will have known him, I suppose?" said Oddie, looking around. He felt rather than could have pinned down a flicker come into someone's eye.

"Several of us knew him," said Colonel Chesney, his voice hard with distaste. "Happy-go-lucky type, practically a hobo—a very irreverent bloke."

"Maybe he found the atmosphere of . . . admiration for Ranulph Byatt not to his liking?" suggested Oddie.

"Maybe."

"And have any of you had any contact or communication with him since?" Oddie asked. They all shook their heads.

"Wasn't the sort who sent Christmas cards," said Chesney. "Wouldn't have been in any hurry to make contact again. He thought us all a bit of a joke."

"I see." Oddie began to turn away, but as he did so Charlie asked, "Which of you have driving licenses?"

"Or can drive, whether or not you have a license," amended Oddie.

"I do," said Mellors. "I've always borrowed the car here when I wanted to take canvases to galleries."

"I do too," said Colonel Chesney. "In the British Army today you can't *not*."

"I have one," said Charmayne, "but I don't. Drive, that is. Ranulph always says it's impossible to *see* landscapes, let alone *feel* them, when you're whizzing by in a car. How right he is!"

"Rather ignores the fact that you might want to use one to stock up in a supermarket," Charlie pointed out. "And you, sir?"

"I don't have one, and I can't," said Ivor Aston. "I've never in my life sat behind a driving wheel."

"And I don't and can't either," said Jenny Birdsell.

"Didn't you use to be a district nurse?"

"Long ago. Used a bicycle. It's how we all got around then. They were just beginning to talk about us having cars when I decided to give it up."

Charlie nodded, and this time he and Oddie did turn away, and left the little group. They made their way back to the farmhouse, nodded to the constable standing on sentry duty in the hall, and then took over the gloomy dining room, with the two windows that looked out on most of the surrounding cottages. Out in the lane the little group of acolytes was dispersing.

"They're off to digest things," said Oddie.

"So are we," said Charlie. "I hope we understand things better than they're likely to do. We need to think where all this is taking us. In other words, what really has been going on here since the Byatts moved in?"

"You think we should go in for a conjectural history?" Oddie asked. Charlie nodded. "All right, I'll begin."

But he had to sit there for a while before he could collect his thoughts and guesses into a suitable narrative sequence.

"Round about 1981," Oddie began, "Ranulph Byatt found himself as an artist. It happened when he witnessed the crash which killed his daughter and her new husband, or arrived to view the wreckage. Doubtless in one part of his mind he was horrified and grief-stricken, but in another part he was excited, aroused."

"Could he have been unaware of the sadistic side of his nature?" Charlie asked.

"Probably not. But he'd never allowed it to get into his art, or maybe never found a way to use it in his art. This experience showed him the way. When he moved here he threw himself into an orgy of painting that liberated that side of him, harnessed it for artistic ends. He was releasing the fascination that pain and destruction had always had for him. And those pictures made his name."

"And they began to get him the sort of admirers that worship unreservedly," contributed Charlie. "What was released in him, they recognized in themselves."

"Yes, I think so. But unacknowledged. You notice when the disciples talk about his painting they use words like *power, imagination.* Never words that would really define the appeal." Oddie paused a moment before he took up the sequence of events. "The vividness of the memories gradually faded. The productive burst was over. But he'd recognized the source of his real genius as a painter, and so had Melanie, who had always been the totally uncritical supporter and source of inspiration. He needed a fresh stimulus, and they both knew it. And by what must have seemed a stroke of fate, he found he could both satisfy his fascination for horror and justify it by presenting it to himself and her as a piece of justice. He had the idea that his son-in-law Morgan Mates, also traveling north to Ashworth, was the cause of the accident that he had already exploited so successfully."

"Yes—I can see how the idea originated. I've been through the case reports again, and checked with the Vehicle Registration Office in Cardiff. A witness said that the car that was speeding and cut in on Catriona's car had a number plate something like CXN and the suffix Y, and it was a sports car. Someone in the police must have relayed this information to Byatt. The car didn't stop, of course. Mates had a BMW, with the number plate CXW and the suffix Y."

"Rules about what could and could not be revealed to interested parties in a case were looser then," said Oddie. "I did things in those days I shudder at now. This would have been another police force, and there would have been no reason for them to check the cars in Byatt's own family. How long that grisly pair nursed their suspicions, we don't know, nor whether there was any basis for them, but they took advantage of his wife being away to exact 'justice.' I'd guess it was poison, something like cyanide. Cyanide is a lot less instantaneous, as a rule, than it is in detective stories."

"Would they need help in getting it down him?"

"That's the crucial question, isn't it?"

"We can't be sure they would," Charlie said, after reviewing in his mind the little they knew about Martha's husband. "They were still pretty able-bodied. Stephen was told that at Oxford his father was fond of cars and practical jokes. It could have been presented as a joke. They'd found out he'd been unfaithful to Martha. A mock trial. Sentence: forced to swallow an emetic. Pure guesswork, of course. But Byatt loved the consequences—the long-drawn-out, agonized death."

"Yes. We mustn't assume an accomplice, beyond Melanie, of course, in that one."

"But the next one, probably a hanging. Hanging someone is *not* easy. They would need all the help they could get, especially as they were by now badly weakened by arthritis, and even though a botched job might be more to Byatt's taste than a clean and quick one."

"One of those already here," mused Oddie. "Not Mellors, then. If we're right about the victim—chosen for his irreverence, and his hoboism, which made inquiries unlikely—Mellors came in for the cottage later."

"I don't see Mellors as a likely executioner."

"If we're right they are *all* possibilities, all people with sadistic undercurrents to their personalities. A man would seem to be the obvious choice."

"Aston says he wasn't out until later in 1990, when the last creative burst was already in full swing, if Briscott is correct."

"That we can check," said Oddie. "Chesney is the obvious possibility. I wouldn't have thought that Charmayne Churton would be much use in carrying out a hanging."

"Don't be too sure," said Charlie. "She's built like a tank."

"True. And if malevolence is a requirement, she has sufficient and to spare. What about Mrs. Max?"

"I don't see her as a disciple at all. She's never shown any sign of responding to Byatt's art. She's here because what's convenient to the Byatts, having a live-nearby housekeeper and cook, is also convenient to her. She seems like a simple countrywoman—sturdy, common-sensical, unimaginative. I can't see her even understanding what's been going on here, let alone participating."

"Maybe. A big maybe. That's her surface. Then there's the younger generation. We can rule out the Birdsell girl, can't we? She wouldn't have been old enough, would she?"

"About ten at the time of the murder we're talking about. Joe Paisley would have been about—let me think—say sixteen."

"Not inconceivable. A strong, capable lad, isn't he?"

"Very much so. And grew up here."

"I suppose we keep him in the frame, then," said Oddie thoughtfully. "You said he claims to dislike and distrust the Ashworth set, didn't you?"

"Yes, but there's a more decisive argument against him than that. If he took part in the killing of Patrick, why didn't he also dispose of the body? If the car had broken down for Joe, he'd have got out and fixed it and then continued on to Bingley Moor, or wherever he had decided to dispose of the body."

"True. There's one thing that puzzles me about that, though. If they needed someone to get rid of Patrick's corpse, why did Melanie and Ranulph decide on Stephen? Why not one of the disciples?"

Charlie thought about that.

"Well, the only ones they could really call on would be Chesney or Mellors. No one would seriously consider entrusting their safety to Charmayne Churton. And the fact that Chesney and Mellors were more reliable—safe, middle-of-the-road men, aside from their kinks—made them unsuitable. Being part of an unspoken consensus that Ranulph needed violence of some kind as a stimulus to do his best work is very different from letting yourself be involved as an accessory after the fact of a murder. I expect they discussed it, but in the end thought Stephen was a better bet."

"Young, weak, impressionable, fond of money. Yes, fair enough. Though they ought to have realized that if he was leaned on he would prove to be a broken reed. I suppose he was the best of a bad bunch—fit punishment for them for having collected such a bad bunch around themselves."

They were interrupted by the phone ringing in the hall. "Take it, Martin, will you?" called Oddie to the man on duty. A few moments later his head came around the door.

"Lady for you, sir. One of this mob here, name of Churton."

"Oh, Lord. Right, I'll take it." Oddie stood up reluctantly, but he managed to keep his voice neutral when he got to the phone. "Oddie here."

"Oh, good!" came the unlovely voice. "I did want to speak to the head man, though your second in command is de*light*ful, of course. Look, I hope you boys weren't taken in by Mrs. Birdsell's claim never to have driven. Because you're too young to remember, but let me tell you a district nurse—which is what she was, and one *does* wonder how she came to give it up, doesn't one?—would *have* to have driven, just to get around her patch."

"I see. Do you know how old Mrs. Birdsell is?"

"Oh, early fifties, I think. Mary Ann was a bit of an afterthought, or a late accident. Never heard the father mentioned. No, I'm afraid she's not the most truthful of persons. Always rather flaunts the fact that she's been here so long, claims to know Ranulph and Melanie better than all the rest of us—though that's really a matter of affinity, isn't it, rather than length of acquaintanceship?"

"I would think you're right. Of course, she'd use her experience as a nurse to help with Ranulph Byatt, in his condition."

"Oh, yes, she *does!* Always ready to help with her cheery smile when Mrs. Max isn't around."

"Did you see her go there on the weekend Declan disappeared?"

There was no hesitation on the other end.

"Oh, she'd certainly have gone then. Martha was away, so Melanie would have needed *some*one's help."

"What I asked," Oddie said with an appearance of patience, "was whether you'd seen her going there."

"I certainly saw her going there one evening. I don't remember which."

"Weren't you at Cliff Richard's show on the Saturday?"

"Of course I was! So it must have been Sunday. Yes, I saw her go there around half past seven."

Only she wouldn't really have been needed, thought Oddie, as he thanked her and put the phone down, since Patrick was there to give any necessary help.

"Silly woman," he said, going back into the dining room. "One just doesn't know when she's lying."

"What did she want?" asked Charlie.

"Wanted to land Mrs. Birdsell in it by saying that, having been a district nurse, she must have been lying about never having driven. The vicious bitch doesn't realize we're more interested in her if she *hasn't* ever driven than if she has. Rivalry for Byatt's affections there, I'm afraid, or at least his notice, which seems the most any of them ever get. She says I'm too young to remember, which is the clumsiest bit of flattery I've ever attracted. My impression is that thirty years ago, especially in flat places like Essex, and in the little villages there, a district nurse was probably thought not to need a car."

"Easy to check, anyway, whether she's ever had a license or not. What else did she say?"

"Said she saw Jenny Birdsell going to the farmhouse on Sunday evening. Also said she usually helped there on weekends, and she would certainly have been needed that weekend, with Martha away."

"What would she be needed *for*, that's the question," said Charlie.

"It goes against the grain," said Oddie, "even to consider the possibility of a nurse doing what was done to that lad."

"Come off it," said Charlie brutally. "Haven't you learned anything from all those children's homes scandals? Some people get jobs in those places because they genuinely want to help kids who've had a raw deal. And some are attracted to work there because they want to abuse the kids who've all their lives had a raw deal and are troubled or defenseless. Most nurses go into nursing because they genuinely want to alleviate pain and suffering. Others . . ."

Oddie put his head in his hands.

"Christ, yes, I suppose so. Gives a new slant to some of the monster matrons of yesteryear, who gave the impression they learned their trade in Auschwitz or Dachau. Though to be fair they reserved their main bestialities for the nurses rather than the patients. . . . Do you think we should have another talk with her?"

"She didn't mention going to the main house when we asked her what she'd done on Sunday."

"No, she didn't. Hence the affectation of disorderliness and forgetfulness—in case anyone remembered seeing her. That's something that could have made the daughter suspicious, if it was a new assumption, but she didn't take her up on her having gone to the farm."

"Mary Ann was at Bible class, remember," said Charlie. "She may have had her suspicions about that too, though, if her mother would have been expected to go there on weekends."

"Seems to me there's grounds for another little chat."

"I suppose we'll have more of that 'Goodness me, how can you expect me to remember all those days ago,'" said Charlie. "Come to think of it, that doesn't go with the rest of her personality, does it? Nor with the district nurse past. They would need to be brisk and efficient."

"I suppose there are district nurses and then again district nurses, same as in any other profession. By the way, the lovely Charmayne suggested we should check how she came to give it up. It's a thought." He looked through the window. "Hey, is that the younger generation arriving home?"

Outside, approaching the gate, Mary Ann Birdsell, walking home, had been overtaken by a car. It had stopped, and she was speaking earnestly with the driver. Charlie walked over to the window to see better.

"Yes, that's Joe Paisley. Looks like it's a serious conversation. Shall we go out?"

"I think so."

They went out into the lane, and walked slowly toward the Birdsell cottage. Faces appeared in windows. Inevitably they were noticed. Every action they took in public in Ashworth was noticed. As they approached the gate of her mother's cottage, Mary Ann came running toward them from the lane.

"I'll let you in," she muttered. "I don't know if my mother's at home or not." She rummaged in a little patchwork bag for the key. Turning her head toward Charlie she continued her muttering. "Go through the cottage and out the back door. Look at the thing for the birds."

"The what?"

"The brass ring with the coconut inside. Mother always

says she picked it up in an antique shop in Spain and has no idea what it is. Joe says I should tell you."

She found the key and put it in the door.

"Come in. Oh, Mother's here," she said in her normal voice—clear, loud, a wayside pulpit voice.

"Oh, dear," Jenny said, bustling forward. "I was just making a cake. Could you make it quick, please? I thought that Ranulph might fancy—"

As Oddie led her to the settee and Mary Ann darted upstairs, Charlie slipped out the back door. On the step he paused and looked around him. There it was—he'd noticed it from the lane on his very first visit. Attached to a pole with a little crossbar at the top, which now his mind transformed grotesquely into a gallows, was a broad brass collar, within which was suspended a quarter of coconut. Two sparrows were quarreling over the remains of white inside.

Charlie went over to it. It was tied to the crossbar with string, and the coconut inside was suspended on more string. When you looked closely the collar was not like a dog collar, but had an element of wraparound to it, which could be tightened by a screw. It was this screw that the collar was tied to the post with, and to its lower portion the nut was tied too. The end of the screw was sharpened, and to Charlie's gaze it seemed that the screw and its thread had recently been oiled.

19

THE FINAL PICTURE

It was a day Charlie would want to put out of his mind for the rest of his life, but would never quite be able to. The end of a case often brought policemen more a sense of horror than of triumph, but this was exceptional. The first chilling spectacle was the matter-of-fact manner that Jenny Birdsell assumed when they confronted her with the evidence of the garrote. The matter, it seemed, was of no greater moment than if a packet of tea bags had found its way into her purse rather than her grocery cart.

"Of course I wouldn't expect you to understand," she

said, when the hideous implement had been put under her eyes. She was sitting in her easy chair, her fingers knitted together, a smile on her lips. The oiled screw brought no pity to her voice or eyes. "Nobody could who stands *outside* the artistic temperament, the creative urge. All of us who know Ranulph are privileged in our understanding. We have explored the wellsprings of his inspiration—an education in itself, a true spiritual experience. When I was asked to help, of course I didn't hesitate. The very existence of great pictures was at stake."

"By help," said Oddie, "I suppose you mean you were asked to be the actual instrument of Patrick O'Hearn's killing?"

"Oh, not killing! Of course not!" Her round, bunlike face did show pity now, but at the crudity of his understanding. "What was to stimulate Ranulph's inspiration was just a pantomime, a performance. Patrick wouldn't have been an easy man to kill if he hadn't gone along with it. He was so different from Declan! So much more sophisticated, so much more aware of the world and its ways. I believe he understood at once when they told him about . . . about Ranulph's sexual inclinations. Didn't shock him at all. Almost as if he understood it from inside himself. They all laughed about it, Melanie said."

"And it was presented to him as a sort of mock execution that he would participate in as the victim."

"Of course. That's what it was," said Jenny composedly.

"I see," said Oddie, keeping the doubt out of his voice. "And I suppose there was money involved?"

"Of course. I'm not sure how much. And in the event—"

"Yes. The event. Tell us about that."

She looked at them, wide-eyed, almost like any other criminal who wanted to convince them it was just bad luck.

"Well, it was the most terrible miscalculation. I blame myself, having been a nurse—but of course so rusty now! You mustn't hold Ranulph responsible in any way. Melanie rang me, as I said, and of course Ranulph's tastes are no secret from *me,* and I said to her that naturally I'd help."

"How long had Patrick been there?"

"Since Saturday afternoon, I believe."

"How many people knew he was there?"

"I . . . I really don't know. Possibly some did. But he busied himself around the house, helping Ranulph and Melanie, and he didn't go out to tramp the countryside or anything like that. Anyway, Melanie and Ranulph knew about my little instrument."

"The garrote, you mean."

"Yes."

"An instrument of *execution.*"

"Yes," she agreed composedly. "A memento of a trip around Spain. It was used there until *quite* recently. It was a little secret, a little joke between us, especially in view of the use I'd put it to. And it was agreed we would all do a performance for Ranulph—a mock garroting. Patrick was a rough, good-natured boy, none too sensitive. He thought it was a huge joke. Ranulph directed the details. The boy was naked . . . though afterward we put a pair of under-pants on him, for decency's sake. He played up tremen-dously—he was really quite an actor. We tied his hands and his legs, and I played the sadistic executioner. I put the collar round his neck, and got the screw in place in the hole. He pleaded for mercy—all part of the scenario, and *awf*ully well done! Then I began to turn the screw, and the collar tightened around his neck, and quite soon he was gagging and trying to scream, and I thought it could be tightened just a little bit more, and I'm afraid the sharp tip of the screw must have penetrated the spinal column—well, that was it for him."

She might have been describing a tea party at which the fish paste in the sandwiches had been found to be slightly off. Oddie found he had an overwhelming urge to put an end to the charade.

"Jennifer Birdsell, I am arresting you . . ."

She remained quite calm, practicing the sort of expression she imagined martyrs assumed, and nodding at the import of his words. As the three of them got up to go out to the car, Mary Ann appeared at the top of the stairs, then followed them down into the sunlight. She said nothing, watching without emotion. A little knot of Ashworth people had gathered in the lane. Mary Ann went over and stood by Joe Paisley.

"I knew she was evil," she said, in her clear, piercing voice. "I always recognized the Devil peering out of her eyes."

Joe Paisley put his arm around her.

"Come on, little chicken. You're coming back with me and Mother to Burnley."

Charlie, watching, realized suddenly that they had been children together. He waited for her reaction, hoping she would not plead an engagement to preach the Word in Keighley market. But after a moment she nodded, then buried her head in Joe's chest.

As Charlie helped Jenny Birdsell, still smiling pityingly, into the police car, Oddie bent over and had a word in his ear.

"Go and bring in Byatt. There's no way we can avoid that now."

"I wouldn't want to," said Charlie. "Would you?"

But he was conscious, as he watched the car disappear up the lane and then started back toward the house, of hostility in the group of Ashworth residents, a stony-faced, implacable sort of hostility, mitigated by personal apprehension—he guessed they were conscious of the part their own passivity had played, and wondered whether that passivity amounted to complicity. The exceptions were Joe and Mary Ann: Charlie could almost feel the force with which they were egging him on to do his duty.

The front door was unlocked as they had left it, and he let himself in. Almost immediately Martha appeared in the sitting room door.

"You're going to arrest him, aren't you? You *can't* think—"

"Will you go back in, please?"

"He's ill. Can't you hear?"

He *could* hear. From upstairs came sounds that were like grunts, interspersed with small cries. Charlie was up the stairs like a flash. The sounds got louder. In the door of Byatt's bedroom he paused.

The policewoman had allowed him watercolors. Her eyes showed her regret and her bewilderment. He was sitting at a little table in the center of the room, paper covering the top of it, and on the paper a picture was taking shape. The lower part of it, a burnished brown-yellow, was circular, forming the shape of a broad collar. Above that the outline of a face was beginning to appear, with the only features so far realized a hideously prominent pair of protruding, terrified eyes, almost popping out from the face and from the paper, and a mouth, torn apart in an agonized shriek, from which a blackened tongue was protruding.

Gradually Charlie started to make sense of the cries.

"Tighter. Turn the screw. Tighter. Kill him! Kill him!"

The old man's face was straining, the eyes filled with a corrosive lust, the feeble old limbs trembling with excitement, only the hands still applying paint being under some semblance of control.

"He'll be sectioned," said Charlie. "There's no way they'll let him stand trial."

Charlie was not a vengeful person, but he found he could not keep the regret from his voice.

Declan wondered whether he was choosing the wrong songs, or whether he had chosen the wrong street entirely. "The Mountains of Mourne" had gone down like a lead balloon, and so had "Danny Boy." The passersby had bustled on with no reaction on their hard or harried faces. Declan had chosen Bond Street because he'd understood—mainly, it must be said, from the Monopoly board—that it was one of the resorts of the well-heeled in London. Perhaps it was true what he'd read: that the rich were rich because they had no taste for giving away money.

His eye was caught by a notice on the side door of the building that he had stationed himself outside. It was Christerby's, the art dealers. He strolled over, still plucking the strings and turning the tuning screw of his guitar. The handwritten notice read:

WANTED
Capable young man for packing and deliveries

Underneath there was an arrow pointing to a still more obscure door. Declan went back to his pitch thoughtfully.

He launched into one of his favorites. His voice, had he but known it, was particularly responsive to the pathetic.

> *The Minstrel Boy to the war is gone*
> *In the ranks of death you'll find him.*

The picture of the innocent musician in the midst of carnage and horror had always touched him. It seemed to touch the passing public too. An elderly woman, heavily made up, actually smiled, and one young man began feeling in his pocket when he was still yards away. The chink was a substantial sound. Declan refrained from looking down, but thought it could be 50 pence, or even one pound. He thought he might try "The Last Rose of Summer" next.

His mind went back to the handwritten notice. Christerby's—that was a fine firm, he was sure of it. He could just fancy working in the art world, learning more about it. Would it be a plus for him if he mentioned he'd worked for Ranulph Byatt, even mixed his colors and generally helped in the artistic process? Not if they rang Ashworth and heard how he'd decamped without warning, that was sure. But perhaps he could explain how he'd found the whole setup there unsettling, even a little sinister.

"And that's no more than the truth, so help me God," he said to himself.

"The Last Rose" and "Home, Sweet Home" went down just as well. Several preoccupied faces betrayed by a flicker that the songs said something to them, brought back something in their past, maybe their childhood. His little cap on the pavement clinked several times, twice with satisfyingly substantial rings.

He was just bringing the song to a yearning close—for he did yearn sometimes for home, which had been a good home to him after his father had died—when he saw approaching from the direction of Savile Row a policeman with a purposeful tread. Quick as a flash he scooped up the money, popped his guitar back in its case, and, on an impulse, instead of walking up toward Oxford Street or down toward Piccadilly, turned and went to the door around the side of Christerby's that the notice directed him to.

It opened directly onto a staircase leading down. The basement, where the packing and unpacking would be done. Declan started down, wondering who it was he would have to charm or impress. He was surprised when he heard the door behind and above him open again, and heard a voice with authority.

"Excuse me."

He turned reluctantly. It was the policeman he had seen approaching.

"Are you Declan O'Hearn?"

Declan's face showed his surprise.

"Yes. How—"

"Look, could you come back up and come with me? We can't talk here."

Declan stood his ground.

"Why do you want to talk to me? I've moved on."

"Could you just come up, please?"

Declan cast a regretful look back down the stairs. Perhaps it would be better to come back without his guitar. He started up the stairs again. When they got into the open air Declan looked at the policeman. He was a young man with an insignificant mustache but compassionate eyes.

"What is it?"

There was a break in Declan's voice, perhaps the result of a twinge of fear.

"Look, I think you'd better come to the station. I'm afraid I've got bad news for you."

And, well trained, he set off, his arm on Declan's, at a cracking pace that did not allow the boy to protest that if there was bad news he would prefer to hear it there and then. As they made their way through the bustling streets a conviction came to him: this was something to do with Ashworth. A shiver went up his spine, as it several times had done while he was there. It was as if this moment marked the end of his youth, the dawn of adult understanding, the coming of darkness.

9 780743 224277